THE EX

THE EX

M.I. HATTERSLEY

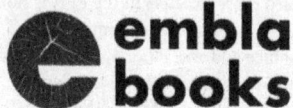

e **embla**
books

This edition published in 2025 by

**embla
books**

An imprint of Bonnier Books UK
5th Floor, HYLO, 105 Bunhill Row,
London, EC1Y 8LZ

A CIP catalogue record for this book is available from the British Library.

ISBN: 9781471420023

Also available as an ebook and an audiobook

1

Typeset by IDSUK (Data Connection) Ltd
Printed and bound in Great Britain by Clays Ltd, Elcograf S.p.A.

MIX
Paper | Supporting
responsible forestry
FSC® C018072

The authorised representative in the EEA is Bonnier Books
UK (Ireland) Limited.
Registered office address: Floor 3, Block 3, Miesian Plaza,
Dublin 2, D02 Y754, Ireland
compliance@bonnierbooks.ie
www.bonnierbooks.co.uk

For Alba & Suzanne

Chapter 1

It was one of those evenings that got dark in an instant; the day turning to night before anyone realised. When Lucy Meadows had last looked up from her work, bright sunshine shone in through the office windows, but now those same windows were inky black squares and the only light in the office came via the blue glow from her computer screen and the ones belonging to John and Paula. She sat back in her chair and stretched her arms up over her head.

"When did it get so dark?" she said.

John raised his head but didn't take his eyes off his screen or his hand from his mouse. "The nights are drawing in, my dear," he bellowed, in a dramatic voice. "Winter is just around the corner."

"All right, babe," Lucy replied. "Let's keep it light."

John glanced over at her with a smirk. "Just saying. *Babe*."

Lucy shot him a grin. She called everyone 'babe' these days, but it was a relatively recent addition to her vocabulary and symptomatic of living in East London. And of working in the media. Back when she first moved here and caught herself saying it, she'd cringe a little, but now she hardly noticed. And with the number of new people she'd been meeting with lately, it meant she didn't have to expend extraneous bandwidth remembering everyone's names.

She pushed back from her desk and scanned the room. She liked the ambience created by the low glow of the computer screens. It made the sparse office space look more impressive than it was and as though the work they were doing was of the utmost importance. So engrossed were they in what they were doing, they didn't even have the time to walk over to the light switch. It would also save them money in electric rates, which, as a new design company struggling to hold their own against all the other design companies here in Hoxton, East London, was always a good thing.

Lucy lifted her phone to her face and it lit up to show the time was four minutes after seven. She also saw she'd got a message. A thumbs-up emoji and the words,

See you there. Looking forward to it!

No kisses, but that was okay. People used so many kisses in texts these days that they'd lost all meaning. She liked it when guys didn't type out 'xs' like they were going out of fashion. Because it meant when they did, they were more significant.

Not that Lucy had much to go on relative to this theory. Over the last few years, she could count on two fingers the number of guys who'd sent her romantic texts of any kind, with kisses or not. But that was her decision. She'd been putting all her energy into starting Blue Fish Design. She knew that, if they were to make a strong go of it, there wasn't time for romantic trysts or worrying if someone was going to text back or not. Those matters were trivial compared to the reality of keeping their heads above water as a new company in an already saturated industry. But they were making it work. Things were finally happening. As of a few hours ago, Lucy had signed her fifth client this month. A big job, too. A full rebrand, including logo and website design, for a juice bar and wellness company based in East Finchley. It would bring in a lot of money to the agency and finally ease them out of the red with the banks.

So, she deserved a little celebration, didn't she?

Things were going well.

She placed her phone down, resisting the urge to text back. It was now 7:10 p.m. She had hoped to go home and freshen up prior to the date, but that wasn't going to happen now. Thankfully, she'd foreseen this eventuality and dressed this morning in her good jeans and a nice top. And besides, this wasn't a date, it was just old friends meeting for a drink. No kisses. No romance. Just a thumbs-up emoji and a catch-up.

Still, as Lucy put her iMac to sleep and rolled her chair out from under her desk, she couldn't help but feel a brief pang of excitement. Maybe it showed on her face because as she looked over, Paula was watching her with a half-smile-half-smirk dancing across her lips.

"Are you getting off?" she asked.

Lucy shrugged. "Yeah. Can't be arsed, really." She stood up and stretched her back. "I've said I would though, so . . ."

Paula nodded knowingly and shot her a wink. "Of course. Have a good time, won't you? Where are you meeting him?"

"The White Lion, near Hoxton Square."

At this, John looked up from his screen. Whether this was out of interest in Lucy's evening plans or the mention of a pub, she wasn't sure, but she suspected the latter.

"Well done for today," he said. "You stormed that meeting."

Lucy grabbed her coat from the back of her chair, trying to hide the grin spreading across her face. She had stormed that meeting. She'd smashed it out of the park.

"And be careful," Paula said, lowering her chin to regard her over the top of her oversized glasses. "I know he's an old flame and all that, but he's still a man. And you haven't seen him for what – six years?"

"Nearly seven."

"Yeah, so, people change. They grow up. They get more confident and solidified in their ideas about who they are, what they think they deserve. I know you said he's a nice guy, but nice guys can turn into pricks if they watch enough of the wrong YouTube videos."

John chuckled at Paula's statement. "Not everyone's as paranoid or down on men as you are, Pauls." He sat back in his chair and grinned at Lucy. "Have a good time. See you tomorrow."

Paula sighed. "Whatever, Trevor. But yeah, Luce, have fun. Be safe." She waved her away. "And well done for today, seriously. You should be buzzing. We both are."

"Thanks, babe," Lucy said, heading for the door. "And don't work too late, yeah? We're getting there. We don't want to burn out."

Her two partners waved her away and returned to their respective screens. Lucy watched them from the doorway a moment, smiling to herself as she surveyed the office of the agency she'd helped create. Then she turned and pushed through the door. A few blocks away there was a large glass of wine with her name on it and she damn well deserved it.

The White Lion was a ten-minute walk from the Blue Fish Agency. She walked down Bateman's Row, past the London College of Fashion, and then took a right onto Curtain Road. The streets around Shoreditch and Hoxton seemed unusually quiet, but it was only a Tuesday night and early. She glanced at her phone: now almost twenty past seven. They'd arranged to meet at 7:15 p.m, but that was okay. It was a girl's prerogative to be a few minutes late. She didn't want to seem too keen. It wasn't a date, after all, just a few catch-up drinks.

The air was cool but welcoming on her skin as she shoved her hands in her coat pockets and quickened her pace. Behind her she could hear footsteps, someone walking almost in time with her. At the corner of Old Street, she stopped and was surprised to hear the footsteps stop as well, almost in unison. She moved against the side of the nearest building and took out her phone, pretending to read a text and throwing her gaze down the street behind her.

Idiot.

There was no one there. Whoever it was had probably cut down a side street or had gone into one of the many bars or eating places that lay along this strip of road.

She carried on, heading across Old Street and up towards Hoxton Square. But as she passed alongside the old courthouse building, she heard footsteps again, quicker now, but so were her own. They were still matching her step for step. It could have been a man, but her instincts told her it was a woman. Not as worrying perhaps, but still weird. When she stopped, they stopped, and this time Lucy didn't wait to shoot a look over her shoulder. A dark figure stood on the street corner on the other side of the road, silhouetted against the brightly lit front of a tapas restaurant. They were wearing a long coat and had their hood up, shrouding their face. Although they weren't looking directly at Lucy, she felt a quiver of panic all the same. Under the large coat, they were probably of average height and build, so it was hard to tell what gender they were. But as she watched, they turned around and walked the other way, heading towards Old Street Station.

Lucy blew out her cheeks. "Stupid cow," she muttered to herself.

This was Paula's fault, filling her head with paranoid thoughts. That and the fact she'd been working herself too hard and her nerves were shot to pieces. But that's all it was. No one was following her. Across the street, she saw a couple walking towards her. The man had his arm around the girl and the two of them were laughing at a shared joke. Up ahead, two men with long hair were vaping outside a kebab shop. It was fine. She was around people. No one was going to drag her into some dark alley and strangle her. Lucy turned on her heels and with a renewed focus, hurried up Hoxton Street towards the White Lion.

The old pub looked so welcoming standing on the corner, that by the time she got up to the door and heard the dull throb of noise coming from inside, she'd put all thoughts of being followed by shadowy figures behind her. As she got through the door, she saw him sitting in a booth towards the rear of the bar. His hair was shorter and neater than the last time she'd seen him, but other than that, he looked the same as he always had. Those same blue eyes. As she walked over, he stood up and threw his arms wide. "Wow, Lou. You look great. You haven't changed a bit."

She smiled. "Babe, stop it. But same to you."

They stared at each other. It felt longer than six years. "I got you a Pinot," he said, gesturing at the large glass of wine on the table. "Is it still your favourite? Sorry, I should have waited, but I got here early and—"

"It's fine," she told him. "Thank you."

They sat down and she pulled the wine towards her. It wasn't her favourite. Not anymore. Lucy liked to think her sensibilities and taste for the finer things in life had grown since university and these days she'd have gone for a red given a choice. A nice Malbec. Something like that. But in pubs like the White Lion, Pinot Grigio was probably a safe bet. She took a big gulp. It was ice cold and tasted of melon and freedom.

"So, babe," she said, regarding him with narrow eyes. "Tell me what you've been up to since we last saw each other."

For the next half hour, they talked non-stop, reminiscing about their time together at Oxford, discussing mutual friends and acquaintances, laughing at – and getting rather nostalgic over – past events, and generally filling each other in on what they'd been doing since leaving university. He'd done so well for himself that she was a little wary of telling him about her own work. But he seemed genuinely interested, and even excited, as she told him about starting her design agency in the heart of London.

"That's awesome. Really awesome." He looked into his drink (a whiskey and coke, the same as always) and when he looked back there was a glimmer of mischief in his eyes. "It is great to see you, you know. It's been far too long."

"I agree." She surprised herself by letting out a giggle and coughed to cover it. "I am sorry though . . . about everything that happened. I'm glad we can still be friends."

His smile grew wider and his presence warmer. "We were young. All water under the bridge." He finished his drink and hit her with an intense stare. "Do you ever wonder, though? Whether we made the wrong decision all those years ago?"

She swallowed, hoping the fluttering in her belly didn't register on her face. "About me and you?"

He shrugged. "Yeah. What if we'd stayed together? Where do you think we'd be now? Married? Kids?"

"Jesus, babe," she scoffed. "I bloody hope not. I'm not ready for kids just yet."

"Fair enough, but you know what I mean."

She smiled, unable to draw herself away from the tractor beam pull of his eyes. "I do know what you mean. And who knows? But I am glad you got in touch. Very glad."

He nodded and so did she, both of them perhaps sensing the heavy subtext in the air. He pointed at her now empty glass. "Same again?"

"What?" She sat upright. "Oh, no, babe. I'll get these."

But he was already standing over her, holding his hand out for her glass. "It's fine. I want to. Another Pinot?"

She flashed her eyes at him and handed over the glass. "Go on then."

He took the glass and headed for the bar, weaving through the crowds of people who now occupied the space. She'd been so engrossed in their conversation that she hadn't noticed the pub filling up, but now she did she was aware of the noise as well. For a Tuesday night, it was certainly busy.

Twisting around, she could see the back of his head as he waited to be served. For such a busy pub, he'd managed to get to the front of the queue rather fast. But that didn't surprise her. He was tall, handsome, forthright. He'd always been a bit that way, but he seemed to have very much stepped into his power over the last six years. She giggled to herself, dumbfounded at the crazy thoughts running through her head. Could this be the start of something? Could she see herself with him again, after all these years? Glancing down at the table, she saw she'd shredded a beer mat into fine confetti and quickly brushed the pile onto the floor. Not a moment too soon either, as he appeared through the crowds.

"That was quick," she said, as he placed the drinks down in front of her.

"Yeah, I don't mess around." He glanced back. "Listen, can you excuse me? I just need to go to the bathroom."

"You are excused," she replied, bowing her head majestically. "But hurry back, okay?"

"Absolutely."

As he left her alone, she closed her eyes and let her shoulders relax. She had been a little apprehensive about meeting up again after so long, but it was going better than she'd imagined. A lot better. Hell, maybe there still was something there between them. Something she'd like to explore.

"Ooh, shit, do you mind if I perch here?"

She opened her eyes to see a woman sitting opposite her. "Oh? Erm. Someone is sitting there."

The woman was about her age and was slim, bordering on skinny, with long dark hair parted down the middle. She might have been good-looking if her face wasn't all screwed up in a tight grimace. "It's okay, I'm not nicking his seat," she said. "I just need to sort my shoe out."

"Ah okay. No worries."

The woman leaned forward and rummaged around under the table for a few seconds before straightening up. "That's better," she said. "Must have got a stone in there or something."

"Argh, nightmare."

The woman stared at her. "That your boyfriend, is it?"

"Excuse me?"

"The man you're with. Is he your boyfriend?"

Lucy sniffed, a little thrown by the woman's directness. "No. He's not. We used to go out, but a long time ago."

"I see. Well, if I were you, I wouldn't let him go a second time. Looks like a real catch, if you ask me."

Lucy frowned and picked up her glass of wine. She took a big gulp. "Maybe he is a catch, but I'm too busy for a relationship. I've got an empire to build."

"Is that right?" The woman got to her feet and laughed. "Well, good for you. You have a good night, anyway."

"Yeah, babe. You too."

The woman sauntered away, lost quickly amongst the crowd and Lucy returned her focus to her glass of wine. But as she moved her head, her vision blurred and warped.

What the . . .?

She shook her head, opening her eyes wide to focus, but it didn't do any good. She glanced around the pub. There was a fuzzy aura around everything and when she moved her head from side to side, the light fittings in the walls had trails. She sucked back a sharp breath, her heart rate quickening as she became more disorientated.

What was going on?

Grabbing hold of the table, she pulled herself to her feet. The room spun as she did. Damn it. It was her own fault. She'd not eaten since this morning and even then, she'd only had a yoghurt and a small apple. Drinking wine on an empty stomach always made her woozy. She needed to eat. That was it. Pushing through the crowds, she headed towards the door, hoping that fresh air would sort her out.

The cool breeze felt good on her skin as she stepped out onto the street, but her vision was still hazy and her arms and legs felt heavy. She walked a little way from the entrance, holding onto the side of the building to steady herself and pulling in more deep breaths.

"Hey, you all right?"

She spun around to see the woman from the pub. She moved towards her. "You look dreadful."

"No. I'm fine." That's what she tried to say at least, but it sounded more like a slurred grunt. She tried again. "I just need some air. Drinking on an empty stomach. Silly of me."

The woman frowned. "Yeah, I know what that's like." She continued to watch her with a concerned expression and, feeling self-conscious, Lucy stumbled away. In a few steps, she found herself in the alleyway that ran down the side of the pub. It was dark here and the ground uneven. It also stunk of stale urine. She reached out to the side of her, searching for a wall, something to lean against, but found nothing. She stumbled over as a powerful wave of dizziness spun the world on its axis.

"Careful there," a voice boomed in her ear. It sounded slowed down and like it was coming from a different room. A different time.

She tried to respond, but her mouth wasn't working anymore. Her tongue felt fat and alien. She tried to walk, but her legs gave way and hands grabbed her under her arms.

"It's okay, I've got you."

Feelings of panic washed over her, replaced quickly by relief and then detachment as her thoughts slowed down and her mind cleared.

"There we go."

The voice was warm and fluffy and the hands holding her were growing bigger and softer by the second. Confusion ebbed away. Sleep beckoned her close.

This was fine.

She was fine.

Everything was fine.

Her arms and legs were floating now, and her head was too heavy to hold up. She closed her eyes and drifted away, sensing the benign embrace of sleep enveloping her like the comfiest blanket ever. Here the world was soft and golden, and nothing mattered. She would sleep now. Sleep for a long, long time. She deserved it.

She liked sleep.

Sleep was good.

Chapter 2

The little boy was still staring at her. The same way he had been doing ever since he and his mum and baby sibling had settled into the booth next to hers fifteen minutes earlier. It was very off-putting, to say the least, and she didn't need the distraction right now.

Oh, great.

Now he was aping her too, pretending to type at an invisible laptop with a cheeky grin plastered across his chubby face. If his mum hadn't been so occupied trying to stop her baby from crying, she might have noticed and told him to stop. *Might have.* But no. It was just more distractions and not what she needed right now. At all.

Camille shook her head and returned her attention to her screen, trying to dispel all interferences from her awareness. But a few seconds later, she found herself glancing up at the boy through her fringe. Yep. He was still tapping away at his invisible keyboard. But fine, let him play. She needed to get on. She needed to work.

She glanced at the word count at the bottom left of her word document – something she'd promised herself she wouldn't do until she'd finished for the day – and was disheartened to see she was still in three figures. Seven hundred and forty-nine words. Pathetic. A glance across to the other side of her screen told her it was almost three. That meant she'd been sitting here for almost two hours and had written less than a hundred words. She needed to do better. Much better.

But maybe the environment was all wrong? She'd read somewhere that it was important for writers – especially freelancers like herself, who didn't have a set office – to distinguish their writing space from their everyday living space. The idea was if you had somewhere that you specifically went to for the act of writing, then each time you visited you put yourself instantly in 'the zone'. Only it wasn't happening that way. This café, on the corner of Kingsland Road, was dour and uninspiring and after sitting on one cappuccino all afternoon, she was now getting dirty looks from the proprietor.

Screw it.

She needed a break anyway. Grabbing up her bag, she made her way over to the counter, monitoring her laptop as she did.

"What can I get you?" the woman asked as she approached.

Camille pulled out her purse, ready to order another coffee. But on opening it up, her heart sank. She thought she had a five-pound note in there, but apart from a smattering of low-denomination coins, there was nothing.

"Oh?" she mumbled. "Sorry, I thought I had more money than I do."

Ignoring the fact that these words could well have been her mantra ever since leaving her job to become a freelance writer and blogger, she scrabbled around inside her purse before lowering it and offering the woman a crooked smile.

"Sorry, I don't suppose you have anything for seventeen pence?"

The woman didn't look amused. "You can have a sachet of ketchup."

"Hmm. No thanks. But you could join my Patreon page," Camille added, attempting to make light of the situation. "The whole vibe of the subscription is 'why not buy me a coffee.' It only costs five pounds per month. Supposed to be the price of a coffee in one of those big coffee places. Not here."

This was met with a scowl. "Patre-what?"

"It's a website. A blogging site. Sort of. I write things on there and people pay to read them. It's a way for creators to be reimbursed at source by the people who consume their work. It's a good idea really, I . . ." She trailed off, the woman's scowl drying up her words. Plus, she'd heard herself just now and maybe the woman's reaction was the right one. "Sorry," Camille added. "I'll finish up now."

She slunk back to her table as the mother of the staring kid leapt to her feet, a wet patch spreading across the lap of her grey jogging trousers and her baby screaming in her arms.

"Oh, great," she said. "All I need."

It looked to Camille as if the staring kid had knocked a glass of water into her lap. The mother picked up a handful of napkins and dabbed at the baby in her arms as the little boy looked on with a worried expression.

"Look what you've done," she yelled at him.

The Ex

The poor woman looked to be at the end of her rope. Her hair was lank and her eyes were red with what Camille assumed to be a lack of sleep or too many tears cried. Before she knew what she was doing, she'd leaned over to her.

"Excuse me, why don't you go to the bathroom and sort yourself out? I can watch your son."

The woman glanced at her and it looked like she was going to burst into tears. "Are you sure?"

Camille smiled. "Yes. Of course. We'll be all right, won't we?" she smiled at the little boy, who nodded cautiously.

"Thank you," the mother said with a release of emotion that was halfway between a laugh and a sigh. "I'm having a bad day today. He doesn't help, but it's everything. This one needs changing too, I think." She was already side-stepping over to the bathroom door next to the counter. "I'll only be five minutes. Thank you."

"Take your time, it's fine," Camille called after her, meeting eyes with the woman behind the counter. She didn't look pleased, but she didn't look angry anymore.

Camille watched the mother and baby disappear through the bathroom door and then turned her attention to the kid. "Don't worry, she won't be long," she told him.

He shrugged. "Are you playing a game?"

"What?"

"On your computer."

"Oh, that. No, I'm writing. Well, trying to. I'm not getting very far today, to be honest, but—"

"What are you writing?" the boy cut in. "Like, stories?"

Camille laughed to herself. "Sort of like stories. What's your name, by the way?"

"Toby," he replied with an air of triumph. "I'm six."

"Six? Wow, that is *soooo* old."

"What's your name?" he asked.

"It's Camille. But you can call me Cam – or Cami. All my friends do. Is it school holidays right now, Toby?"

"Yeah." He sniffed. "But we don't get to do much fun stuff now that my sister is around. Mum's too busy looking after her all the time."

"I'm sure your mum wants to do nice things with you, Toby. She's just trying to make sure everyone's happy."

Toby wrinkled his nose. "What sort of stories do you write? Do they have pirates in them? I love pirate stories."

"No. Not really," she told him. Then, to herself. "Maybe I should write pirate stories." She glanced at the collection of dull, uninspiring words on her screen. Pirates would certainly be more fun to write about than the pros and cons of a gluten-free diet.

Despite the lexical quagmire in which she presently found herself, Camille still had big dreams for her writing career. She hoped one day to make it as an investigative journalist. A hard hitter, who wasn't afraid to expose the truth, no matter what the cost. Failing that, she'd be happy to make a decent living as a well-being blogger. Failing that, anything that kept the wolf from the door and food on her table and meant she didn't have to hang up her laptop and go back to temping in an office.

Because right now Camille was barely making ends meet writing for a small group of subscribers on Patreon. In the past, she'd written online articles for Women's Health and Splendour Magazine, but despite sending her best efforts, no one had commissioned her for almost a year. Not exactly the glamourous path she'd imagined for herself all those years ago. She'd studied hard and gotten a 2:1 in English from Oxford, but at times like this, she wondered if she'd have been further forward in her career if she'd spent the three years honing her craft. Putting pen to paper. Finger to keyboard.

"I'm actually writing a book," she told Toby. "But I'm finding it hard to motivate myself." She sighed as the little boy stared at her with a puzzled expression on his face.

It wasn't a lie. She had been working on her book – a sort of hip, self-help manual for millennial women – for the last three years. Her vision was that it would be the go-to tome for young women, a wry but vital exploration of women's issues, mental health and relationships in the modern world. Not because she was particularly skilled at negotiating these areas in her own life (not yet anyway), but she prescribed to the old adage – you teach what you need to learn most.

But who was she kidding?

As she looked into Toby's innocent, confused face, she felt more of a fraud than ever. What if her inner voice was right? What if it wasn't anxiety and self-doubt crushing her spirit and telling her to give up, but rather a deeper wisdom? Was it time to listen to it? Did she have what it took to be a proper, grown-up writer? Or was she just another millennial loser who thought the world owed her a living? What was certainly true was that life was passing her by. She was strong on all the socials, had plenty of followers, but in real life, she couldn't remember the last time she'd had a good laugh with a close friend.

"Oh, thank you so much. You're a lifesaver." Camille looked up as Toby's mum returned from the bathroom, his little sister slung over her shoulder, but quiet now and gurgling happily. "Was he good for you?"

"Yeah, the best," she said, giving Toby a wink. "He's been giving me some advice about my writing."

The woman raised her eyebrows as she looked at her son. He nodded proudly. "Cami is going to write a book about pirates. They're the best stories."

She was about to respond when her phone vibrated noisily on the table. She picked it up to see it was a text message from . . . Erica Ross, of all people.

"Sorry," she said, raising her head and smiling at Toby and his mum. "I just got a message from an old friend I haven't heard from in a while. But, yes, pirates. Thanks, Toby. I'm on it."

"We'll leave you to it then," the woman said and smiled. "And thanks again."

"No worries." She was already opening her phone as the woman grabbed Toby's hand and led him away.

She swiped on the notification and it opened to reveal a brief text message.

Hey hun. Sorry I've been a shitty friend lately but been busy as hell! But have you heard the news? We need to talk! ASAP!

Camille wracked her brain. What news? She clicked open the BBC app but there was nothing of note on there. As she closed it down, a notification popped up telling her she had a low battery and, on checking, she saw she only had two per cent left.

No. Not now!

Erica needs to talk. ASAP!

She texted back.

What news? What's happened?

Erica must have had her phone out waiting because the thought bubble with the three dots popped up almost instantly, informing Camille her friend was typing a reply. She held her breath, her mind working overtime. Was she pregnant? Getting married? Had some mutual friend from university disgraced themselves or (perhaps worse) achieved something amazing? When the reply came, she felt her heart sink, but it was no less intriguing.

You haven't heard? Shit. Ring me! Can't do it via text.

A furtive glance over at the woman behind the counter told Camille there was no chance she would let her plug her phone in to charge and her laptop was running on fumes by this point as well. She'd choose a better writing environment next time, but for now, she needed to get home. She fired back a quick reply to Erica, telling her she needed to charge her phone and then she'd call her. Once done, she folded up her laptop, placed it in her backpack and hurried out of the café towards home.

Chapter 3

Camille made her way along the grey, rainy streets of Dalston, the weather seemingly matching her mood as she pulled her coat tight around her and quickened her pace. Off in the distance, she heard the rumble of thunder and wondered if this was some sort of foreshadowing relative to Erica's news. Camille had felt a sense of unease as she'd read the message and as she got nearer to home, she became more and more certain that whatever her old friend was about to tell her, it was going to be bad. She felt it in her bones. This, despite knowing deep down that this kind of magical, superstitious thinking was silly and often meant she needed to take a time out from the constant emotional drain that came from trying to succeed as a writer.

Yet this had always been the dichotomy at the heart of Camille's creative existence – and indeed, her existence full-stop. Depending on her state of mind, or the time of day, she could be super pragmatic or totally idealistic, believing in the truth and nothing but the truth one minute and asking the universe for help the next. Was she hedging her bets? Probably. Did it matter? Who the hell knew anymore?

It took her twenty-five minutes to get to her house and once inside she threw off her coat and ran upstairs to her bedroom.

The Ex

"Ant?" she called out. "Are you home?" There was no response, but she wasn't expecting one. Her flatmate Anthony was an actor, but if he wasn't working in his dream job (his 'sexy work' as he called it) he was engaged in his 'pay the bills work' which was waiting tables in a Soho bistro.

Camille went into her bedroom, ignoring the piles of clothes on the floor and the unmade bed. Reaching down the side of her desk, she pulled up the end of her charger and plugged in her phone. The screen was completely dead, so she left it to wake up and got undressed. The house was freezing, but they'd agreed they wouldn't put the heating on until seven each day (another of the reasons Camille was writing in cafés). Once down to her underwear and a vest top, she went to her wardrobe and pulled out some dark navy sweatpants and an oversized hoody. Pulling them on, she saw her phone was now charged enough she could use it. So, sitting down at her desk, she opened it up and scrolled through her contacts until she found Erica's name. A shiver ran down her spine, but she couldn't be certain whether it was due to feelings of trepidation or simply the lack of heating as she tapped 'call' and held the phone to her ear.

Erica answered on the first ring. "Cami. How are you doing?"

"I'm good, thanks. Long time no speak. Are you still up in Scotland?"

"Aye. I am that," she replied, affecting a bad Scottish accent. "But enough about me. Have you seriously not heard?"

"Heard what? Tell me."

"It's Lucy," Erica said.

Camille rolled her eyes. "God. What about her?"

"She's dead, Cam."

Camille sat upright. It felt like the last bit of warmth had been sucked out of her. She swallowed. "*Lucy* Lucy? Lucy Meadows? Our Lucy?"

"Yes, mate. It's awful. I'm still friends with her sister, Meg. She called me this morning. They found her in her apartment last Wednesday afternoon. She'd hung herself."

Camille chewed her lip. She had no words.

Suicide.

Bloody hell.

"Did she leave a note?"

"No, nothing. She had a bit of booze in her system, but not loads. They think it was an impulsive act, but Meg had no idea she was even struggling. She had just started a new business and was pretty stressed, so they think that might have something to do with it but, I don't know. It's just horrible, isn't it? When was the last time you spoke with her?"

Camille paused, as if thinking. But she knew exactly when it was. Right before she'd found out that Lucy had been seeing Mark behind her back. "A long time ago," was all she said. Then, "Listen, Erica, can we catch up again soon? It's just, I've just got things going on and ... Sorry ... This has thrown me somewhat. I need to take a moment."

"Yes, of course. You're still processing, I get it. Why don't I text you later and we'll try to arrange some kind of meet up soon? Are you still in London?"

"Yeah. Oh, shit. Funeral. Will you be going? Where is it?"

"I'm not sure yet. I'll let you know."

"Thanks," Camille said. "And thanks for calling to let me know. I've got to go." She hung up and held her phone on her lap. *Bloody hell.*

Lucy Meadows had committed suicide. Lucy. She always seemed so positive and easy-going. But it only went to show – you never really know someone until it's too late. She flung her phone back on the desk to finish charging and went downstairs.

The front room felt too quiet as she entered and headed straight through into the kitchen. She'd promised herself she wouldn't drink in the week anymore, but it wasn't every day you found out your friend had killed themselves. Besides, she'd already ruined her pledge on Monday when she'd found out she'd lost two subscribers on her Patreon page and shared a bottle of cheap rose with Ant.

She flung open the cupboards, believing there to be a half bottle of vodka squirrelled away behind the half-empty boxes of cereal and economy bags of pasta. But all she found was a bottle of cheap imitation Amaretto liqueur, called *Almondetto*. She lifted it out and screwed off the top. The flaky residue of dry sugar syrup around the rim of the bottle was rather off-putting, but it smelled okay, of sweet almonds and booze. She placed it down and grabbed a glass tumbler from out of another cupboard before heading for the fridge freezer.

She yanked the door open and knelt to pull out the bottom drawer where the ice cubes would be if there were any.

"Bugger."

There was no ice. She checked the other freezer drawers just in case but was left wanting.

25

"Bugger," she said again, louder now because she really wanted that drink. Or at least, she wanted to get tipsy enough that the harrowing news about Lucy was easier to deal with.

She was about to glug out a large measure of the sweet liquid regardless, when she heard the front door open and Ant entering the hallway.

"Cami?" he shouted out. "You home?"

"I'm through here," she replied, going into the front room. "You had a good day?" It was a linking question, her asking him about his day so she could offload about hers. But he ignored the question and a moment later, she heard him running up the stairs. "Where are you going?"

"Two seconds. I'm dying for a piss!"

She went out into the hallway to see him disappearing around the corner at the top of the landing. With sagging shoulders, she wandered back into the front room and sank onto the couch. She had hoped Ant's presence could bring her out of her thoughts, but alone and with no drink, she was left to face the crushing reality of her friend's death. Poor Lucy. What must she have been going through to think that was the only option available?

Camille often felt despondent about life – especially in the last few years once she'd realised her life was well and truly on a plateau – but she'd never considered what Lucy had resorted to. Her problem was she'd been on a clear and prescribed path from an early age. Being clever had helped. So, for her there was never a question that she'd sit her GCSEs, then A-Levels, then a degree at university. And not just any university either, Balliol College Oxford to read English. She'd been on an upward trajectory her entire life, always moving towards the next milestone. Then, suddenly, she found herself adrift, floating in space with no milestones and no safety net to catch her. Was that how it was for Lucy too? Camille had heard from mutual friends that she'd started her own business, but that didn't mean she had life any more worked out than Camille did or was even happy.

Because clearly, she wasn't.

"Cam, come up here, will you?" Anthony's voice snapped her out of her thoughts.

She lifted her head. "What is it?"

"Come up here." He sounded angry.

She stood and hurried into the hall and up the stairs. "What's wrong?" As she got to the landing and moved around the corner, she saw him standing outside her bedroom with his arms folded and his tongue jabbing into his cheek like he always did when he was annoyed.

"I'll tell you what's wrong," he said. "The fact you're trying to burn our bloody house down. Not to mention wasting electricity."

Camille frowned and joined him at the door. "What do you mean?"

"I mean them. You stupid sod," he waved his arm the way of the hair straighteners that were laying on her bedside table. A tell-tale orange flashed on the side of them. "You've left them switched on. Again. When are you going to learn, Camille?"

"Shit." She barged past him into the room and switched them off. She wanted to tell him the top of the table was made of metal, so it was fine, but she knew that wasn't the point. "Sorry."

Ant looked at the ceiling. "It's ridiculous Cam. I'm sick of telling you off. And I mean, who straightens their hair these days, anyway? It's all about big curls and waves, babe."

Camille sniffed. "I said I was sorry. Don't get at me, please." She waved the air in front of her, attempting to stem the tears she sensed were coming – before waving Ant away, who'd noticed and had turned to face her.

"Oh, come on. I was only half-serious. Don't do that." His perfectly sculptured eyebrows rose to meet each other above his nose. "Come here."

He reached out and she pulled away before wilting into his arms. "It's not you," she whimpered. "I've just had some bad news. A friend of mine from uni. She's killed herself."

"Oh, fucking hell," Anthony said. "And there was me going off on one to you like a stupid prick." He held her at arm's length, tilting his head to look her in the eyes.

"I'm fine," she said, looking away and dabbing at her eyes. "Just had a shitty day all round. It was the last straw."

"Right then," Ant said. "Go wash your face. We're going out."

"Ah, no, I can't. I'm skint until the end of the month."

"Well, lucky for you, it's my treat then, isn't it?" he said, his eyes widening devilishly. "Come on. We'll have a few wines, and you can tell me all about it."

Chapter 4

She stole your man?" Anthony cried, a glass of wine hovering inches from his lips. "Bloody hell, Cami. I know she's dead and everything, but that's a bit much. And before that, you were best friends?"

They were in The Huntsman, a large pub a fifteen-minute walk from their house. It was a nice enough place, old-fashioned but perfect for chats and Sunday afternoon sessions. But they hadn't had one of those for a long time.

Camille shrugged. "Yeah, we were a close bunch. Me, Lucy, Erica, Mark and Stephen." She smiled to herself at the memory of them all. They'd met in fresher's week at Balliol College and, despite them being from different backgrounds and all studying different subjects, they'd grown close. It had got rather messy on certain nights out, with people getting drunk and snogging other members of the friendship group, but it was all good fun. When Camille and Mark became a couple, she had worried it might affect the group dynamics, but it didn't, not really, not at first. That came later.

She glanced at Anthony, who was shaking his head as if he'd just heard a terrible scandal.

"Come off it," she said, nudging him. "Boyfriend swapping? That's a typical Sunday afternoon for you, isn't it?"

He flicked up an eyebrow. "Hey, I resent that comment. Maybe once. But Tim and I are serious now. No more messing around."

Camille grinned. "That's good to hear. I'm pleased for you. You deserve to be happy."

"Stop trying to change the subject, missy," he said, leaning over the table. "Tell me more. Did you kick off when you found out about the two of them?"

She curled her lip. "Not really. Mark and I were coming to the end of our relationship, anyway. It was an overlap, more than an affair. That doesn't excuse it, I know. And I'm not going to pretend it didn't hurt. But it was more the fact they hadn't told me that made it worse. I couldn't trust either of them after that. I wanted nothing to do with them."

"And now she's dead."

"Now she's dead."

They both drank. Camille, staring into the middle distance, looking at nothing but seeing so much. Despite everything, she'd missed Lucy and the gang since leaving Oxford to move back to London. But that was almost twelve years ago. If she'd really wanted to get back in touch with Lucy, she would have done.

"Are you in touch with any of the others?"

Camille sniffed at the idea. "Erica, yes. But not Stephen and certainly not Mark."

"Because of what happened?"

"Sort of," she smiled and shook her head, preparing herself to explain.

Anthony frowned. "What is it?"

"Mark Kennedy. The golden boy of Balliol. He was so handsome when I met him. Well, he is still. Only last time I saw a picture of him, his whole appearance was much neater and more corporate than when I was with him. He's one of them, you know . . ."

Another eyebrow shot up. "One of them?"

"Part of the establishment. *The Man*. I should have known, really. He was doing politics, philosophy and economics at Balliol College. It says it all. But he had a real artistic soul as well. I never thought he'd go into politics."

"I see. And he has?"

"After Oxford, he worked as a journalist for an online politics and culture magazine called Vivid Stance. It was a bit poncey. But last I heard, he was making his move into politics for real. He's a clever man and was always very charming. He'll do well."

"Wow. But fuck him for cheating on you as well, right?"

Camille giggled and took a drink of wine. "Absolutely. He could be a real shit too, at times. Especially if he'd been drinking." She lowered her head, the remembrance of that night hitting her like a freight train. She hadn't thought about it for so long, it was almost like it had happened to someone else. Maybe in a way it had done. She shook the thought away and raised her glass. "Anyway, good luck to them all. And here's to Lucy. Rest in peace, darling."

"To Lucy." Ant clinked his glass against hers. "Poor cow. It's so sad when someone feels that's their only out."

They fell silent again and drank to cover it. It was strange for Camille, to talk about her old friendship group again after so long. She tried not to think about any of them too much and if she was honest with herself, it was because she was jealous. Well, not jealous exactly, that was the wrong word, but she longed to have her life in order the way Erica did. Or to have an exciting future in front of her the way Mark and Stephen had. Even Lucy had her new business. And yes, that might have been one reason she was so stressed out she drove herself over the edge, but at least she'd got there. She'd succeeded. In a way.

And what had Camille done with her life? Nothing. She always told herself she'd be a famous writer by the time she was twenty-five, a fully professional one at the very least. Now here she was at thirty-two, scraping a living, writing generic articles for a subscription site and becoming more and more disillusioned by the month. Desperation was the death of art, but she had nothing else to fall back on. Despite her late mother's insistence that she get on the career ladder as soon as possible, she'd focused on her writing and creative exploits to the detriment of everything else. If it had worked out, she'd be a hero. Now that it hadn't, she felt like a phoney and a loser. So, when do you admit defeat?

"Well, well, he is a looker, isn't he?"

Camille pulled herself out of her spiralling mood to see Anthony ogling his phone screen. He turned it around to show her a photo of Mark he'd found online.

"Ah, yes. There he is. Mr Right. In more ways than one."

Anthony pursed his lips. "I see. Tory boy, is he?" He squinted at the screen. "I like me a bit of posh now and again. It says here there's a strong rumour going around he may stand as an MP in the next election. For Barking, of all places. Woof, woof."

"Stop it," she told him. "We're having a drink in remembrance of my friend, remember? Besides, the last thing I need is to know how well everyone else is doing."

She had heard little from Stephen over the preceding years, but she suspected he'd be doing well for himself. He was from a good family and already had plenty of contacts in the world of finance. She'd have bet good money on him being a banker or a city trader. That's if she had any money.

"Hey, stop that now," Ant scolded. "They aren't any better than you."

"It certainly feels like it sometimes."

"Oh my god, stop feeling so sorry for yourself. You're young, you're gorgeous, you're alive. You've got everything going for you, Cam. You just need a break. And it will come for you. I can feel it." He glanced at his phone and pulled a face. "But I need to make a move, I'm afraid. I said I'd go around to Tim's place. You going to be okay?"

"Yes, I'll be fine. I'm going to finish this drink, then walk back. And thanks, Ant. I needed that." She raised her glass.

"Don't mention it." He got to his feet and looked out the window with a frown. "Are you sure you're going to be okay walking back on your own? It's got dark since we left. Do you want me to walk you home?"

"No. I'll be fine. Go!"

"Okay, but stick to the main road, yeah, and don't talk to any strange men."

"Yes, thanks, Dad."

"Oh, piss off, will you? Right, I'm gone. See you at home. Tim has a class first thing, so I won't be late."

She waved him off and watched as he left the pub. Then she downed the last of her wine and got to her feet herself. It had been a strange day. The best thing she could do now was go home and put all this behind her. Hope tomorrow was a better and more productive day.

Chapter 5

The rain had stopped, but it was a chilly night and the air still felt wet as Camille left The Huntsman and made for home. She was glad she'd worn her long coat, which she fastened all the way up, and had also brought her woollen hat, which she put on and pulled down over her ears. Swaddled in the warm clothing, she felt safe as she walked down Kingsland High Street. Night had most definitely arrived since they'd been in the pub, but the main strip was still busy with people. As Camille passed by her fellow pedestrians, she wondered where they were going. Some of them were no doubt heading home after a long day's work, some on their way to meet with friends and lovers, perhaps some had received bad news, too and were so discombobulated all they wanted was to get inside and run themselves a warm bath. That's what Camille was telling herself at least – that it was the news of Lucy's passing that was making her feel like this – not the fact she'd hardly written anything of worth today, and that after reflecting on the successes of her old university friends, she was doubting herself more than ever. But like everyone else walking the streets tonight, she kept her eyes down and a dogged expression on her face, displaying an outward message of determination even if her internal workings were in tatters.

At the end of the high street, she turned the corner onto Sandringham Road and here, away from the main strip, the streets suddenly appeared darker and more imposing. Gone were the bright lights provided by the kebab shops and late-night off-licences. On this deserted street, the only light came from the dull orange glow of the streetlamps overhead. As the rows of houses stretched out in front of her, she regretted turning Anthony's offer down.

No. Don't do that.

She was being silly. Letting her imagination get the better of her. She didn't need someone to walk her home. She was a grown woman. But that didn't stop her from stuffing her hand into her pocket and finding her house keys, slipping the main door key into her fist so it protruded between her index and middle fingers.

It was quiet as she walked along. So quiet she could hear footsteps some way behind her. They were only faint at first, but the more she focused on them, the louder they seemed to get. She quickened her pace and they seemed to speed up at the same rate.

Was someone following her?

Without stopping, she risked a furtive glance over her shoulder. Across the street twenty metres behind her, a dark figure was walking the same way. They had a big coat on, and their hood was up over their face, so she couldn't make out what they looked like or even their gender.

Camille turned and walked faster, clutching the keys in her pocket tight as her heart beat loud in her ears. She was about ten minutes from home. But a lot could happen in ten minutes. Her mind swirled with dark thoughts and troubling memories – of all the reports she'd heard over the last few years. Of women her age or younger getting snatched off the streets and their burnt or dismembered bodies found on wasteland.

She coughed and wasn't sure why. Maybe it was an attempt to get out of her head and back into the moment. Maybe she was trying to alert this shadowy figure that she was a human being, not a prize or a trophy.

She hurried on, the footsteps still following on behind. As she got to St Mark's Rise, she could either carry on down Sandringham Road towards her house or take a right and follow the curve of the road around to meet Downs Park. It was a split-second decision (she wasn't going to slow down to ponder which direction to take) and she opted for the right, taking it at the last second in the hope her sudden shift would throw off the person following her.

She headed quickly down the road, doing that kind of skip-run-walk that people did when they didn't want others to think they were in a rush. As the road met at the intersection with the grounds of the new academy up ahead, she slowed her pace and threw her gaze back over her shoulder. Gone. There was no one on the other side of the road. Her shoulders sagged and she allowed herself to exhale. But as her sense of awareness grew, she let out a gasp of panic.

They were still behind her. But on her side of the street now, around twenty metres away but gaining on her with every step.

Shit. No. Please no.

Camille put her head down and strode on, breath clasped in her chest and her whole body tight with tension. The metal key in her fist dug into her fingers, but she hardly noticed. As she crossed over the road she glanced back. The person following was crossing over too.

That was it.

That was the sign she'd been waiting for. The sign that this wasn't her being silly or over-thinking things. She was now in a dangerous situation, and she needed to remove herself from it. Fast.

She pulled her hands out of her pockets, seeing both were now clenched in tight fists. Gripping her keys to her chest, she broke into a jog, then into a run. As she raced past the rows of houses, she glanced into their windows, praying to the universe that some benevolent soul might be watching out the window and beckon her inside to safety. But no. Thick velvet curtains and blackout blinds hid the innocuous scenes of domesticity, those in the warmth and safety of their homes oblivious to her plight. Camille had lived in the big bad capital for many years now, but this was the first time she'd felt this scared for her life.

Stupid bloody idiot.

Why hadn't she let Ant walk her home?

Their house was only a minute or two away now, around the corner and the second street on the right. Cecilia Road. Good old Cecilia Road. She could see the edge of the road sign poking around the side of the house on the corner. Crossing over to the other side, she hurried along as fast as her legs could take her. She wasn't sure how far away the person behind her was, but she didn't want to know. She could no longer hear footsteps, but she was panting loudly, and her ears were full of pressure, so that was no proof they'd gone. As she turned onto her street, she slowed her pace a little, heading straight for her house, number nineteen. She still had her keys in her fist as she vaulted the low fence and fell into her front door. Glancing back, she saw the figure standing on the corner of her street. They'd stopped. They were watching her.

Scrambling her keys into her grip, she got the one for the front door into the lock and twisted it open, so very glad Ant had forgotten to lock the Mortis lock further down. He always forgot it and she was always telling him off. But she wouldn't anymore. She pushed into the safety of her hallway and slammed the door behind her.

She was home. She was safe.

Chapter 6

Camille leaned with her back to the front door, her chest rising and falling rapidly as she gulped back large mouthfuls of air. She remained like this for another half a minute before the adrenaline subsided enough so that she could move. When it did, she laughed, which sounded a little hysterical, but it was a good release.

Had that just happened? She shook her head and another laugh erupted from her belly and this time it sounded more joyful. The sound of relief. Moving over to the mirror above the shoe rack that no one ever used, she took in her reflection. She looked tired and a little wired, but as she smiled and told herself it was all going to be fine, another wave of blessed relief washed over her. She even felt a little silly now, here in the warm comfort of her house. The heating had come on since they were out and with the outside world locked outside where it belonged, it seemed ridiculous that she'd come so close to being attacked just now.

Had she come close?

It had certainly appeared that way to her, but the mind was very good at playing tricks, especially when your guard was down. Maybe she'd put this one down to a close call and leave

40

it at that. No point telling Ant and worrying him unnecessarily. She'd learnt her lesson. Next time, she'd stick to the main strip or get a taxi home.

She slipped her shoes off and stuffed her hat into her coat pocket before hanging it up and moving into the front room. As she entered, she could see through into the kitchen and her gaze fell on the bottle of Almondetto on the worktop and the empty glass beside it.

"Screw it," she muttered to herself. "When in Rome . . ."

She walked over and poured out a decent serving and took a sip. It was like thick sugar syrup mixed with ethanol, but it was alcoholic and would settle her nerves, she reasoned. She took the drink upstairs to her bedroom and switched on the light.

"Bloody hell, Cam."

With her senses heightened, it was like she was seeing the mess for the first time. She took in the piles of dirty clothes, the piles of clean washing, the creased shirts that needed ironing but as they didn't own an iron, were hanging over the back of her chair. Scraps of paper and magazines littered the floor, along with notebooks filled with scribbled ideas that would never be realised or explored. It wasn't good. In fact, it looked like the bedroom of a teenager, or someone with serious mental health problems. Camille placed the drink down on her bedside table and lifted her laptop off her desk and onto her bed. There was no point starting anything now, but first thing tomorrow she would sort her life out, starting with this bedroom. She had to. She'd been treading water for far too long. It was time to make some changes.

She opened her laptop with the very real aim to register with a few job sites before going to sleep. The idea of another banal office job was anathema to her, but times were hard and seeing what was out there couldn't hurt. Yet as she opened a new browser window, she instinctively clicked on her bookmarks and then onto Facebook.

It was rather passe now, of course, Facebook, but she was a member of a few freelance writers' groups, which she found useful. Plus, a little research into what people were talking about often gave her ideas for articles. Tonight, though, her attention was drawn immediately to the top of her news feed and a new post about Lucy Meadows. Some girl called Paula Bates, whom Camille had never heard of, had written it but someone from Balliol had tagged all of Lucy's university friends in the comments section. The post was the usual sort of thing people wrote when someone died young and unexpectedly. Paula explained how kind and funny Lucy was, how creative and ambitious and driven she was too (yeah, okay, Paula. Don't rub it in). Then she urged people to check up on each other and to reach out to someone close if they were going through dark times. It was a well-written piece, not too poignant but touching all the same. Paula wanted to remember Lucy as the vital, fun-loving person she remembered her to be, and that sounded like a good idea to Camille. She was about to click off when her gaze fell to the comments section under the post. One comment, in particular, stood out to her, written by someone called Douglas Mathers, whose name she didn't recognise. It stood out because most of the other comments were single lines of text, people expressing

their sadness at losing Lucy, wishing her to 'RIP' – yet Douglas
Mathers' comment took a very different slant:

Nice girl. But does anyone else think this is very strange?
This means two of Mark Kennedy's girlfriends have died
in mysterious circumstances in the last year. Makes you
think . . .

The comment was met with a barrage of angry replies, mostly
telling Mathers he was sick or jealous and being ridiculous
bringing this up, especially in a post about Lucy. But others
asked him to clarify his points, which he did a little further
down.

Lucy Meadows and Ophelia Andrews. Both dead within 3
months of each other. Both ex-girlfriends of Mark Kennedy.
I'm not saying he had anything to do with their deaths, but
it seems odd to me. You know what they say: there's no
smoke without fire.

Camille stared at the words. She had goosebumps running
up both arms, but the heating was on. Ophelia Andrews. She
didn't recognise the name, but it was rare enough that she
found her Facebook profile easily. From a quick scan of her
feed, it appeared she'd died at the start of the year, around the
eighteenth of March. Three months ago, like Douglas Mathers
had said. It was sad. Her page was full of messages from friends
and loved ones she'd never get to read. Camille read a few of

them before clicking open a new browser window and typing her name into the search bar.

After a few dead ends, she found a local news site that reported that the poor girl had been found dead in her flat. The article didn't mention the cause of death, only that there was no foul play involved. In Camille's experience, that usually meant one of two things: a drug overdose or suicide. The article said she was from London originally and had recently returned there after a year living in Paris. Poor girl. There was just one photo of her in the article. Her graduation photo. She was grinning at the camera, but the more Camille stared into her eyes, the more she saw a sadness behind her smile. At least she thought she did. She was probably projecting. It had been a weird few days.

It didn't help matters when she found herself opening a file of old photos and clicking on a folder marked 'Oxford 2009.' Her second year at university, when she and Mark had first got together. As suspected, the folder contained mostly photos of the two of them. They looked so young and happy. So in love. The people in the photos looked out at Camille across the years and as she flicked through them, she was reminded of the camping trip they took up in Scotland, their summer holiday to Ibiza, the party at Stephen's house where afterwards Mark had . . .

She clicked off that photo, glad when the next one was of their whole friendship group – her, Mark, Erica, Stephen and Lucy. They were at some formal dinner party but were all making goofy faces at the camera. She couldn't remember who'd taken the photo, maybe one of Mark's posh PPE classmates. It looked like that kind of party.

The next photo was one of Camille on her own, with the Parthenon in Athens over her shoulder. Mark must have taken it. They'd gone there for a weekend soon after they became an item. Mark had paid, or rather, as she'd suspected at the time, the bank of Mummy and Daddy had paid. But she never complained. She was happy to get away, to be alone with this amazing sexy boy who was so confident and charming and treated her like a queen. Well, most of the time.

She snorted loudly as a way of dispelling the thought and returned her attention to the photo on the screen. The girl staring back at her looked so vibrant, so full of life, that it made her sad. Where had that young girl gone? When had that light in her eyes dimmed so greatly?

The next photo was of Mark. It was on the same holiday, but he was sitting outside a taverna in a town square. His blue eyes sparkled in the hot Greek sun as he grinned devilishly at the camera. He was a handsome guy, all right. Camille moved her face closer to the screen.

Was that the face of a killer?

Could Mark really have had something to do with Lucy's death?

She sat up and closed the folder. She was being stupid, letting her mind race into dark territory that it had no reason to be in. Forget this, she told herself. Move on. She reached for her drink, but a loud bang from downstairs startled her and she knocked it over.

What the hell?

She froze, listening intently at the door. What if it was the person who'd followed her home? What if they'd broken in and were here to . . .?

"Hey. It's me."

She relaxed as Ant's voice carried up the stairs, then groaned as she saw the sticky liqueur had spilt over a pile of clean washing. She picked up a jumper from off the top and brushed it down before quickly admitting defeat and chucking it into the corner. "Did you get home okay?" Ant called up.

"Yeah," she lied, sliding off the bed and moving over to the door. She grabbed the handle, knowing she should go down and tell him about being followed – maybe even about what Douglas Mathers had said – but for some reason, she felt weird about doing so.

But why wouldn't she feel weird?

She had no proof that anyone was following her. The figure she'd seen was most likely some guy taking an evening stroll, wondering why the hell the girl in front of him kept looking back at him like she did. And the Mark thing was even more preposterous. It was just gossip and hearsay. Douglas Mathers was probably an internet troll. Some loser who'd been jealous of Mark. There'd been plenty of those about.

She let go of the door handle. "You're home early," she shouted down.

"I know. As soon as I got to Tim's flat, he got all funny about some assignment he has to complete. I said I'd leave him to it. The bloody idiot."

Camille smiled. More than glad he was home. "Sorry, mate. Are you okay?"

But Ant didn't reply. He must have gone into the front room out of earshot. She thought briefly about going downstairs, but she was settled here. She went back over to her bed and closed the laptop. That was enough silliness for one day. She placed it back on the desk and got undressed for bed. Tomorrow was another day. And why couldn't it be the start of a new era as well? Yes. This was the universe giving her a sign. Showing her that, not only was life precious and she shouldn't waste it, but that she too could achieve what her friends had done if she only pushed herself. She was as clever as any of them. She'd got a two-one from Balliol, for Heaven's sake. And she was more than dedicated to her dreams. She only needed to work harder on manifesting them. But she realised that now. She was done living like a slob, existing from payday to payday like some pathetic hack. It was time for Camille Fletcher to grow up and step into her power. But tomorrow. Right now, she was too emotionally drained to do anything but climb into bed and pull the covers up over her head.

Chapter 7

Anthony was already dressed and eating breakfast in front of the TV when Camille got downstairs the next morning.

"You're up early," he mumbled through a mouthful of toast before looking her up and down. "And you're wearing actual clothes rather than those saggy-ass flannel monstrosities. What happened? Did you piss the bed?"

"Shut up. I set my alarm," she told him. "This is the new me. Up and at 'em. Seize the day and all that. I've decided I'm going to get myself a job. A proper job."

"Bloody hell. You sure you want to do that?"

She perched on the arm of the couch. "It's not about what I *want* to do, Anthony. That's been the problem for too long. I need to think about what I *need* to do."

He sniffed. "What about your writing? You can't give that up, Cam. You're a brilliant writer and I'm not just saying that. It keeps you going, doesn't it?"

"Only just. But I feel like it's become a chore, almost. I'm not writing what I want anymore, just what I think will get me more clicks, more subscribers."

"And what do you want to write about?"

She shrugged. "Not sure yet. Something important. Something with weight to it. But while I figure that out, I'd rather have

48

my 'pay the bills work' be something that doesn't involve me prostituting my creativity."

It sounded pretentious, even to her. She was waiting for one of Ant's usual pithy comments, but an advert for the new Tom Hardy film had flashed up on the screen to distract him. With her housemate's attention elsewhere, she got up and moved through into the kitchen to make some coffee. They only had instant, so she spooned out a large helping into her mug and poured a glug of milk on top to dissolve the granules. As she waited for the kettle to boil, she walked over to the window. The weather outside was miserable. How dare it? Today was supposed to be a new start. That meant sunshine and bright skies were needed.

"I've been reading about that ex of yours."

Camille turned to see Ant leaning against the doorframe. "Oh? And?"

"Yeah, I was Googling him. There are loads of articles online. He seems like he's going places. But he's not got any social media, which is a bit weird, don't you think?"

"Maybe not," she replied. "It makes sense if he is moving into government. A misjudged tweet from ten years ago can kill your career fast these days. He's probably just being careful."

She didn't know who she was trying to convince the most. She'd also had no intention of telling him about what she'd seen on Facebook, but he was waiting for her to say more and perhaps it would be good to share. If not just to hear how ridiculous the allegations sounded out loud.

"There are some rumours kicking around about Mark actually," she started. "I saw a post about Lucy and someone had commented underneath, pointing out that two of his exes had died within three months of each other. Both in *suspicious circumstances*."

"Are you joking?" Ant's eyes grew wide. "Do you think he had something to do with their deaths?"

"Why would he?" The kettle clicked off the boil and she walked over and filled her mug with the hot water. "Thanks for eating all the bread, by the way." She nodded to the empty plastic wrapper on the side.

"Sorry, but forget the bloody bread. Tell me more." She pushed past him and he followed her into the front room. "Did you know this other girl as well?"

"Ophelia Andrews, she was called. And, no. I think he met her after university. I looked her up. She seemed like a decent enough girl. It's just a tragic coincidence, that's all."

"Yeah, but what if it isn't?" He was getting excited now and she already knew he wouldn't leave it alone. "Maybe you should investigate, Cambo? Maybe this is that 'something with weight' you've been looking to write about?"

She sipped her coffee, mentally kicking herself for ever opening her mouth but also wondering whether he might have a point. "Leave it, Ant. I only told you because it was such a stupid comment. Just some troll trying to upset people."

"Hmm. Maybe. But there's no smoke without fire."

There was that phrase again. She took another sip of her coffee. It didn't taste any better. She looked at Ant. "You haven't got a fiver you can lend me, have you? I need to go buy the jobs papers and I might get some breakfast while I'm out."

"Yes, no worries. I suppose it's fair seeing as I ate the last of the bread."

"Exactly."

He rummaged in his jeans pocket and pulled out a balled-up note. He held it up. "There's a tenner. Give it back whenever. When you've sold your big story about Mark Kennedy to the papers."

"Stop it," she told him. "I mean it."

*   *   *

Camille opted for the café around the corner this time. It was nearer and there was always a full set of the day's papers for the customers to read. Besides, her usual café was the place she went to write and if she was using today to focus on her future and find a job, it made little sense to go there. It already felt like she was cheating on her tenacious, creative side with this much more boring and responsible version of herself.

After ordering poached eggs on toast and a large latte, she selected the Hackney Gazette and a copy of The Guardian and found a seat near the window. She lay the Gazette open on the table and flicked to the jobs section. She didn't remember the last time she'd read a print newspaper, but it felt grown-up to do so and that was probably a good start.

But that was about as far as she got. As she scanned the adverts, she found nothing that excited her and even less for which she was qualified. They all seemed to want job-specific diplomas or heaps of experience. She closed the paper and replaced it with The Guardian, spreading it out in front of her and gazing at it as if it held the answers to all her problems. It did not. It being a Thursday, the jobs section was vast but, even here in what most people considered a leftie-liberal kind of broadsheet, few jobs caught her eye. An ad agency in East London was looking for a copywriter, but they wanted someone with at least five years' experience. Camille didn't have any experience. She had experience in life. In getting her heart broken. In struggling to keep her head afloat while she focused on her dreams. It was experience enough, perhaps. But not in the world of work.

How the hell do people do this?

How did Erica do it? How did Lucy? How did Mark and Stephen?

She sniffed, angry at herself for letting envy get the better of her. It was a destructive emotion and it never helped. The story she often told herself was that her old friends had wealthier families and more contacts, but the truth was they'd achieved success on their own merits. It wasn't their fault Camille had been raised by a single parent who had passed away not long after she graduated. But it wasn't hers either. She'd done damn well to get to Oxford to read English. She should be proud of herself for that alone. Like her mum had been before she died.

Jesus.

Why was she thinking about mum all of a sudden? Where had that come from? She sat upright and shuddered. She had to think of the future. That was all that mattered.

She pulled out her phone – eager to check the online job sites – when the waitress appeared by the side of the table holding a plate and a large mug. "Eggs on toast and a latte?"

"Yes. Thanks." Camille hurried to clear the table of papers so the young woman could place her food down.

"Job hunting, is it?" she asked, sliding the plate in front of her.

"Unfortunately, yes. I'm not having much luck, though."

"Mary is looking for someone to do a few shifts here, I think. Fridays and Saturdays. You should speak to her."

Camille laughed. But when she glanced up at the waitress, her face was serious. "Oh. Yes. Great. Thank you, I might do that."

She looked down as the young woman sauntered back into the kitchen. She could feel her cheeks burning.

Jesus, Cami. Shall we add terrible snob to that list of negative personality traits as well?

But the eggs smelled good, and the coffee was creamy and just the right side of strong. She gulped down a large mouthful before picking up her knife and fork to start on her food. Before she had a chance to take a bite, her phone vibrated on the table next to her hand.

"Oh, for f . . ."

She glanced down at the screen to see it was Anthony calling her. She'd only said goodbye to him half an hour ago. What could he possibly want? She considered letting it ring out, but she didn't like to do that. It wasn't fair and it could be important.

She placed her cutlery down and picked up the phone, swiping it open as she did.

"Hey. Everything good?"

"Well, depends on your definition of good." He sounded out of breath. He sounded serious.

"What do you mean?"

"I mean, I've been doing some more digging since you left. I think your internet troll might have been right."

Camille glanced around. The walls of the café felt like they were zooming in on her. "Ant. What are you talking about?"

"I'm talking about Mark Kennedy and those two girls. I think you need to come home, Camille. Now. I've got something here you need to see."

Chapter 8

Camille chewed on her bottom lip, unable to take her eyes off the screen. She reread the tweet from Ophelia Andrews for a fourth and then fifth time. It made her blood turn to ice water.

"What do you think?" Ant asked.

They continued to stare at Ant's laptop screen, which he'd placed open on the coffee table in front of them. Beyond this, the TV showed the news on mute, but neither of them was taking any notice of it.

"What do I think?" she mumbled. "I think this is messed up. How did you find it?"

He shrugged. "With a name like Ophelia Andrews, I figured she'd be easy enough to search for on the socials. She's not been very active on Facebook or the 'Gram for a while, but she liked Twitter. She was posting a few times a day, right up until six months ago."

"When she died."

"Exactly. I've read everything she posted for the last year and there's nothing to indicate she was depressed or struggling with any alcohol or drug problems."

Camille sat back. "But that doesn't mean she wasn't suffering behind closed doors, Ant. I mean—"

"Yes, yes, I know. Don't get all woke on me, I'm just saying. But then there's this one tweet, posted on the sixteenth of March. Two days before they found her dead."

Camille glanced back at the screen. She'd read and reread the missive so many times in the last five minutes she could probably recite it off by heart. It wasn't a long message, just two lines. But what it said was chilling.

I got followed home tonight. Some guy in a hooded top. I didn't see his face. Was scary as hell, though. If you're a woman and in the Wood Green area, be vigilant. Don't go out alone.

She ended with a selection of relevant hashtags. But the post had got thirty-six likes and two retweets, as well as a reply from someone with a picture of a dolphin for their profile picture saying the same thing happened to them. But there it was, in black and white. Ophelia Andrews had been followed home. Right before she died. A chill ran down Camille's spine as she recalled her own experience the previous night. She swallowed, wondering if Lucy had a Twitter account, wondering if she'd written anything that indicated the same had happened to her.

She shook her head as if this would somehow unjumble her thoughts and make sense of all the scary, conflicting notions whizzing around in her brain.

"It's pretty scary, hey?" Ant whispered, leaning into her. "What do you think?"

Camille continued to stare at the screen. What did she think? She thought this could very well be proof that something weird was going on. Had the police seen this message? Had they investigated Ophelia's claims before pronouncing her death as not being foul play? She shook her head again and braced herself. She had to say something.

I was followed home too, Ant. Last night. By a man in a hood.

She had the words queued up, ready to come out, but she had trouble putting any sound behind them. She opened her mouth but shut it again. Jesus. What was this? Ant was her best friend. He could help her navigate this terrifying experience.

So, tell him.

She opened her mouth.

"Do you want a brew?" he asked, getting up and breaking her focus before she had a chance to speak.

"Umm. Yes. Please. Coffee."

"Coming right up. I think we're going to need it. There's more."

"There's more?" She glanced up at him and he raised his eyebrows with a nod.

"Oh yes. Give me two minutes."

Whilst Ant busied himself in the kitchen, Camille clicked off the macabre tweet and scrolled through Ophelia Andrews' timeline. She seemed a cool girl, funny in places, but none of it really sank in. Camille's mind was too fogged with other things. She was thinking about Mark, about the possibility that he might have something to do with these poor girls' deaths. It still didn't add up. But there was that one time. She'd told no one about it, not even Erica. But maybe she should. It could cast things in a new light. The only problem was, like with being followed, her recollection was unclear, and she worried her stressed brain might have made up a lot of what she remembered. It happened. It happened a lot. Plus, she was embarrassed. That was a big part of it too. Because to admit to these things happening was to admit she was weak and scared and much more vulnerable than she ever liked to think about.

"There we go," Ant said, placing a steaming mug down on the table next to the laptop and settling back beside her, clutching his own mug. "I put some sugar in it. It's horrible, this coffee."

"Yeah, it is," she said, making no move to pick up her mug. "So, what else did you want to show me?"

"Take a look at this," he leaned forward and clicked on another tab on the laptop screen, showing an article and a photo of Mark's face.

Camille stiffened, having already seen too much of him this week. She narrowed her eyes at the screen. "What is it?"

"After I finished looking up Ophelia, I did some more digging on golden boy too. He's doing very well for himself, Cam. Very well."

All right. Thanks a lot. Isn't everyone? Move on.

Ant turned to look at her as if expecting more of a reaction. "This article is about him moving into politics. It sounds like he's got a lot of people behind him. Kingmakers, they call them. Private funders, business owners. He's being set up as a big player. Maybe the next London mayor, they're saying."

She shrugged. "Great. Good for him. He'll do well. He's ambitious, charming. But it doesn't mean he's a murderer."

"No, it doesn't. But the more I investigated him, the less I could find. Now I'm no clever investigative journalist like you." As he said this, he nudged her. It was playful, but any encouragement just felt bittersweet. "But there's hardly anything about his past. He's squeaky clean. If he's on social media at all, then it's new profiles starting around March 2020 and dealing only with his bid for Parliament."

"Still doesn't mean anything."

"I know. We said that. But if he's cleaned up so much of his past, what's to say he's not trying to erase everything linked to him pre-2020 ... Or *everyone*?" He raised his head and grimaced. "Do you have any dirt on him?"

Camille looked away but clearly couldn't hide the resentment on her face, because Ant leaned around to catch her eye.

"What is it?"

She waved him away. "It's nothing. It's stupid. I don't even remember what happened. Not properly."

"But something happened?"

She drew in a deep breath. Was she doing this? "Mark was always a forthright guy," she started, unsure how she was going to present this but hoping the words would come to her. "He liked to be number one. A real alpha male type. He was the oldest of three boys and from a very rich family. I don't think he'd ever had anyone say 'no' to him."

Anthony sat back and made a low, growling noise. "I see."

"Yeah, but the thing is, he was a proper gentleman. Most of the time. He was sweet, accommodating, seemed to really care about my feelings. Only one night we were drunk after a party and I remember he got kind of rough." She looked into her hands, which were clasped together in her lap. "As I say, I was drunk too, so it's sort of hazy. And even now I'm not sure how much of it actually happened or whether it was a dream or my mind playing tricks or . . ." She trailed off and rubbed at her lips with the heel of her thumb. It wasn't coming out the way she wanted. It sounded worse than it was.

Or did it?

Was that her making excuses for him like she always had?

"Rough?" Ant said. "What do you mean by rough?"

She sighed. "As I say, we were both steaming drunk. I remember we had sex, but that it wasn't nice. It didn't feel right. I don't think I told him to stop exactly, but I wasn't into it, you know?"

"Did he know you weren't into it?"

"I don't know. It's all too blurry in my memory. It's why I've never talked about it. And next to what some women must go through, it was nothing. And this sort of thing happens, doesn't it? I was drunk. So was he. He probably didn't realise."

Ant sat forward and steepled his fingers under his chin. "It shouldn't have happened, should it? People like Mark. They think they can take from people with no consequence."

"Hey, come on. You're talking like he's guilty of killing those girls. They were both ruled as no foul play involved, remember?"

"He's guilty of something." He had this in his teeth now, she could tell. Anthony Campbell was a very loyal friend and he loved a bit of drama as much as anyone. He glared at Camille. "Something's not right, don't you think?"

"Maybe." She closed her eyes, sensing what she was about to say next.

Should she tell him?

She didn't want to get him more riled up than he already was, but things had stepped up a gear.

"The thing is, Ant, I think I was followed home too. Like Ophelia."

"What?"

"Last night. On my way home from The Huntsman. A dark figure in a hood. Same as in her tweet."

"Bloody hell, Cam. Why didn't you tell me?"

"Because I wasn't certain! I'm still not. It could have been someone out for an evening stroll. And I'm fine."

"Aww, babe. That's bad. Were you scared?"

"Yes. I was terrified. But I wonder now if I was just scaring myself. It happens, doesn't it?"

"Maybe Ophelia thought the same thing. Then she ended up dead."

He had a point. "What should I do? Go to the police?"

"We could." But he grimaced at the suggestion. "But not yet. We need more evidence. You know what the police are like. They'll dismiss it out of hand with nothing concrete. Then you're labelled a kook and anything you say after that will be taken with a pinch of salt. No. We need to do some more digging." He turned to her with an almost manic expression on his face. "You need to write that article, Cam! Expose the fucker. This could be your big break. You could get a book out of it. A Netflix docuseries. Think of the fame."

"Stop it," she told him. "Two women have died. It's not funny."

"And I'm not trying to be. I'm serious. Come on, you agree with me, don't you? Something is off here. We need to get to the bottom of it."

"I don't know, Ant." She leaned forward and picked up her mug of coffee. It had cooled down sufficiently for her to take a big gulp. It was still bitter, even with the sugar, but the caffeine was needed.

What to do?

Because maybe there was a story here. She didn't want to write about her own experience with Mark, but maybe if she spoke to Lucy's friends, Ophelia's too, then she could find out what happened once and for all. It would appease Ant if nothing else. Because he wasn't going to let this go. She closed her eyes and could see Ophelia's tweet imprinted in her mind's eye.

She was followed home.

They were both followed home.

Then one of them died two days later.

She shuddered and opened her eyes. What was the next step? Contact Erica to see if she had any more information? Then it hit her. Of course.

She placed her mug down and pulled Ant's laptop onto her lap.

"What are you doing?" he asked as she opened a new browser window and logged onto Facebook.

"Hang on. You'll see."

The Ex

She found Stephen's profile straight away. They were still friends on the platform despite not speaking in years. She opened his page, Stephen Ainsworth. It said he lived in South London.

"Who's that?" Ant asked.

"He was part of our friendship group at Oxford," she said. "Mark's best friend. I think they stayed in touch after university. I'm wondering if he still knows him."

She clicked on the blue 'message' button and began to type. Her message was brief – *Long time no speak. How are you? What have you been up to?* – that kind of thing, but she finished off saying she needed to speak with him about something important and enquired if they could meet up soon.

"There," she said, sitting back. "He probably won't reply. He probably doesn't even remember me. We were close at one point, but then we—"

"Wait. Look. He's online."

She craned her neck to see that indeed the three dots in the bubble had appeared. A moment later, a reply popped up on the screen.

Hi Camille. Good to hear from you! I'm good thanks. And yes, it would be awesome to meet up. How's tomorrow at 1? My work is just around the corner from Spitalfields Market. We could meet there, get some lunch?

She replied, saying she'd meet him outside Liverpool Street Station and was looking forward to it. She thought that would be the end of their messages, but when he replied a few seconds later, it felt like all the air had been knocked out of her.

I'll see you then. I think I know what you want to talk about. And if I'm right, I agree. It is important. Very important.

Camille raised her head to meet Ant's gaze.

Shit.

Maybe his theory wasn't so fantastical after all. She closed the laptop. Come tomorrow, she'd know more. But she was already feeling wired, and a heavy cloud of anxiety had appeared on the horizon of her soul. For now, she had to try to put all thoughts of Mark and what he may or may not be capable of out of her head. Otherwise, she was going to drive herself mad with worry.

Chapter 9

Camille watched Stephen as he peered across the market hall and waved at the food stall owner, who was walking over with a tray of food and two plastic cups of water.

"You've got to try these tacos," he said with a wink. "They're amazing." He sat upright and smiled at the woman as she placed the paper plates on their table. Three tacos on each plate and piled high with slaw and hot sauce. "Thank you ever so much. They smell a-mazing. As usual."

The woman smiled as she handed over the cups of water before strolling back to her stall. Stephen turned back to Camille and raised his eyebrows eagerly at the plates of food.

"Looks good," she said, eyeing her plate greedily.

"The avocado and black bean ones you've got are fabulous," he said. "I'd say as good as the pork carnitas, if not better. I come here at least twice a week. It's so good." He scooped one of his tacos off the paper plate and attacked it without any glimmer of self-consciousness.

Camille smiled to herself. She didn't remember Stephen being this confident and charismatic back in their university days. But then maybe that was because Mark was such a big character, he'd been in his shadow the whole time. They ate in silence for half a minute before Stephen sat back and picked up a napkin, dabbing at his mouth.

"You know, it's funny," he said, waving a finger in the air, seemingly to help him swallow down the food in his mouth. "I'd thought about contacting you recently. It was daft that we ever fell out of touch."

Camille placed her half-eaten taco down. "I know. Time flies, doesn't it? What is it they say? Life is what happens to you when you're busy making other plans?"

She cringed internally at the words. That might be true for her but, like the others, Stephen had done well for himself. Very well. She took a bite of the taco. It was salty and spicy and tasted delicious. She munched it down as she took in her old friend.

He was now an investment banker at Matrix Advisory Partners and was about to be made vice president. Not bad going, considering he was one of the youngest working there. He'd told her all this as they'd walked here from Liverpool Street Station, with her offering up impressed noises at the news of his success and him playing it down in typical Stephen fashion. He dismissed the banking industry as being full of sharks and wannabe alpha-wolves, saying he had no chance of surviving amongst them, but she could tell he was only being modest. Whether that was for her benefit (she'd been so vague about her own career, it was probably clear to him she wasn't doing so well) or him not wanting to be associated with that brutal, ruthless world, she wasn't sure. But it was endearing, either way.

He frowned at her as he placed the rest of his taco in his mouth and chewed it down. "So come on then, Cam," he said, once finished. "What's this important matter you want to talk about?"

She sniffed, feeling embarrassed suddenly and a little confused after the way he'd responded online. "I don't know. It's silly perhaps. It's just . . . Mark. Are you still in touch with him?"

"I see." He glanced around before leaning over the table. "I knew this would be about Mark. Everything was always about Mark, wasn't it?"

It was Camille's turn to frown. "We were a good group, I thought. All equal."

"I know. I'm joking. But that's why I knew what you wanted to talk about. Mark Kennedy. You've heard the rumours, haven't you?"

Wow. Despite his cryptic message, she hadn't really been expecting him to bring this up. Perhaps, too, she'd been hoping the rumours were all just pie in the sky. Or her and Anthony looking for things that weren't there to bring a little excitement into their mundane lives.

"What do you know? Have you heard something?"

He twisted his mouth to one side, head swaying side to side. "Yes and no. I've been on social media and read what a few keyboard warriors are saying about him. But you've got to appreciate, Cam. He's a relatively young and privileged white man doing very well for himself. He's going to have his detractors."

She nodded. Yes. That's what she'd thought too. She was about to tell Stephen this when he raised his hand.

"But, then again," – she almost thought he was going to say there was no smoke without fire, but he didn't – "that's three ex-girlfriends that have died in the last year. It does seem a bit odd. Whichever way you look at it."

"Three?" she cried out, before catching herself and lowering her voice. "Three ex-girlfriends? I only know about Lucy and Ophelia. Who's the third?"

Stephen's hand hovered over his remaining two tacos. "A girl called Charlotte Browning. Mark met her during his gap year in Thailand. She seemed nice. They dated for about six months."

Charlotte from Thailand. She'd heard Mark mention her once or twice. She'd tried to not listen. "What happened to her?"

"This is the thing you've got to remember, Cam. None of these deaths are being classified as anything other than tragic accidents or, in Lucy's case, tragic stupidity." He sighed. "That was nasty, sorry. I didn't mean it. I just can't believe it. Poor Luce. It's so sad."

"I know. And me neither. She had everything going for her."

"Were you two still in touch?" She shook her head and he baulked. "Oh, shit. Yeah. I remember now. Her and Mark. Sorry."

"It's fine. There's been a lot of water under a lot of bridges since then. But tell me, what happened to Charlotte?"

"Fell down the stairs in her house," came the reply. "Awful business. Fell and broke her neck. Died instantly. But she had alcohol in her system, apparently. They think she slipped on something."

Camille sucked air through her teeth. "Yikes."

"I know. Grim, isn't it? But it does sound like it was an accident. I know it's easy to jump to conclusions, but we can't go labelling the guy a murderer just on a couple of coincidences."

"Three exes though. In one year. It makes you think." She finished the food in her hand and swallowed it down with a drink of water. In front of her, Stephen was attacking his next taco. He caught her watching him and shrugged.

"It's a messy business."

"What, eating tacos or all this about Mark?"

He laughed and so did she. It felt good, but she stopped herself. "I take it the two of you are no longer close."

"No. I moved back to London straight away after I graduated, but he stayed in Oxford for a while, if you remember. When he moved here himself, we met up for a few beers, but our friendship had already withered on the vine. I've not seen him in over five years now. I keep tabs on him though, of course, like you do, wind myself up about how well he's doing." Camille couldn't help but let out another chuckle. "Yeah. I do the same. But with the entire group. Erica, Lucy. And you're not doing too bad for yourself. I feel like the runt of the litter."

"Ah, come on. You're a writer. That's amazing."

"I'm a blogger," she said, giving the word as much derision as she felt it required. "And I haven't written a decent article in months. My housemate thinks I should write about Mark, about the rumours. But I won't."

"Yeah, that's probably not a good idea," Stephen said, picking up another napkin and wiping at his hands and face. "Mark is on the rise and has some powerful backers. If you write anything remotely libellous or defamatory without evidence, they'll be down on you like a shit storm. I'd leave it alone if I were you.

The only people who can corroborate any of these rumours are dead. So, you be careful."

The way he said *be careful*, the way he looked at her, made the hairs on the back of her neck stand to attention.

"Oh shit. Is that why you wanted to meet me? Because of Mark? Because I'm one of his exes too?"

She sat back, her mouth hanging open. Fucking hell. This was getting serious.

"Sorry, I didn't want to worry you," Stephen told her. "I'm being over-cautious, that's all. He would never ... Not Mark. You know him. He's not a murderer."

"You sure of that?"

"Pretty sure. Yes." He balled the napkin up and flung it on his plate. "Forget about it, Cam. You aren't on some creepy hit list."

The way he said it, she could tell he was making light of the concept, but it had the opposite effect. "How many others are there?" she asked. "Do you know?"

He sighed. "Three more. You and two others. Leila and Harriet."

"Leila, yes. He was with her before me."

"That's right. She was a nice girl from what I remember. A good laugh. Not that you weren't nice or a good laugh as well." He tilted his head to one side and considered her. "I've freaked you out, haven't I? I'm sorry, Camille. That was the last thing I wanted to do. Please don't dwell on this. It's a few people on the internet putting two and two together and making ten thousand. Mark might be a bit of a prick these days, but he's harmless enough. Until he gets into the government, at least."

"Yes. You're right." But Camille's mind was already working overtime. "Remind me again. Leila . . .?"

"Leila Bloom and if I can remember correctly, it's Harriet Knight. She was a bit of a weird one. He was with her after Lucy. For about a year. She was quite controlling from what Mark told me."

"He'd know all about that."

Stephen tilted his head again and smiled. "It is good to see you again, Cam. I know this is a bit out of the blue, but do you want to get a drink sometime? Tonight maybe?"

"Oh? Umm. I can't. Not tonight. But . . ."

"As friends, I mean," he quickly added. "Just friends. It'd be good to catch up properly. We always had a good laugh, me and you. Why not? And no more talking about Mark Kennedy."

"Can I get back to you? My head's all over the place today. I don't want to say yes and then have to cancel."

"Sure. I understand." He reached into his jacket and came back with a business card. "My details are all on there. Send me a text."

Camille accepted the card and held it up. "Thanks. I will. But I should really get going." She stood and gathered her bag and coat up. "It was nice to see you again."

"It was." He stood and they engaged in an awkward hug before Camille stepped away.

"Best go."

She turned and walked away from the table, sensing his eyes on her as she did. Despite her growing unease, she couldn't help a smile teasing at her lips at the thought of him watching her.

It had been some time since anyone asked her out for a drink. Maybe she'd take him up on his offer.

Just as soon as she was sure her ex-boyfriend wasn't out to kill her.

Chapter 10

She knew Anthony would be waiting by his phone, eager for her to call. So, it didn't surprise her when he answered after one ring.

"Go on then," he said. "What did he say?"

"There's another girl," she said, lowering her voice to a whisper. She was walking back to the house from Hackney Downs station and there were still quite a few people around. "Another dead girl. Another ex of Mark's."

"You are kidding me?"

"A girl called Charlotte who he met on his gap year. She fell down the stairs and broke her neck. She'd been drinking. The authorities ruled it death by misadventure."

She knew this because she'd googled Charlotte Browning the second she'd left Spitalfields Market and read the news report whilst weaving around other pedestrians on her way to the station.

"Stephen said there were three more exes that he knew about," she continued. "Me and two others. Do you think I should be worried? Do you think I should contact Mark and put my mind at ease?"

"How would speaking with him put your mind at ease?"

"I don't know." She gasped. Dusk was around the corner and despite sticking to the main roads, her pace had quickened almost instinctively. "I still think this is all the stuff of conspiracy theories and bored internet trolls."

"And what about what he did to you? What about being followed? No. Screw that. You need to tell someone. You need to tell the police."

"The police? No, Ant. What would I say?"

"You tell them everything we know and let them do the rest. If there's a link between three recent deaths, then they need to know about it. It's too much of a coincidence, if you ask me. You owe it to these women, Cam."

She could see what he was doing, appealing to her sense of morality and sisterhood. But it was working. She pulled her phone from her ear to check the time. It was a few minutes after four. "Okay, fine. I'll go tomorrow."

"We'll go now. Where are you?"

"Making my way up Amhurst Road. I thought I'd stick to the main roads."

"Good girl. I'm just checking now. The nearest police station is that one up on Stoke Newington high street. The one we went to when I got mugged last year. Do you want to meet me at the house and we can walk up together? It'll only take us fifteen minutes."

"I don't know, Ant. Are you sure this is wise? I worry we might have gone down the rabbit hole with both feet if we involve the police. We aren't just getting overexcited about this, are we? Because . . . you know . . . we're bored and out of work?"

"Hey, Miss. Speak for yourself. I'm not bored. And I'm not out of work."

Which was true, he wasn't. He had his job at the bistro. But he hadn't had an audition in at least three months, and she didn't remember the last time he'd had a paid acting role.

She ran her tongue along her bottom teeth. "Fine. I'll be home in five. Get yourself ready."

"Don't worry about me, Cambo," he told her. "I'm always ready."

*   *   *

Thirty minutes later and the two of them were sitting in an interview room at Stoke Newington police station exchanging furtive glances as a gruff middle-aged man who'd introduced himself as DI Richard Shaw continued to stare at them.

"You do know wasting police time is a crime, don't you?"

He sounded northern and had a world-weariness to him that was evident the moment he'd approached them in the waiting room and instructed them to follow him. It was like he already suspected they were wasting his time.

"I do. We do," Camille answered, putting on her poshest voice. She didn't know why. "But you must understand, sir, we didn't know what to do. These three women have all died in mysterious ways. As well as this, other things have been happening that seem awfully strange and too much of a coincidence not to be investigated . . ."

She trailed off as the police officer let out a loud sigh. His pen was still poised over the yellow notepad in front of him with the words 'three women' and 'Mark Kennedy' up top, but he had written nothing for the last ten minutes. "All I'm hearing, Miss Fletcher, is that some of your friends have died, tragically – and I am very sorry for your loss – but you said yourself, the deaths *have* already been investigated."

"But what about the links to Mark?" Ant asked. "He knew all these girls at one time. They were his ex-girlfriends."

DI Shaw eyed him with a neutral expression, but Camille noticed the contempt and frustration bubbling under the surface. The same way it did when he looked at her. "Why would Mr Kennedy risk being tied to these deaths?" he said. "If he is, as you suggest, removing people from his past who might cause him problems, don't you think if there was any evidence at all he was involved, we'd find out? Surely killing three women is going to look worse on his CV than anything they have on him."

His eyes flittered between the two of them, a wry smile twitching at the corner of his mouth. It made Camille want to flip the table over, made her want to grab the pen from him and stab it into his hand.

But this was what she'd expected coming here. And the main reason she didn't want to inform the police of her suspicions. Because they were just that – suspicions, theories – and the more she'd spoken them out loud, the more crackpot and paranoid she'd sounded. There was no evidence that Mark was involved. There wasn't even any evidence these girls died in any other way than what had been reported. A suicide and two deaths by misadventure, with no one else involved or anyone suspected of being at the scene when they happened. If the police didn't consider them as murders, there was little point in searching for a murderer.

Camille flinched as her phone vibrated and chimed from her bag on her lap. DI Shaw glanced at her with a withering look on his face. He nodded at the bag. "Do you need to get that?"

She shook her head. "No. Sorry. I should have switched it off."

DI Shaw pulled in a long breath and exhaled the air slowly down his nose. It felt like he wanted them to know he was being patient with them. But in doing so, it kind of had the opposite effect. And maybe that was his actual point.

"I'm sorry, Miss Fletcher. But these are all closed cases. My colleagues didn't view them as anything other than what they were: unfortunate deaths of young women. And as far as the link to Mark Kennedy is concerned," he shrugged his shoulders, "who knows? Maybe he attracted a certain kind of person. Someone a little unhinged and unsettled, who struggled with their own demons. It happens, doesn't it? Hell, what do I know? This Mark Kennedy chap may have broken these girls' hearts, which eventually led them to suicide or drinking so much they didn't wake up or fell down the stairs. And if that's the case, maybe he is to blame in some way. But as far as what I can do, and what the police can do, I'm afraid there's no case to follow up here. The rulings have been made and the cases are closed."

"Broke their hearts?" Anthony repeated. "Jesus. It's like the last five years never happened. You do know we're all watching you now, don't you? Mr MET police officer."

Camille dug a sharp elbow into his ribs. This wasn't helping. Not one bit. In turn, DI Shaw leaned back in his chair and laid his pen down. "I think this interview has reached its conclusion, don't you?"

"What about what Cam told you about how Mark was with her? About that night? He's not a nice man. He's got form."

DI Shaw regarded Camille with heavy-lidded eyes. "Do you want to make a statement, Ms Fletcher?"

"I don't know. I—"

"Because, let me tell you, if you are going to report an historic attack of this kind, there will be a lot asked of you. Are you prepared for that? For the fallout? I'm not trying to discourage you and if you do want to report it, we shall take it extremely seriously" – he glanced at Anthony – "as we always do. But you need to make sure you're one hundred percent certain of your story."

He looked back at her, waiting for her reply. He didn't blink. A few seconds went by. Camille looked into her lap.

"No. I don't want to report it. I'm still not sure exactly what happened and I couldn't say for certain."

"Are you sure?" DI Shaw asked.

She didn't look up, just nodded. There were tears in her eyes, but they were there for many reasons and remembrance of what Mark had done that night was only a fraction of it. Mainly, they were tears of shame and embarrassment. She suddenly felt vulnerable and foolish. Like she was a child playing at being an adult.

"I'm sure," she said, finally.

"Okay then. Thank you for coming in. I understand why you did, but let me assure you again, if there had been any suggestion at all that these women were murdered, we would have investigated it fully."

Anthony 'tsked' loudly beside her, but Camille ignored him. "Thank you," she told the police officer. "We're sorry for wasting your time."

"That's fine," he said, screeching his chair back and standing, gesturing for them to do the same. "It's better to be safe than sorry about these things. And I'd rather people were vigilant than not."

Camille and Ant both got to their feet and DI Shaw led them out of the interview room and through into the reception area. None of them spoke until they got there and then it was only a polite goodbye before the two friends shuffled out into the chill of the early evening air.

Once outside, Anthony tutted again and shook his head. "Can you believe that? What a fucking joke."

Camille set off walking. She'd had enough of all this. "But he's right," she called back. "It's all hearsay and gossip. We need to drop this. I mean it, Ant. Come on, let's go home."

"But those girls . . .?"

"What about them?" she snapped, spinning around to glare at him. "Don't you think it's a bit sick what we're doing? It's starting to feel so to me. It's as if we want this to be true for our own sense of drama or something. The best thing we can do for Lucy and the others is let them rest in peace."

"That's what he wants."

She turned around and carried on walking. "Seriously, Ant. Give it a rest." Her fists were balled up tight and her jaw was rigid with frustration. At Ant, but mainly at herself. For getting caught up in believing those poor women had lost their lives in nefarious circumstances. They were real people with real lives and problems, and they deserved to be honoured as such, rather than being reduced to elements of some salacious story.

As she headed down Stoke Newington Road, she felt the tension leaving her shoulders and her face relaxed. By the time Ant caught up with her as she turned down Amhurst Road, she was feeling a little more positive.

It was awfully sad that Lucy and the other two women were dead, but it wasn't anything to do with Mark. And she wasn't in danger. The feeling she felt now was as if you had gone to the doctor with severe back pain and discovered you had a slipped disc, rather than spinal cancer or something more serious. The pain was still there, but you didn't seem to suffer as much with it when you knew it wasn't going to kill you. The Buddhists had a term for it – the two arrows of suffering. The first arrow is the actual pain and the second is all the destructive thinking you have about the pain. She was bored and desperate for something to happen and she'd been overthinking things.

But that stopped now.

Yet as she pulled her phone out of her bag and checked the message that had arrived whilst she was in the police station, the ground was once more pulled from under her. She stopped dead, her heart pounding as she stared at the notification on her screen.

"What is it?" Ant asked.

She didn't respond. She was too busy opening Instagram and going to her direct messages. There it was. One unread message.

The Ex

From Bl00mer33. Camille already knew who this was, but clicking through to her profile page confirmed it. Leila Bloom. The girl Mark had been going out with before her. She clicked back and onto the message without taking a breath. What Leila had written was brief and to the point. Just two lines. But as Camille read them and re-read them, she felt dizzy and sick all at once.

Hi, you don't know me, but I think we both know the same man. Mark Kennedy. Can we meet tomorrow? We REALLY need to talk!

Chapter 11

It was a pleasant day as Camille exited the tube station and headed along Cranbourne Street towards Leicester Square. She'd arranged to meet Leila in a coffee shop in Soho, so Oxford Circus was probably the nearest tube stop, but as she was early, and the sun was shining, she felt the walk would do her good.

Taking a right down the side of the Prince Charles Cinema she stopped to take in the upcoming features. She loved visiting the old art-house cinema, with its sloping floor and art deco features, but hadn't visited in such a long time. They were showing *On the Waterfront* in the coming week. Maybe she'd ask Ant if he wanted to come and see it with her. A bit of Brando on a Wednesday evening would be a real treat. But more than that, a trip to the cinema was an agreeable and innocent pastime. The sort of thing regular people did. Not those obsessed with whether their ex was a killer. If nothing else, it would take her out of her head and inject some much-needed normality into her life.

Though as she left the cinema behind, she realised no amount of positive thinking or future projections could shake the feeling of dread that lay heavy in her stomach all morning. She wasn't sure what Leila was going to say when they met, but she didn't expect it to be encouraging or make her any less paranoid. There had been a moment this morning, on waking, when she'd considered cancelling the meeting. She meant what she'd told Ant last night. They had to put this morbid business behind them and move on, stop being ridiculous. But her innate writer's curiosity had quickly trumped these notions. So, here she was.

Unfortunately, that same writer's curiosity and ability to create monsters out of shadows was with her as she turned off Wardour Street and found herself in a deserted passageway. Away from the cut and thrust of the main strip, it felt too quiet and her footsteps echoed off the buildings on either side of her. She quickened her pace, trying to stay present and away from her own toxic thinking.

She was being silly.

No one was following her.

But as she got to the end of the row, she heard a second set of footsteps behind her. Hurrying to the end of the passageway without looking back, she took a right down Berwick Street and found, to her relief, the thoroughfare busy with people on both sides of the street. But as she risked a glance over her shoulder, she saw a figure emerge from the side street behind her and any relief she'd felt turned to abject concern. The person was wearing a large coat and had the hood pulled up over their head. Considering it was such a nice day, they already looked out of place on this street, full of people in short sleeves and summer jackets. But the way they had their head down so the hood was obscuring their face made them look even more sinister. Camille let out a yelp and hurried onwards, looking back every few seconds to check if they were still behind her. Each time she did, her heart did another somersault. They were walking at a steady pace and keeping their distance, but they were still behind her, still coming.

She ducked down a narrow side street and ran to the end, hoping to throw them off. Coming out on Hopkins Street, she took a right onto Broadwick Street and stopped on the corner to catch her breath.

Jesus.

Was this actually happening?

Again?

The answer came as she peered down the street and was horrified to see the hooded figure was still following her. She carried on, running now as she travelled along Broadwick Street and veered right onto Poland Street. A small book shop stood a few doors down on her side of the pavement and as she approached, she saw through the window it was full of people. Almost instinctively, she went inside.

A man standing near the entrance looked up from the book he was reading as she stood panting in the doorway. Regaining her composure, she moved further into the shop and over to the counter. From this position, she had a clear view through the large storefront window out onto the street. Picking a book up at random, she held it in front of her face, peering over the top as she watched and waited. A second went by. Then another.

Shit.

She stiffened as the hooded figure appeared, but whoever it was walked straight past the window. They were moving at the same speed as before and didn't seem to be searching too hard for her.

Was this just another coincidence, or was she going mad?

She lowered the book from in front of her face, seeing she'd picked up a hardcover copy of Edgar Allan Poe's short stories. She flicked back to the page she'd opened it on, her stomach turning over as she saw the title of the story, *The Man in the Crowd.*

Jesus.

Another coincidence? Or was this the universe trying to tell her something?

Was it a warning from the cosmos?

She flicked through to the contents page, her gaze falling on more troubling titles: *A Descent into the Maelstrom. The Premature Burial.*

"Bloody hell."

She slammed the book shut and placed it back on the shelf before hurrying out onto the street. The hooded figure was nowhere in sight, and she allowed herself a moment to relax and settle herself. This had to stop now. She was becoming a nervous wreck. She pulled out her phone and was dismayed to see she was now ten minutes late for her meeting. Should she text Leila to say she couldn't make it? This felt like the final straw for her, as she had already been having doubts.

If the universe was sending her such blatant signs, shouldn't she pay attention to them?

A Descent into the Maelstrom? Jesus.

She certainly felt like she was descending into something – madness, maybe. And the last thing she wanted was a premature burial.

She went to turn back but stopped herself. No. That wouldn't be fair. And La Petite Place, the coffee shop where they'd arranged to meet, was only a minute's walk from here. Besides, she'd come too far now. She needed to know. Otherwise, she might be jumping at shadows for the rest of her life. Turning around, she set off walking towards the coffee shop. She'd hear what Leila had to say. She owed her that, at least.

Chapter 12

Leila must have recognised Camille from her Instagram profile because she raised her hand and waved her over as soon as she entered the coffee shop.

"Hey there," Camille said, her stomach knotted with nerves as she sauntered over to the table. "Leila, yes?"

She smiled and held out her hand. "That's right. Hi Camille, nice to meet you."

"And you. Call me Cami, please. Everyone does."

"Great." They shook hands before Leila gestured for her to sit.

"So, were you in the same year as me?" Camille asked, shuffling onto the seat and placing her bag down on the adjacent chair

"I think so. I graduated in 2010. I was at St John's. History of Art. You were at Balliol, right? Same as Mark."

Camille tensed. She hadn't even taken her jacket off and they were already getting into it. "Yes, same as Mark. Studying English."

Leila nodded knowingly. "I remember you. Well, I was aware of you, you know. Mark's new girlfriend. People liked to point you out to me." She stopped and frowned. "Sorry, are you okay? You look like you've seen a ghost."

"Do I? No, I'm fine." She took the time to remove her coat and folded it on top of her bag. It was an attempt to compose herself, but it didn't work. "I'm just curious what it is you wanted to talk about, that's all."

Leila's eyes widened. "Well, isn't it obvious? You must have heard by now, surely. Mark! And more specifically, three of his ex-girlfriends winding up dead."

"I see. Yes. That's what I thought." She glanced about her, noticing her surroundings properly for the first time. The coffee shop was old-fashioned with dark beams over their heads and orange floor tiles that looked like they were from the seventies. Black and white photos adorned most of the wall space. On the table in front of Leila was what looked like a cappuccino, but Camille saw no sign of any wait staff.

"So, you know why I asked to meet?"

Camille bit her lip as she met Leila's gaze. Her dark eyes were wide and intense looking and appeared to be piercing into her soul. But other than that, she was attractive. Slim, full lips, with naturally blonde hair cut into a shaggy bob that ended just over her shoulders. Her eyes grew wider as if urging Camille to respond.

"You think Mark had something to do with those women's deaths?"

"Don't you?"

"I don't know. I've seen what people are saying online. But it's just trolls, isn't it? Mark would never hurt anyone."

Leila sat forward and spoke in a low voice. "Has anything weird happened to you recently?" When Camille didn't respond straight away, she continued. "Because someone followed me home. A week ago. It was dark, so I didn't get a good look at them, but it was terrifying. Every time I slowed down, they did too. Every time I speeded up, so did they. In the end, I panicked and jumped into a black cab. Ever since then, I've not been able to get it out of my head that these things are all linked. Then you popped up in my 'suggested profiles to follow' section on Instagram and I knew I had to connect. Just to see and . . . What is it?"

Camille sat back. Clearly, her expression had given her away. "I was followed too," she whispered. "Definitely once, a few days ago, and maybe just now on my way to meet you. Someone in a big coat with their hood up. I was terrified. Both times. But I've been trying to put it down to paranoia. My imagination running away with itself."

"Yes. That's what I was doing as well. At first. But that's how society conditions us to act and think, isn't it? We play down our fears. We pretend everything is fine because we don't want to make a fuss or risk looking like a hysterical crank. But maybe a lot more women would be alive today if they hadn't played down their concerns."

Camille nodded. Leila was certainly convincing. She liked the way she talked. She was rather scary but seemed bold and strong-willed.

"It's easy to dismiss these ideas as just paranoia or whatever," Leila went on, picking up the spoon from the side of her coffee cup and waving it in the air. "But something is going on here, Cami. I know it."

"Do you think it was Mark?" she asked. "Who followed you, I mean. I didn't see the person's face either time. But their build was about the same as his from what I remember."

"It could have been him. Could have been someone he paid to do his dirty work. People do that. I'm sure of it. Those with enough power and money. And you say Mark would never hurt anyone, but I know different."

"What? Really?"

Leila threw a furtive glance around the café and Camille followed her lead. Most of the tables were occupied, but everyone seemed too submerged in their own life dramas to be interested in them.

"He was horrible to me," Leila started. "Especially towards the end of our relationship. Cruel and nasty and certainly abusive emotionally."

"Oh no. I'm so sorry," Camille said. "That's awful."

"Yeah. There were a couple of times I wondered about reaching out to you when you and he started hanging around together. And more so when you became a couple. But I didn't want to appear like the wronged woman. You know how it is. Another role society casts us in." She shrugged. "But I saw a really different side of him. He could turn in an instant if things weren't going his way. I saw him hit a guy once, too. In a bar."

"Whoa. Was he violent to you?"

"Not as such. But a few times he'd do violent things when we were arguing. Punch the wall, smash a glass. Things that made me think the potential was there." She suddenly looked up and locked eyes with Camille. "Was he violent with you?"

"No." The word fell out of her mouth before she had a chance to really consider the question. It was a stock response. But she saw now Leila was right. It was the way she'd been conditioned to act. And maybe it was time to stop letting the world dictate her behaviour so damn much. She swallowed and tried again. "I mean, I'm not totally sure. There was one night when we were both drunk and he got rather rough with me in the bedroom. I told him to stop but . . . It was a long time ago and I was pretty far gone, so it's rather hazy. I just remember it not feeling right."

"Well, that's enough, I'd say," Leila said. "Have you told anyone about your worries? About being followed?"

"My best friend Ant knows. He's a good guy. He actually made me go to the police, but I felt they were very dismissive. The police officer I spoke with made me feel stupid."

"The fucker," Leila whispered. "It's brave is what it is."

"I even told them about Lucy and the other girls. How I thought their deaths were linked."

"Let me guess. He said the police didn't consider their deaths to be suspicious. If they weren't murdered, there was no murderer to look for."

"Something like that."

"Yeah. That's what they said to me, too. Talked to me like I was that same wronged woman. A crazy ex-girlfriend trying to get her ex into trouble because he dumped her. But that's not who I am. I know it." She leaned forward. "Well, that settles it, Cami. If the police won't do anything, then we'll have to do it ourselves."

"What do you mean?"

"I mean, we need to gather our own evidence. We need to find out what really happened to those poor girls. Prove Mark Kennedy is responsible. Or, at the very least, we prove conclusively that he isn't, so we don't have to look over our shoulders for the rest of our lives. We have to step up, Camille. We have to do what the police won't. Are you with me?"

Camille swallowed again, but it caught in her throat and when she spoke, it came out in a strained croak. "Erm. Yes. I think. But the police—"

"Don't you want to get the bastard for what he did to you?"

She spat the words out and they hung in the air between them as Camille studied her new acquaintance's face. It sounded as if Leila was making this personal, maybe even using the women's deaths as some kind of excuse to get back at Mark. She'd hardly blinked the whole time they'd been sitting here and the muscles at the edge of her jaw were pulsing with tension.

Did she want to punish Mark?

Was that it?

Camille looked away, admonishing herself for thinking that way. Because whatever Leila's motivation, something wasn't right here. And if that was the case, maybe they did need to take matters into their own hands. Leila was certainly intense and somewhat daunting, but she was also on Camille's side. And it was true what they said, there was safety in numbers.

Camille sucked in a deep breath and straightened her back as she made a mental commitment to herself. She'd do it.

She'd work with Leila to find out the truth. That was what a real investigative journalist would do after all. What a proper grown-up writer would do. Besides, she was in too deep to turn back now. What if their suspicions were correct? Not only did these women need justice, but her own life was in danger. Either one of them could be next on Mark's hit list.

She leaned forward. "Yes, I want to get him," she whispered. "I'm in."

"Great." Leila pushed her cup of coffee to one side and placed both hands on the table. "Now let's go get a proper drink and talk about how we nail this fucker."

Chapter 13

Camille sipped at her gin and tonic and watched Leila as she scribbled down names in her notebook.

"That's everyone then," she said, underlining the last name on the list. "In chronological order of when Mark dated them. Unless there are other exes of his you know about."

Camille cast her attention down the page. There were six names, three with an ominous line crossed through them. "No. That list looks conclusive. But there could be more we don't know about. After he was with Ophelia. Mark always struck me as the sort of man who didn't like to be single for too long."

"Have you read anything anywhere about a partner?" Leila asked.

Camille shook her head. "No. Everything online just talks about his political career and he's not quite famous enough yet for it to be common interest. One feature on him that I read said he was quite guarded about his private life."

Leila looked up and waved her pen at her. "Exactly. Another red flag. But this is why we're here, right? It's why we need to do this. If there are more women on this list, we need to warn them. That's if they're not already dead."

She said this in a sarcastic tone, but Camille suspected it was a defence mechanism more than her being flippant. She took a big gulp of her drink. It wasn't the nicest gin and tonic she'd ever tasted, but the pub they'd chosen to begin their investigations in wasn't the nicest pub she'd ever visited. Yet The Unruly Cow had been the closest establishment that sold alcohol and the apt name appealed to them. It was also quiet and large enough that they could sit away from the handful of other lunchtime drinkers and talk without being overheard.

"We have to be careful, though," Camille said. "There isn't any evidence tying Mark to these deaths, so we need to be one hundred per cent certain before we go public. He's got friends in high places and from what I've heard, he's become very litigious."

Leila pointed the pen at her and closed one eye. "No evidence . . . yet! But we'll get some. Then we'll get him. Don't you worry."

"Are you so sure he's got something to do with it?"

It was a pointless question. There seemed no doubt that Leila believed whole-heartedly that Mark was involved. But that self-assuredness was partly what had attracted Camille to her and a big reason she was sitting here now. Leila was bold and loud and angry and full of momentum, and she certainly talked a good fight. If she believed Mark needed taking down, then so did Camille. And she was ready to follow her new friend into the lion's den.

"Of course I'm sure," Leila replied. "Men like Mark think they can do whatever they want, to whoever they want, with impunity. As he's gained more power and influence and gathered more 'yes men' around him, I can only imagine that belief has grown astronomically. Why wouldn't he want to erase those who posed a threat to his meteoric rise?"

"But *do* we pose a threat? Are we really on his radar?" She couldn't help smiling to herself, proud she'd contributed to Leila's use of space metaphors. But her new ally didn't seem to notice.

Leila set her pen down and leaned over the table. "How do you think it would look if we both told our stories to the press? He's a violent man with a short temper who takes what he wants when he wants it. That doesn't look good on the ballot papers, does it? And who knows what these other girls had on him?" She sat back and shook her head. "No. He's a toxic and dangerous man, Camille. We need to expose him for what he is. We need to take him down. It's the only way we can be certain he won't come for us next."

Camille exhaled slowly. Everything was happening so fast, but she suspected Leila was right. She also realised now what had been troubling her this whole time, ever since she'd read that Facebook comment linking Mark to Lucy's death. Because despite her misgivings about whether or not he was responsible, she'd never once questioned whether he was actually capable of killing. Yes, she'd been unsure of his motives and unclear whether he would have done it given his situation, but the actual act of putting his hands around someone's throat and squeezing until the life left them? She could easily see him doing that. There'd always been a darkness behind his eyes, and, behind closed doors, a ruthlessness in his demeanour that had excited her briefly but quickly became too intense. It had been a shock when she'd found out he'd been cheating on her with Lucy, but her overriding emotion wasn't heartbreak but betrayal that her friend had done that to her. But even these feelings had quickly turned to relief. And maybe even a passing concern for Lucy's well-being.

What Camille still had trouble imagining was Leila and Mark as a couple. But maybe that was why they hadn't lasted. Even back when he and Camille had been just friends, he was exhibiting signs of someone who didn't like his authority being called into question. He needed to be in control and hated being challenged, especially by women. What Leila had said about him being violent to her made sense.

"Okay, so here's how it looks," Leila said, turning the notepad around so they could both look at it. "We know about Charlotte before me and Lucy, who came after you and, more recently, Ophelia Andrews. Which leaves just one more woman on the list unaccounted for. Harriet Knight, who Mark began a relationship with after Lucy, but while still in Oxford."

"How do you know about her?" Camille asked.

Leila shrugged. "I've done my research. I'm a member of a few Balliol alumni groups and I messaged a girl who was a classmate of Mark's. They never went out, but she knew him. She mentioned your name and Harriet's, too."

"Who was it? Who messaged you?"

"I can't remember." She screwed her face up. "A girl called Joanne, I think. Does it matter?"

"I guess not. Have you spoken to Harriet?"

"Not yet. I messaged her at the same time I messaged you, but she's not gotten back to me as yet. I've engaged in some research on her though, as I'm sure you're not surprised to hear by now." She grinned impishly at Camille, which made her cheeks feel warm. She sat forward as Leila continued. "She and Mark were together for about eight months. But that's another thing. All of Mark Kennedy's relationships last about the same amount of time – between six and eight months. Which, I'd say, is enough time for the honeymoon period to fade away and him to show his true colours."

Camille finished her drink and placed the glass down, considering Leila's words. She was a savvy girl and made a lot of sense. "It's a shame she's not got back to you. Has she read the message?"

"No. Not yet."

"We need to talk to her. Is she in London?"

"Sheffield. I know she works as a solicitor. But that's all I've got so far."

Camille chewed her lip. "There is another possibility here. Isn't there?" She eyed Leila, wondering if she should voice the thought forming in her mind. She decided to go for it. "What if Lucy and the others were murdered, but it wasn't Mark?"

"What? No! Why say that?"

"I don't know. It's just an idea that came to me. Mark is still the linking factor, of course. But what if it's not him but someone who knows him? You hear about it, don't you? It could be one of his investors. Or a jealous girlfriend."

"Seriously? You're blaming a woman?" Leila drained her glass and waved it at Camille. "So, is it you, Camille? Are you killing off your old rivals? Or perhaps you think it's me? Jesus."

"No. I'm not saying that. But if we're agreed on the fact these deaths are more than a coincidence, then surely it's critical to explore all the options. I want to get to the bottom of this once and for all like you do. But . . . well . . . I suppose I still don't want to believe Mark – someone I loved once – would do something like this. Or that anyone would."

She looked away as Leila continued to stare at her. She felt stupid and guilty, too. Because it was true. Mark's star was on the rise and if he'd behaved with these other women anything like he had done with her and Leila, then it would be in his best interests to silence them. It was doubtful anyone had any actual proof of what he'd done, but if enough voices spoke out against him, people would listen. Because there was no smoke without fire. If they spoke out, the world would see he was a violent and toxic individual and they cancelled people for far less these days.

"Listen, Cam. I like you," Leila said. "And I need your help, but if you have any doubts about what we're going to do, you need to tell me. The more we dig into Mark's life, the more dangerous it could get."

"I know that. And I do want to know what's going on. I was even considering writing an article about it all." She laughed, but Leila didn't. "Sorry. I'm not making light of it. I suppose I've just been of two minds about everything up to now."

"Yes. I can see that," Leila said. "But it's time to step up, Cam. Don't you want to know the truth?"

She examined Leila's face.

"But what if the truth is that Lucy did commit suicide? What if Ophelia and Charlotte did die in tragic accidents?"

"Then we'll know for sure. And we'll walk away. But, right now, there are too many unanswered questions for me to leave this. If there's even an ounce of uncertainty about the nature of those women's deaths, then I want to find out exactly what happened. For my sanity as well as my safety. Because if it is Mark killing these women, then I could be next. Or it could be you. And the police have made it very clear to us both they aren't interested in exploring any other theories. So, Camille, I'm only going to ask you this once. Are you in? Do you want to help me find out the truth about those deaths, whatever it may be?"

A shudder shot down Camille's spine. Leila certainly knew how to rouse a person's spirit. And that's what she needed right now. Someone to take the lead. To push her into action. Because Leila wasn't just a great motivational speaker, what she was saying was important. Lucy and Camille might not have been friends towards the end, but they were close once. She owed it to her to find out the truth.

She raised her head, teeth chattering as a shiver of adrenaline flowed through her. "Yes," she said. "I want to help. So, what do we do now?"

Leila looked at her watch. "Do you have anything you need to do this afternoon?"

Bloody hell.

If only she knew.

Camille wished she could say she had plenty on, but the reality was she didn't have plans for the rest of the week or even the month. "No. I'm free."

"Good," Leila replied, getting to her feet. "Me too. So, how do you feel about a trip to Sheffield?"

Chapter 14

Camille leaned back in her seat, watching out of the window as the 14:02 train to Sheffield left St Pancras and sped through North London. Everything had happened so fast she was still struggling to process it all, but she was excited about the prospect of getting out of London for a while, even if the circumstances surrounding her trip were rather peculiar and not a little grim.

She glanced across the table at Leila, who was scrolling through her phone with a scowl creasing her features.

"Thanks again," she told her. "I will pay you back, I promise." It had been rather awkward at the ticket booth when she'd realised she didn't have enough money to pay for her ticket, but Leila had come to her rescue and paid for both fares.

"Don't worry about it. I'll put it on my expenses." She looked up from her phone and smiled. "Perks of being self-employed."

Camille smiled back, despite the hollow feeling in her stomach. She was supposedly self-employed, too. "What is it you do? Sorry, I should have asked."

"It's fine. I'm an events planner. Weddings mainly, but I do some corporate stuff now and again. It pays well and with this time of year being slow, it means I've got free time to investigate."

Camille pulled her shoulders back before releasing them. "I feel nervous for some reason. But excited too. Sorry, I don't want to make out this is a game or anything."

"No, hun, it's cool. I get what you mean. This isn't how I'd normally be spending a weekday afternoon, either. It is rather exhilarating. But we need to keep our heads screwed on."

"Yes, of course." She nodded at Leila's phone. "Any word yet from Harriet?"

She curled her lip. "No. She's not even read the message. But I've got the address of her work. We can wait for her."

"What? Just approach her cold as she's heading home? Isn't that a bit forward?" But then another thought hit her, and she gasped. "Shit. I hope she's okay. What if she's . . .? Oh, shit!"

Leila's mouth twisted into a grimace. "Yeah. I was thinking the same thing. But let's not jump to any conclusions until we know."

"Yes. You're right." But it was hard for Camille not to let her imagination run away with her. To distract herself from the bad thoughts, she pulled her phone out, seeing she had a new message from Stephen. They'd been messaging each other ever since they'd met up and she'd told him about her meeting with Leila today. In his message, he said he remembered her and that she was a nice girl. But he also warned her to be careful. A smile spread across her lips as she read the message and the sign-off, where he asked again if she wanted to meet for a drink.

She fired off a quick reply, telling him she was on her way to Sheffield to meet with Harriet and that she'd text him later. As she pressed send, she raised her head to see Leila looking at her.

"Boyfriend?" she asked.

Camille frowned. "God. No. What makes you say that?"

"Just the way you were smiling."

"No. I was just messaging Stephen Ainsworth, actually. Do you remember him?"

Leila's eyebrows shot up. "Steve? Whoa. Yeah, I remember Steve. Nice enough guy. Have you stayed in touch all this time?"

"No, not at all. I only got in touch recently. After seeing that post about Mark and Lucy. I wondered if he'd heard anything similar. He told me to leave it alone. Said it was just silly rumours."

"Yeah, well. He's not in danger of being killed if he's wrong, is he?" Her tone had turned serious and the way she was looking at Camille made her uneasy.

She opened her mouth, praying words of appeasement might miraculously fall out of it. But before that happened, Leila's phone buzzed.

"Shit."

"What is it?" Camille asked.

"Harriet's just replied to my message." She glared at her phone, eyes darting over the screen. "Well, well."

"Is she okay?"

"Seems to be," she said. "But she's not playing ball."

"What do you mean?"

Leila held the phone up to show her the message on the screen. There was no introduction or greeting, just two lines of text.

I have nothing to say about Mark Kennedy. Please don't contact me again.

"Oh no," Camille said. "What do we do now?"

Leila wrinkled her nose up. "Same as what we were doing. We go to her workplace and speak with her, face to face."

"But she said—"

"I know what she said, Cami. But doesn't that strike you as odd? Doesn't it make you want to speak to her more than ever?"

"Well, I suppose so."

"Right then. So, buckle up, hun, because I'm guessing Ms Knight isn't going to be the affable third musketeer that we were hoping she might be."

* * *

It was close to 6 p.m. as the taxi pulled up on Queen Street in the north of Sheffield. "Anywhere here is fine, thanks," Leila told the driver, shoving a twenty through the slot as he pulled up at the side of the road. She nudged Camille's arm. "There, look. Randall and Jones Solicitors. Come on."

Before she could respond, Leila had flung open the door of the taxi and was marching across the small square, with Harriet Knight's office situated over on the other side. Camille mumbled a thank you to the driver and clambered out after her.

"Get a move on," Leila called back. "We're going to miss her at this rate."

"Coming." She hurried across the paved square, catching up with her in front of the solicitors' building. Before she had a chance to ask what the plan was, a woman appeared in the doorway. She was tall and slim, with dark hair scraped back from her face. She was also about the same age as her and Leila. Despite never seeing a photo of Harriet Knight, she knew it was her. There was something about the way she nervously glanced around, and the tension in her neck and shoulders, that echoed her own physicality. Camille's intuition was proven to be correct as the woman stepped out onto the street and Leila made a beeline for her.

"Harriet. Hi there."

The woman froze and clutched her leather satchel to her chest. She was looking Leila up and down with wild eyes as Camille joined them. "Who are you?"

"It's me, Leila Bloom. I messaged you before. About Mark Kennedy."

Harriet's expression switched from confusion to scorn. "I told you I had nothing to say. What the hell are you doing here?"

"We need to talk."

"No. We don't," she snapped, before turning away and striding off.

The two new friends watched her go with open mouths.

Camille's instinct was to let her go. It was clear Harriet didn't want to get involved and they should respect her wishes. It was crappy that they'd come all this way, but if she didn't want to speak to them, what else could they do?

But Leila had other ideas. Slinging her bag defiantly over her shoulder, she marched after Harriet and, after waiting a moment, Camille did too.

"I take it you've heard?" Leila asked as she got alongside Harriet. "All we want to do is talk to you. See what you know. Don't you think it's weird how three of Mark's exes have wound up dead in the last year? Three are dead. Three are still alive. You, me and Camille here. But any one of us could be next. It could be you, Harriet. Doesn't that worry you at all?"

"I said, leave me alone." She stopped walking and turned on Leila, hissing the words in her face. She had fine features and kind eyes, but with her hair scraped back, coupled with the power suit she was wearing, she cut a formidable figure. "This is ridiculous. I have nothing to say to you."

She stomped off once more, but this time Leila didn't follow.

"Bugger," Camille said. "That's it then."

"Is it?"

"Well, yeah? You heard her. She won't talk to us."

"What do you think's going on with her? Do you think she knows something?"

"I don't know." Camille's stomach was in knots, but she wasn't sure if it was anxiety or embarrassment or just plain fear causing it. "I think we should go home."

Leila narrowed her eyes as she stared after the fast-departing Harriet. "Not yet," she replied. "She knows something, I can tell. We need to know what it is."

"But how? I think the best thing we can do is head back to London and have a rethink."

"Au contraire, my nervy friend," Leila replied with a half-smile. "We've come all this way. I'm not leaving yet."

"But she won't talk to us. What are we going to do?"

Leila hit her with a manic grin. "We're going to follow her," she said.

Chapter 15

Camille quickened her pace to keep up with her forthright new friend as they weaved their way through Sheffield city centre in pursuit of the mysterious Harriet. On their way, they passed through the impressive Peace Gardens and along what appeared to be the main shopping area, featuring many well-known retail outlets. This was Camille's first time in the city, and it appeared to be a pleasant enough place, but her mind was elsewhere.

What was the deal with Harriet?

Putting herself in the same position, she'd have been slightly perturbed at being approached out of the blue by two strangers. But she would have heard those people out. Especially if what they had to say involved the possibility her ex-boyfriend was a murderer. And not only that, but that he was murdering the very women he'd once shared a bed with.

If Harriet knew all these things, and from her actions, it seemed to Camille she did, why wouldn't she at least talk to them?

Up ahead, Leila stopped at a pedestrian crossing and spun around to glare at Camille, her stern expression willing her to keep up.

"I think she's heading for the train station," she said, as she got closer. "I'm guessing she lives outside the city."

Camille stood up on her tiptoes and peered over the people in front of them. "Where is she?"

Leila did the same. "There," she said, pointing. "On her phone. Shit. She's crossing over the road. Come on."

As Camille watched, Harriet glanced around her before racing across the dual carriageway to the other side of the street. It might have been Camille projecting her own feelings onto her, but she seemed scared, pensive, as if she knew she was being followed.

A hand grabbing at Camille's wrist snapped her back to the moment as Leila dragged her across the road. Once there, they headed down a side street after Harriet, but keeping a safe distance, lest they alert her to their presence. Camille barely took a breath as they followed her through a network of zigzagging pedestrianised streets before coming out onto a main road opposite the university. She could see Harriet was still on her phone, talking rapidly to whoever was on the other end.

A thought hit her that maybe she was talking to Mark and as soon as the idea formed, more followed. Were they in this together? Was Harriet telling him they'd been rumbled and that Camille and Leila needed to be taken care of?

No.

Stop that.

She shook the thoughts away. They'd bubbled up from her own sense of paranoia and were not helpful. A proper writer stuck to the facts. That was all that was important. Logic, not emotions.

So, what were the facts here?

Harriet had not been happy to see them. Plus, she'd made it very clear she didn't want to speak to them about Mark or the dead women. After letting them know these things in no uncertain terms, she'd fled the scene whilst talking animatedly on her phone. It didn't look good, but it didn't prove she was part of the conspiracy, either.

Leila stopped and held her arm up across Camille's chest as they approached the edge of a building that looked out on the dual carriageway. In front of them, Harriet had also stopped and was waiting for a break in the traffic.

"Stay here," Leila whispered, flattening herself against the building and pushing Camille back with her. "We can't let her see us."

They watched and waited, their chests rising and falling with the exertion as Harriet bounced on her heels at the side of the road. She looked agitated. But a second later she was on the move again. The two women gave it a beat, then followed on behind her. Over the main road they went and into the university grounds where there were fewer people than the busy streets that had brought them here. They hung back a few metres, lest the echo of their footsteps gave them away. But as they turned a corner and found themselves in a large square, Camille let out a gasp.

Across the other side, Harriet was talking to a man in a dark suit. He was balding with a neat beard and, as Camille watched, he reached into his bag and pulled out a red document file. She threw her attention around the area. Apart from Harriet and this man, the square was deserted. Tall buildings surrounded it on every side, concealing them from the roadside and any foot traffic that might be passing by. In other words, it was a perfect place for an illicit meeting.

Camille returned her attention to Harriet as she flipped through the file before placing her hand on the man's upper arm and smiling up at him. She couldn't hear what was being said, but their body language appeared to be relaxed.

What the hell was going on?

Harriet closed the file and placed it in her satchel before giving the man a stern nod and continuing on her way.

"Shit," Leila whispered, leaning back against Camille, as the man walked towards them. As he got closer, she pulled her phone out and showed it to Camille, raising her voice as she did.

"No, hun. I think you've taken a wrong turn." She stabbed her finger at the screen. "See? You're here and the station is around the other side of the building and across the street. If you go back the way you came and take the next right, you'll see the signs . . ."

She trailed off as the man passed by them and disappeared around the next corner. Camille relaxed her shoulders, looking up as Leila hit her with a devilish grin.

"That was too close."

Leila set off after Harriet, but Camille grabbed her arm and pulled her back. "Wait. This is getting weird. Do you not think we should leave? Maybe try to contact her again via social media, explain ourselves properly."

But the suggestion was met with a sneer. "Are you joking? Whatever is going on, I need to know. *We* need to know." With that, she shook Camille's hand from her arm and strode off across the square.

Camille pulled her phone out to check the time. 18:45. Anthony would wonder where she was. She tapped out a brief message, telling him she was in Sheffield and she'd ring him in a while to explain. Then she stuffed her phone back in her pocket and hurried after her daring new chum.

* * *

The two women followed Harriet through the university grounds and out the other side, where she crossed over the road and entered the train station as suspected. They followed her inside but remained out of sight, watching from behind a newspaper kiosk as she made her way over to platform six. A quick examination of the departures board told them the train was bound for Huddersfield and departed in four minutes. Running over to the ticket booth, they bought two returns before heading onto the platform and jumping on the first carriage of the train. From here they crept along the aisle, both wide-eyed and unblinking as they scanned the seats for Harriet. As they got through into the next carriage, Camille stopped. There she was at the far end, sitting facing them but looking out the window. Her face was stern as it had been earlier and her exquisitely styled eyebrows almost met in a heavy scowl over her nose. She looked angry, but Camille now sensed there was anxiety behind the rage. Worry twitched at the corners of her eyes and tightened the skin under her jaw.

Leila must have seen her at the same time, as she grabbed at Camille's arm. Instinctively, they moved on either side of the doorway leading to the carriage so they could stay hidden but monitor Harriet's movements. Which was a good plan, because five minutes later the train pulled into the stop for Meadowhall and she got up and headed for the exit.

The two women exchanged a glance before disembarking, winding around the people waiting on the platform in pursuit of Harriet as she disappeared into the depths of the station building. Meadowhall was one of those large shopping centres that most big cities built in the early nineties to emulate the popular retail malls of America. But like Westfield in London, it looked dated and somewhat of an eyesore to Camille's sensibilities. But, regardless, Harriet wasn't here to shop. She marched straight past the entrance of the mall and out of the building, heading towards what appeared to be a residential area.

Camille and Leila tailed her as before, walking in silence but keeping their distance. Five minutes later, Harriet turned down the side of a post office and disappeared from view.

"Let's go," Leila said, quickening her pace. "We can't lose her."

They hurried over to the side of the post office and Camille risked a furtive glance around the side of it. Harriet was walking down the street in front of them, but had slowed her pace considerably and was scrabbling in her bag for something.

"What's going on?" Leila whispered, shoving into her.

"I don't know. Wait."

As she watched, Harriet pulled out a set of keys from her bag, before veering into the driveway of a large house set back from the road.

"That must be her house," she said, leaning back so Leila could see.

"Yeah. Definitely." She surveyed the scene, mouth twisted in a pout of concentration, before nodding to herself and turning back the way they'd come.

"What are you doing?" Camille whispered, hurrying after Leila as she turned down an alleyway that ran between two houses.

"I want to get a better look at her set-up," she replied, not looking back.

Her set-up?

What the hell did that mean?

Camille slowed down, her heart doing a backflip as Leila strode down to the end of the alley and disappeared around the corner.

"Leila. Wait."

She trailed after her and found herself in an overgrown passage that cut across the back gardens of a row of houses. She figured it was most likely used by the residents as a back route and a way for them to take their recycling bins to the main road for collection. But it was also useful for getting to Harriet's back garden unseen. And that's what Camille was afraid of.

"Leila. What are you planning on doing?" she hissed after her.

But Leila didn't reply. She was bent over, peering through a gap in the fence that stood between the alley and Harriet's back garden. Joining her there, Camille saw a large patio with a patch of grass at the bottom, complete with a slide and a swing. Harriet had children. She had a family. This wasn't right. They'd made a mistake.

But before Camille could voice these feelings, Leila was reaching over the top of the gate and unhooking the latch.

"I just want to get a closer look," she said in response to Camille's glare.

She'd eased open the gate and had one foot in the garden when Camille heard footsteps in the alley to her right, followed by heavy breathing and the feeling of a sudden shift in the atmosphere. As she turned, she saw a dark figure approaching them down the narrow alley. She tried to scream, but the air caught in her dry throat and came out as a desperate gurgling sound. She grabbed for Leila, but she'd already seen. Her usual confident demeanour was gone and in its place a look of servile dread. This only made Camille more afraid. If this usually bold, confident woman looked so petrified, then they must be in trouble.

The figure stormed towards them. She could see now it was a man, a big man, wearing a green wax jacket and an angry expression. There was a real menace in his eyes. Spittle foamed at the sides of his mouth.

Was this it?

Was he here to kill them?

He stopped a few yards away and held his arms out.

"Who the bloody hell are you?" he growled in a strong northern accent. "And what the hell do you think you're doing in my garden?"

Chapter 16

"Shit. I'm so sorry," Camille spluttered, thinking fast as the man stared at her. She could almost see the rage seething out of him. "We didn't know . . . We were just seeing if our friend lived here. We thought she might, but we weren't sure. Were we, Leila?"

She looked at her friend for backup but got nothing. Leila was staring down into her hands like a scolded schoolgirl.

"I saw you from my bedroom window," the man snarled, his demeanour not abating in the slightest. "I saw you following my wife like a couple of freaks, and then what? You come around the back and try to break in? Are you casing the joint? Is that it? You think we've got money? Because I can tell you for nothing, we haven't."

"No!" Camille told him. "It's not like that. I promise. Do we look like burglars?"

The man sneered. "Takes all sorts these days. How do I know you're not working for someone? You could be stooges. I should call the police right now. For fuck's sake, this used to be a good neighbourhood. What is the world coming to? I ought to—"

"Damien!" a woman's voice yelled. "It's fine."

Camille snapped her head over to the source of the voice and saw Harriet standing in the garden a few feet away. Their eyes met and Camille offered her a kind of half-grimace-half-smile. It was the sort of look she hoped expressed how sorry she was and that she knew she was in the wrong.

"We just want to talk to you," she told her, nudging Leila. "Don't we?"

"Yes," Leila said, finding her voice suddenly. "That's all we want. We need your help, Harriet."

"What the hell is going on?" Damien asked, but Camille sensed he was mellowing a little. "Do you know these people, love?"

Harriet snorted softly down her nose. "Not in so many words. But we are linked in some way, I suppose. They used to go out with Mark Kennedy as well."

Damien raised his eyebrows at Harriet. "Oh. I see."

"Are you the husband?" Leila asked.

"Aye."

Harriet gave him a tight smile. "Sorry, love. Can you give us five minutes?"

"You sure?" He glanced at Camille and then Leila.

"Yes. I'm fine. Thanks."

He cleared his throat before shuffling past them into the garden and walking back to the house. As he passed his wife, he paused and kissed her, but Harriet didn't take her eyes off Camille and Leila. When Damien was inside, she stepped forward.

"You don't take no for an answer, do you? What were you thinking, following me back to my house? Jesus Christ. That is not on."

Leila raised her head. "Who was that man you met with?"

"Whoa, slow down," Camille said. Because Harriet was right. This wasn't on. "I don't think that's any of our business."

"We don't know that yet," Leila replied, not taking her eyes off Harriet. "So, who was he?"

Harriet huffed and rolled her eyes. "His name is Geoff. I work with him. I'd left a file at the office and asked him to meet me with it on his way home from work. Is that okay with you?" She glared at Leila. "He's gay and married, if you needed that information for . . . Whatever this ridiculous vigilante mission is."

"Vigilante mission?" Leila repeated, in an incredulous tone. "We're trying to find out the truth behind the fact three of Mark's girlfriends have died in the last year. Two of them in the last three months. Now you clearly know something or think something is afoot if you've already spoken to your husband about it. So, we're here now, we're talking. What's your story?"

Harriet stared at her in silence, nibbling on her bottom lip as she did. Finally, she blew out a long breath. "Okay. Yes. Fine," she said. "When I first heard about Lucy Meadows and then poor Ophelia, I did start to wonder about it."

"And Charlotte Browning. Don't forget her."

"Yes, and Charlotte. Sorry, it was just Ophelia and I were close and I knew of Lucy, but it's tragic what happened to her as well. Of course it is." She stuffed her hands in her pockets. "But the more I've considered the facts, I really don't believe there's anything in these rumours. It's unfortunate and sad, but people die every day. Often, they have ex-boyfriends."

"But they all had the same ex-boyfriend."

"I'm sure it happens. The law of averages. We know about these girls because they all went to Oxford at the same time as we did. And so did Mark. Hell, there might even be other men they all went on dates with whilst they were at uni. It could easily have happened. People have types, etcetera, etcetera. It's a weird coincidence, I'll give you that, but it's a coincidence all the same."

She made a good argument. Camille was beginning to waver before Leila quickly brought her back around.

"We were both followed," she said. "A figure in a big coat with a hood covering their face. It was scary. And it was real – before you tell me it was just my mind playing tricks."

But it didn't seem like Harriet was going to question it. In fact, for the first time since they'd been talking, her unyielding expression faltered. In that moment, Camille saw something in her eyes. It wasn't fear exactly, but it was close to it.

"Have you been followed?" she asked her.

Harriet looked up at the sky and sighed. "I don't know. Maybe?"

"Maybe?" Leila spluttered. "When?"

"Last month, on my way home from work. And then a few days ago." She looked down and twisted her mouth to one side. "I've been trying not to think about it."

"But we have to think about it," Leila told her. "Our lives could be in danger. And you were concerned enough that you told your husband about Mark and these women? Yes?"

Harriet replied with a curt nod.

"We just want to talk to you," Leila said, her voice softer now. "We've both been to the police with what we know and were

120

both told to leave it alone. The officer I spoke with implied I was paranoid and crazy. But what if we're right? What if Mark is killing his exes?" It seemed she had more to say, but she stopped herself as a small girl stepped out onto the patio behind Harriet.

"Mummy," she yelled. "I want some juice."

Harriet turned around and waved at her. "Go ask Daddy, darling. Mummy's speaking to these ladies." When she turned back, her face was stern once more, but her eyes had warmth in them. She sighed again. "You're not going to leave me alone, are you?"

"We only want to talk," Camille said with a smile. "Find out if you know anything we don't."

"Fine," Harriet said. "Come inside and we can talk. But not for long. I have to make dinner."

Chapter 17

In the sanctuary of her home, Harriet appeared to soften. The tense muscles in her face relaxed almost instantly and after taking her hair down, she looked positively welcoming as she made tea for the three of them.

"Come through into my office," she said, leaving the kitchen and leading them along a spacious hallway, past the front room where her daughter and husband were watching cartoons on a large flatscreen television. "We can talk better there."

Camille let Leila go first and followed on behind, taking in Harriet's impressive home, with its tasteful all-white décor and expensive-looking furniture. Here was another success story. Another reminder of how little she herself had progressed since graduating.

"When did you realise the link?" Harriet asked as she opened a door off to the right and stepped back to allow them to enter.

"Someone mentioned it on Facebook," Camille replied, going through into the room and looking around. "I thought it was just a troll at first, but the more I thought about it, the more freaked out I got. Then Leila contacted me and . . . Well, here we are."

Harriet's home office was bigger than Camille's bedroom. Like the rest of the house, the décor here was predominantly white, but a large mahogany desk with a green leather top spanned one wall and, in front of this, a tan leather chair. Harriet pulled it around to face the room and sat down. "Please," she said, gesturing at a two-seater leather couch on the opposite wall, "have a seat."

The two women did as suggested, Camille cupping a mug of tea in both hands as she settled herself on the hard cushion.

"I've got to admit, it freaked me out too," Harriet told them. "A lot."

"How long were you and Mark together?" Leila asked.

Harriet screwed up her face. "Nine months? Maybe a bit longer. Less than a year." She puffed out her cheeks. "It was a bad break-up. Messy."

"Did you ever see any sign that he might be capable of doing something like this?"

"What? Systematically murdering his ex-girlfriends. Being a serial killer. Because let's face it that's what we're talking about if this is true."

"Jesus," Camille muttered to herself. She'd not thought of it like that. But Harriet was right.

"I don't know, is the short answer," Harriet continued. "But the idea that he might have had something to do with Ophelia's death has given me cause to think these past few weeks. As I say, it was messy the way we broke up. We both acted terribly, but there were a few times towards the end when Mark turned really nasty. And I mean *really nasty.* I'd never seen him like that before. He scared me. And if I'm honest, he still does. I think that's why I've been trying to convince myself that this is all just nonsense. And why I don't want to be involved in whatever you're trying to do." She lifted her mug and sipped at her tea, nervous eyes flitting between Camille and Leila. As she lowered her drink, she shrugged. "I've got a good life here. I like my job. Damien's a wonderful husband. And I've got my little princess, Rosie, who you met outside. I left Oxford feeling pretty shitty about many things, but my life is good now. I don't want to rake up the past."

"But you could be in danger," Leila said. "Mark could take all that from you."

Harriet's mouth twisted to one side. "What's his motive, though?"

Leila gasped dramatically. "Well, his political weight is growing stronger all the time, for one thing. Give it a year or two and he'll be big news. That's what everyone is saying in every article I've read. It's not going to be long before he's a regular on the news. A household name. He's getting rid of anyone who might become a problem for him. He's the same as you. He doesn't want the past raked up. He's scared of how it might damage his career."

Harriet frowned. "But surely being linked to the deaths of your ex-girlfriends is more damaging?"

Camille sat back. That right there was the question that had been bugging her. It was the same question DI Shaw had posed to her. But now Harriet had articulated it again, she found she had an answer.

"He's being clever about it," she said. "Because so far none of the deaths has been classed as murder, or even considered suspicious. We've got two accidental deaths and a suicide. All of them closed cases. We've linked them to Mark as have other people who were in the same year at Oxford, but only because we were there, and we know. But there's no reason for the police to look into a dead woman's past relationships if they think her death can be easily explained." She glanced at Leila, feeling energised by her own words. "It's almost the perfect crime," she added.

Harriet didn't look completely convinced, but she didn't dismiss the theory either. Instead, she sighed again and shook her head. "I can't believe I'm getting stressed out and worried about Mark fucking Kennedy. After all this time." She sniffed. "I don't know, Camille. I understand what you're saying, but it all seems a bit of a leap to put all that together and come out with Mark as the murderer."

"Yes. It is a bit of a leap," Leila butted in. "But what if that's what he's relying on? What if that's how he keeps the police off his back whilst he kills the rest of us?"

A silence descended on the room. They each sipped at their tea and Camille glanced from Leila to Harriet. They were both staring off into the middle distance, deep in thought.

"Do you have anything on him?" she asked Harriet.

She raised her head, seemingly dropping out of her thoughts. "Oh, I could crush the bastard if I had any proof. He was horrible to me towards the end. Abusive, nasty. One night when he was drunk, he pulled a handful of my hair out. Another night, he forced himself on me. I can't even say I put up much of a fight, which is the worst thing. I feared him, but I was also resigned to it. I still hate myself a bit for that. He left me timid, broken . . . As I say, I don't want to rake up the past."

"But there you go," Camille said. "He'll know we all have terrible stories about him. He forced himself on me as well. So that's your motive right there. He doesn't want these stories to see the light of day."

"But there's no proof," Harriet said. "No evidence. I know things are getting better in terms of historic sexual abuse cases, but he'll have the best lawyers. He could crush any allegations before they get to trial."

"Not if enough of us come forward," Leila said, sitting up and shuffling to the edge of the couch. "Fucking hell, I'm more certain about this than ever before. He's behind this. He has to be. He's shutting us down. Erasing his past mistakes in the worst possible way."

"But would he really kill?" Harriet said.

"He has done! Three times!" Leila replied, her voice rising. "This is getting scary now. We need to go to the police. All three of us. We need to tell them what he's done and what we know."

Harriet shuddered. "No. I can't."

"Why not?" Camille asked, placing a hand on Leila's arm in pre-emption of her response. "Please. It'll mean so much more if all of us went together. They might actually take us seriously."

"I'm sorry. I've got a good job. A family. I don't want to drag them into this. As I said, I've moved on. I'm happy. I want to keep my past as far enough away from my present as possible."

Leila opened her mouth to speak, but Harriet held her hand up. "I know what you're going to say, and I will help as much as I can. I'll give a full statement if it comes to that. But that's as far as I can go."

Camille squeezed Leila's arm. "Okay. We understand. Don't we Leila?"

"I suppose so."

Harriet smiled. "Thank you. We'll exchange numbers and keep in touch."

"We're going to get him," Leila told her. "We're going to take that bastard down. Make him wish he never messed with any of us."

"Good. I hope you do. If he is behind this, he deserves everything he gets."

Camille tilted her head to one side. "Are you still unsure whether he really is involved?"

"I'm trying to stay sane, that's all, and look at it from a logical perspective. And I suppose there's a certain amount of self-preservation at play too. I don't want him getting back in my head."

Just then, they heard a child's footsteps thundering down the corridor and a voice yelling, "Mummy!"

Harriet raised her head. "Righto. It's time for me to make dinner."

"Yes, of course," Camille said, getting to her feet. "We'll get out of your hair. But thank you for talking with us. For sharing your story."

Leila stood as well. "He really did a number on you, didn't he?"

"Yes." Harriet looked away and for a split second, Camille saw the timid, broken young girl she'd alluded to.

"Well, don't worry," she said as Harriet moved over to the door and opened it for them. "We're going to expose that evil prick and make him pay for everyone he's ever hurt. If it's the last thing I ever do. I'll make sure of it."

Chapter 18

It was dark as they got on the train back to London. The first carriage they entered was all but empty except for a smartly dressed woman with a slim can of gin and tonic nestled between her thighs. She ignored Camille and Leila as they shuffled past her and slumped opposite each other around the first table seats they came to. Neither of them had any energy to speak as they removed their jackets and settled in for the journey, but they'd done enough talking for one day. Indeed, for Camille, it felt like she'd lived a whole week in one day. Was this a case of being careful what you wished for? She'd been bemoaning the lack of purpose and direction in her life. Now she had too much of both.

As the train set off, she felt her phone vibrating in her pocket. Assuming it to be Ant, she was going to let her answer machine pick it up, but as she pulled it out, she saw Stephen's name on the screen. She glanced across at Leila, who was already poring over her phone, so she swiped it open and answered.

"Hey," she said, attempting to sound breezy despite the fatigue. "Nice to hear from you."

"Yeah. I thought I'd give you a quick call and see how you're doing."

She chuckled to herself. "I'm doing all right. Thanks. I'm very tired, though."

"Busy day at the office?"

"Something like that."

"Oh shit. You were going to see Harriet, weren't you?" He sounded shocked he'd forgotten. "How did it go?"

"Good. Well, you know. Not good. But useful. I think meeting with her has solidified a lot of things in my mind. Mark has been a real shit to a lot of women. He's been violent, abusive . . . and the rest."

As she said Mark's name, Leila shot her a glance. Camille mouthed the name 'Stephen' and gave her what she hoped was a reassuring thumbs-up.

"Was he like that with you?" he asked.

She stiffened. She hadn't expected the conversation to go here so quickly. Or at all. "Sort of," she said, hoping he wouldn't push for more information. "But the bigger picture is there's a lot of people – women, ex-girlfriends – with a lived experience of Mark Kennedy and their stories could be very damaging to him if they got out. And now three of these women have turned up dead." Leila glared at her and strained her neck to look down the carriage. But there was no one in earshot.

"It's fine," she whispered to Leila. "Stephen knows."

"Who are you talking to?" he asked.

"Leila Bloom. She's with me."

"Ah, yes. Okay. Give her my regards, won't you?"

"I will." Then, to Leila. "He says 'Hi'."

Leila rolled her eyes at this and returned to her phone.

On the line, Stephen coughed and when he spoke again, his voice was more serious. "Be careful how you move forward with all this though, Camille. Do you understand what I'm saying? Whatever you think might have happened, it's still only a theory. Hearsay in the eyes of the law."

"We're going to get evidence," she told him. "We're going to prove it."

She glanced out the window at her reflection, highlighted by the stark fluorescent lights of the train. The woman looking back at her looked fiery and determined.

"Well, if you can, great. Because right now, to any outsider, to any police officer or jury member, it will seem quite a reach to go from three women dying in tragic circumstances to pointing to Mark as their killer. I don't want you to get into something so deep that you can't get out. Mark's influence is growing all the time. If he gets wind of what you're accusing him of, he could sue you for defamation or even get you arrested for stalking."

The words landed heavily on Camille's shoulders. Ever since they'd left Harriet's house, she'd felt on top of the world. She'd felt bold and strong and ready for action.

"We'll be careful," she assured him. "It's about gathering the facts, I know that." She continued to stare at the window and an idea came to her. Could she? Would he? It was a dangerous move, but the intrepid woman staring back at her said she could.

"As long as you keep that in mind," Stephen was saying. "Because I really think that—"

"Could you contact him?" she blurted out before she changed her mind. "Mark, I mean. I know you've not seen each other for a few years, but you were his best friend once. Can you speak with him, ask if he'll meet with me?"

She looked across at Leila. Her mouth was hanging open but, as their eyes met, she gave Camille an encouraging nod.

"Why do you want to meet him?" Stephen asked. "If he's doing what you think he's doing, isn't that dangerous?"

"We'll meet somewhere safe. Somewhere public. I want to look him in the eyes and ask him what he knows."

Stephen went quiet for a moment. She heard him sigh and then he said, "I'll see what I can do. What shall I tell him?"

"Tell him I'm writing an article on the future leaders of the country, something like that. Say I'm speaking with CEOs of start-ups, scientists, politicians. Be vague, but appeal to his ego."

"Okay, leave it with me. But I can't promise anything."

"Thanks, Stephen. I owe you one."

"Yeah, you do. I'll settle for that drink. One night soon?"

She giggled. "I'd like that. Why don't you text me some potential dates and times and I'll get back to you?"

"Cool, it's a date. Well, not a date. A few friendly drinks. But I look forward to it."

"Me too. Bye."

"See you."

She hung up and held her phone in both hands to her chest.

"Whoa."

She looked up to see Leila grinning at her.

"What?"

"You like him?"

She made a disgusted face. "No. He's just a friend. He's helping us out. He's going to contact Mark."

"And say what? Have you got a plan?"

"I want to test the waters, see what he's like face to face. I think I'd be able to tell if I looked into his eyes."

Leila didn't look convinced. She let her head loll back onto her seat and chuckled joylessly. "Stephen Ainsworth. There's another blast from the past. When did you last see him?"

Camille adjusted herself and leaned her elbows on the table. "Last week, actually. I arranged to meet with him after Lucy died. He's a good guy. Seems to be doing well for himself."

"Yeah, he was a good guy."

"Did you know him well?"

"For a while." She snorted but waved it away. "It's nothing. We had a thing once. After some party. But don't worry, nothing really happened. He was too drunk and he . . . couldn't perform, shall we say."

"Oh dear."

"Yeah. I shouldn't have said anything. Sorry."

She pulled a face and the two of them shared a giggle. But as the laughter dissipated, an awkward silence fell over the table. Camille closed her eyes, feigning sleep.

Why did Leila just tell her that?

She knew Camille had feelings for Stephen.

You like him. She'd said it herself.

Whether these feelings were of a romantic nature or simply platonic, Camille wasn't yet sure, but neither was Leila. And if that was the case, letting slip about her and Stephen's, albeit uneventful, tryst was clearly designed to make Camille feel bad. Whether that was a conscious move or just an aspect of Leila's bold and abrasive personality, it was unclear. But there were a lot of things about Leila Bloom that were unclear.

What was her game?

Camille loved Leila's energy and forthright attitude. But if she really considered it, she was kind of making this whole thing with Mark and the dead women about herself. And if that was the case, a good investigative journalist would have to ask herself why.

Who is the source?

And why are they saying what they're saying?

What do they have to gain?

All good questions. But none with any actual answers.

Camille opened her eyes. She was overthinking this far too much. She smiled at Leila, who was staring straight at her. As she smiled back, Camille felt her doubts fading. Leila's smile was completely genuine, with warmth in the eyes.

"You okay, hun?" she asked.

"Yeah. Sorry. I'm just tired and my stupid brain is working overtime."

Leila raised her eyebrows. "Tell me about it."

Camille sat back in her seat. Yes. Everyone had an angle. But that applied to herself just as much. And she trusted Leila. She had to. Apart from Harriet, she was the only other person in the world who fully understood what Camille was going through.

"Stephen is a nice guy, though," she said as if reading Camille's mind. "Handsome too. I saw a recent photo. He's definitely blossomed since uni."

"I wondered if it's since coming out from under Mark's shadow. The two of them used to be so funny together." She shook her head, remembering. "Shit. Sometimes I still can't believe it."

"Yeah well. You need to start believing. Because we've got work to do."

Leila was right. Camille had to step away from all the second-guessing herself and over-thinking the whys and what ifs. If she was going to survive the next few weeks, even mentally, she had to trust her instincts and open her mind to the real possibility of what Mark was. She had to operate under the belief that Mark Kennedy – her one-time friend and lover, her ex-boyfriend – was a murderer. And if she didn't want to be next on his hit list, she had to prove it to the world. She had to stop him.

Chapter 19

The next few days passed by in a heartbeat. Camille had arrived back at her flat to find an email from Hot Looks magazine that wanted seven-hundred-and-fifty words on dating in your thirties. The tone they wanted was 'edgy but funny' (a fluff piece which she could have written with her eyes closed on a normal week) but although it paid well and she needed the money, she was having trouble writing it. Every time she sat down at her laptop, her mind drifted to Mark and Lucy and his other exes. That was the only story she wanted to tell. The only story that interested her. And it needed to be written.

But first, she needed to know how the story ended.

Ant had been his usual supportive self, listening intently to everything she'd found out from Harriet and becoming excited when she'd told him she was now fully committed to her mission – to expose Mark for what he was and prove that Lucy, Ophelia and Charlotte were murdered. But then he'd got an acting role (an advert for a new credit card aimed at young adults, filming in Bristol) and had been away for most of the week. Although it had given Camille plenty of time to process everything she'd discovered since meeting Leila.

Because there was a lot of processing to do.

She was certain, more than ever, that there was more to what happened to Lucy and the others than mere coincidence. Harriet's point – about them only being in her sphere of awareness because they'd attended Oxford University at the same time – gave her some doubt, but she'd keep this in mind as she moved forward and not let it sway her. It was as important to be aware of your own blind spots when doing this kind of investigative work as it was to be open to hard truths. But those hard truths certainly were taking shape and the more she found out, the more they looked like absolute truths. The only truth. She was ready to do whatever it took to prove what she already suspected.

Harriet had called it a vigilante mission, but it wasn't that, it was a search for justice. And they were getting closer every day. Leila and Camille had agreed to do their research independently and meet up again at the end of the week to share what they'd found. As Camille was the closest of the two of them to Lucy, it had been decided she'd contact Lucy's parents. It had been a hard conversation to have, especially over the phone. She'd met them once when they were visiting their daughter at Balliol College. From what she remembered, they were nice people, quiet and unassuming. From her phone call with them, it seemed they hadn't changed in all these years, but now you could add broken-hearted to that list of attributes.

It had been a hard conversation to have, especially over the phone. Lucy's mum's voice wavered with emotion as she explained how confused she and her husband were, how she never even knew Lucy was depressed. It sounded like she blamed herself in some way and, at first, she was adamant she didn't want to talk any more about it (especially not to some investigative journalist – the way Camille had stupidly described herself), but eventually she'd acquiesced. Camille was to meet both parents – who were now divorced but still close – in a day's time at Lucy's mum's house in Sevenoaks. So instead of writing her article on dating in your thirties, she was spending all available time considering what she might ask them. It was important to her that she didn't worry them unduly or imply their darling daughter was murdered with no real evidence, but there were also questions that needed answering.

She did wonder if, once the truth was out there, Lucy's parents would gain any kind of comfort in knowing that she hadn't chosen to die. What was more comforting as a parent, knowing your child had been murdered or that they'd taken their own life? Camille wasn't sure, but maybe there was no right answer. Because there was no comfort to be gained.

Yet, despite most of Camille's mental capacity having been taken up with their case against Mark, she had done some research for her article – *Dating in Your Thirties* – in that she'd arranged to meet Stephen for a drink (or two) after he'd finished work. Which was why, on this bright Wednesday afternoon, she was currently riding the Overground over to Whitechapel. As the train sped past derelict wasteland and scenes of urban decay, she closed her eyes and engaged herself in a meditative breathing exercise. It was an attempt to calm her nerves and rid herself of the negative energy she'd been encircled in these last few days. Because whilst she was ready to step into her new role as a badass investigator, she also needed to protect herself. And not only physically, but mentally. It was important to look for the goodness in life, especially when most of the day you were focusing only on the bad.

Stephen was waiting at the bar as she entered the Mucky Pig Tavern. He spotted her straight away and waved her over, a welcoming smile lighting up his face. Yes. She'd made the right decision agreeing to meet him. As she weaved her way over to the bar to join him, she felt the stresses and fears of the last few days falling away. At the same time, she made a pact with herself, vowing to stay present and open to whatever the universe had planned for her. At least for the next few hours she'd put all thoughts of dead friends, evil exes and broken-hearted parents out of her mind.

"You look great," Stephen said as she reached him. He leaned down and kissed her softly on the cheek. "What can I get you to drink?"

"Hmm, let me have a look." She leaned over the bar top and squinted at the rows of brightly lit bottles along the back wall. She wasn't entirely sure why she was doing this; she'd already made her choice on the walk here from Whitechapel Station. She pondered the many options for a few seconds longer, sensing Stephen's eyes on her. "I'll have a dark rum and coke," she told him. "Please."

"Good choice," Stephen said, beckoning the barman over. "I think I'll join you."

Once they had their drinks, they found a table towards the back of the pub and sat facing each other. Camille let out a deep sigh as she settled into her surroundings. The pub was warm and cosy with just the right amount of people in it. She'd walked past it many times over the last few years and had often wondered what the interior was like. The answer to that was ancient, with original beams and low ceilings that Stephen had to stoop to walk under at points.

Camille sipped at her drink as she turned her attention back to him. "This is nice," she said. "The place, I mean. But the drink as well." He'd got them doubles and she could certainly taste the rum. But it was good. It was needed.

"Isn't it? I come here now and again. It's got a good vibe."

They smiled at each other, the atmosphere just the right side of awkward.

"How's work?" she asked.

He shrugged. "Work is work. I've got a new client who's a bit of an annoying prick, but other than that it's going well. What about you? Did you finish your article?"

"Not really." She made a shocked face. "I'm finding it so dull I'm having trouble getting my head in the game. But I will." She hadn't told him what the piece was to be about and she had no intention of doing so.

They sipped at their drinks in unison, not taking their eyes off one another.

"What about the other big story?" he asked, placing his drink down. "Any developments there?"

She regarded him as he twisted his glass around on the table. Did he think she was stupid in pursuing these theories? Or was it more than that? Was he concerned for her?

"I've spoken with Lucy's parents," she said. "I've arranged to go down to Sevenoaks tomorrow afternoon to interview them or, at least, have a chat. See if they can throw any more light on what happened to her."

Stephen pulled his lips back and bared his teeth. "That's a tough conversation to have, I imagine. Good luck with it."

"I know. But I'm hoping, in the long run, I'll be able to provide them with better closure than what they have now." A shudder ran down her spine, the way it did every time she imagined talking to Lucy's parents about the possibility of her being murdered. But like the other times, she ignored it. This was important work she was doing. She had to believe that. She tucked a strand of hair over her ear. "I don't suppose you've spoken with Mark?"

Stephen shook his head. "I emailed the last address I had of his. It didn't bounce back, but he's not replied yet. I kept it light – long time, no see and all that – but nothing. I found another email on his website, but I wasn't sure if some administrator monitored it, so I thought it best to try the friend route first."

"Good idea."

"If you want, though, I heard he's setting up a campaign office. I could make some enquiries and go see him face to face."

Camille picked up her beer mat and tapped the edge against the table. All of a sudden, things felt very real.

"No. It's okay. Let's do it slowly at first. See where that gets us?" She took a large gulp of rum and coke. "But thank you. I do appreciate your help and it's so nice to hang out with you again after all these years. You haven't changed at all."

Stephen arched an eyebrow. "Really? That's a bloody shame. I was a total loser at university."

"No, you weren't. You were sweet, funny."

"Sweet and funny? Great. Exactly how one describes their wimpy, platonic friend."

She giggled. "I see. And you don't want to be seen like that?"

"Wimpy?" He blew out a breath, making his lips vibrate. "I work out three times a week. Have you not seen these guns?" He tensed his bicep and Camille giggled again.

"I meant platonic."

He shrugged theatrically. "I'd like to think there might be a possibility of getting out of that cursed friend zone."

"Oh, you're not in the friend zone. Don't worry about that."

"Is that so?"

"Of course. I'm not your friend."

They both laughed, still not taking their eyes off each other. It felt so freeing to be here with Stephen. Yet it wasn't so much their romantic potential that gave Camille a warm feeling inside as the fact that, for the first time since leaving university, she felt in control of her life. It was weird to think, given the circumstances, but she was finally stepping into her power. She had more purpose and drive than ever before, and whilst these were the scariest and most uncertain times she'd ever experienced, it felt like the universe was well and truly behind her. She trusted her intuition. She had to. Often, it was all she had. And right now it told her she was ready to take on Mark Kennedy and then the world.

As the evening progressed, the talk moved to other things. The usual stuff at first, culture and current affairs, but moving quickly on to deeper subjects, their hopes and dreams for the future, where they saw themselves in ten years. The conversation flowed easily and they laughed often. So much so that they'd had two more double rum and cokes each (Stephen insisting on buying both rounds) before Camille glanced at her phone and realised it was almost eleven. She'd been having such a good evening time had run away from her.

"Shit. I need to get off in a minute," she told Stephen.

"Aw, really? Maybe one more drink?"

She swilled the last half-inch of liquid and ice around in her glass. "No. I shouldn't. Besides, they'll be calling last orders in a minute."

Stephen lowered his chin. "We could always go back to my place for a drink. I'm in Limehouse. Not that far from here. Right by the river."

Camille bit her lip. It was very tempting and with the alcohol rousing her in more ways than one, she could readily accept the offer. But no. She had work to do. She was on a mission.

"Sorry. I can't," she told him. "Maybe next time."

"Come on," he said, drawing out the words. "One drink. Then I'll get you an Uber home. It'll be fun." He reached for her hand and gave it a squeeze.

"Stop it," she sighed, looking down. "I do want to . . ."

"Let's go then. Nothing has to happen." He held onto her hand, lowering his head to look her in the eyes. "It's been so good getting to know you again, Cam. I don't want to rush any-thing. But one drink won't hurt, will it?"

She gritted her teeth. It wouldn't hurt. It wouldn't hurt at all.

But no. She'd already had more to drink than she'd intended. She had a duty to show up at Lucy's mum's house tomorrow with her professional head on. She pulled her hand back from his.

"Next time," she said. "When I'm not busy the next day."

"Okay," he said and smiled. "I understand."

"But definitely soon," she added.

"Great."

She drained her glass and got to her feet. "But now I really do have to go. I'll speak to you soon."

"Yes. Let me know how it goes. And good luck."

He looked up at her as she passed by and leaned down and kissed him on the cheek. Then, feeling buoyed by the drink, she walked out into the cool night air and jumped straight in a taxi. She could scarcely afford the fare, but something told her good money was on the horizon. Besides, she needed to get home and go to bed as soon as possible. Tomorrow was a big day for her. It was important she be on top form.

Chapter 20

Camille removed her cardigan and rolled up her shirt sleeves before settling back into the large plush velvet armchair. Mrs Meadows' front room was as hot as a sauna and the bright sun filtering through the large bay windows didn't help. While she and Mr Meadows (or, Anne and Nigel, as they'd instructed her to call them) pottered about in the kitchen next door Camille removed a newly bought notepad and pen from out of her bag and placed them on the arm of the chair.

"Here we go then. A nice cup of tea," Nigel said, appearing in the doorway carrying a tray, which he placed on the coffee table. On it were a teapot, a milk jug and three cups and saucers. Plus, a plate of digestive biscuits and folded linen napkins. The gentle middle-England domesticity of the offering almost broke Camille's heart, but she remained stoic as Nigel met her eye. "Do you take sugar?"

"No. Just milk. Thank you."

Stooping over, he poured some milk into one of the cups, followed by some rather weak-looking tea. "Biscuit?" he asked, handing her the saucer, teacup shuddering on top.

"No, thank you."

She accepted the tea and watched as Nigel made drinks for himself and his ex-wife before waddling backwards to sit on the couch opposite. A moment later, Anne appeared. She looked to have been crying but still smiled sweetly as she settled herself next to Nigel and accepted the tea he offered her.

"We'll do our best to help you out," she said. "But I'm not sure what else we can tell you, Camille. We hadn't seen Lucy for almost three months, had we Nigel? She was very busy with her new design business." She shook her head sadly.

"Yes. It's hard, isn't it?" Camille said, slowly twisting around to pick up the notepad and pen off the chair arm. "Work and life get in the way. Especially if you're living in different cities."

Anne sniffed and pulled a crumpled tissue out of the sleeve of her jumper. "I just wish she'd have come home earlier if she felt . . . like that. We're a close family, we always have been. I always thought she could talk to me about anything. It just doesn't make any sense to me." She dabbed at her eyes with the tissue.

"You were good friends with Lucy, weren't you?" Nigel asked. The same confused expression hadn't left his face. Busy eyebrows knotted together over watery blue eyes. She wondered if this was his default expression now. She didn't blame the poor man. His only daughter, dead at thirty-two. It was enough to break anyone.

"We were close, yes," she replied. "For a few years at least. But we had a bit of a falling out, I'm afraid. No one's fault, really. Not mine or hers, anyway."

"That's a shame," he said and looked at the floor. "Maybe if she'd had more friends around her, she wouldn't have felt so despondent. Sorry, I just can't get my head around the fact that she thought doing *that* was her only option." His face screwed up and it looked like he was going to burst into tears, but he fought through it and his face relaxed as he shook his head. "My poor girl. Such a damn waste."

Camille gave what she hoped was both a comforting and empathetic smile. But really, she had no concept of the extent of their suffering. All because of him. Mark Kennedy. She peeled the cover of the spiral-bound notepad open and readied her pen.

"When was the last time you spoke to Lucy?" she asked, working to maintain a steady tone of voice.

Mr and Mrs Meadows exchanged glances. "I spoke to her the day before she died," Nigel said quietly. He reached over and grabbed his ex-wife's hand, despite it being balled up in a fist of emotion. "She rang Anne first, but she'd misplaced her phone, hadn't you love?"

Anne sniffed and made a face like she'd never forgive herself for missing that call. She probably wouldn't.

"Did she say anything that gave you cause for concern?" Camille asked. Then, pre-empting Nigel's response. "Sorry, that's a stupid question, I know. Because, of course you'd have done something if she had done. I suppose I'm just trying to piece together those final days."

"Why are you doing this?" Anna asked, with a voice threatening to break. "All these questions. What good will it do?"

Camille swallowed. "As I told you on the phone, Mrs Meadows – Anne – Lucy and I were very similar people. We had similar taste in music, films, even boys." She smiled, but it felt wrong and she altered her expression immediately, tapping her pen on the blank notepad resting on her knees. "What I mean is, despite us growing apart, we were very good friends once and I don't believe she was the sort of person who would take her own life."

She paused to let the words sink in, but both Nigel and Anne stared at her. Was this something that had crossed their minds as well?

"As I've already said, I'm a writer – a freelance journalist – and ever since I heard about Lucy's passing, I've felt uneasy about her cause of death. I feel like there's much more to the story than what the police have come up with."

"What are you saying? That she didn't hurt herself?"

"Maybe."

Nigel looked even more confused. "But the way they found her . . . in her bedroom . . ."

"I know. Please, I don't want to drag up awful memories for you. But I do want to honour Lucy in the only way I can. By writing about who she was. And what she was. Which was a vital, brilliant, funny young woman with everything going for her." She took a deep breath. She was going for it. She had to. "Mr and Mrs Meadows, I don't think Lucy took her own life. I think she may have been murdered and, if that's the case, I intend to find out who did it and get justice for your daughter."

Lucy's parents looked at each other with open mouths. Then Anne shut her eyes and shook her head. "No. Let her rest in peace. Please. It's over. She's gone."

Camille pressed her lips together and glanced down at the notepad. She hadn't written a word. "I understand where you're coming from, Anne," she said. "I'm very sorry if my questions have upset you. That's not what I intended. I only want to find out the truth. Even if it happened the way the police said it did, I want to know why. What makes a woman like Lucy do something like that? I promise you the piece will honour Lucy. It won't be salacious. If anything, it will be a testament to her life."

She didn't know where these words were coming from, but she knew she was grasping at straws. With each word, she felt more and more uncomfortable. She turned her attention back to Nigel. "That last time you spoke. Did Lucy say anything to you that might be important?"

The poor man opened his eyes wide and stared at a point in the corner of the room. As if he was staring into the past.

"She seemed all right," he said with a shrug. "Normal, you know. She sounded happy. Her new business was stressing her out, she said, but she was enjoying being her own boss. We didn't speak for long, I'm afraid." He gave Anne's fist another squeeze. "In fact, she was in a bit of a rush, now I think of it. She was going for a drink with an old boyfriend of hers."

Camille froze, gripping the pen she'd been toying with tight between her fingers. "Oh?" She took a deep breath, lest she sounded too frantic in her response. "I don't suppose you remember the name of this person?"

Nigel pursed his lips, thinking. "Oh dear, she did tell me his name . . ."

"It wasn't Mark, was it?"

His eyes narrowed. "Mark? Mark. Yes. I think it was. She seemed eager to see him again. Which is why I can't understand her . . ." He trailed off and looked Camille straight in the eyes. "Do you think he had something to do with it?"

"That's what I'm trying to find out," she said. "Did the police talk to you after Lucy died? Did you mention to them she was meeting with Mark?"

"I think I did. They knew she'd called me that day and asked me what I knew. But as I say, the way they found her . . . It seemed a foregone conclusion."

Camille put her pen down. Yes. But that's what Mark wanted everyone to believe. She raised her head. "Thank you both so much for your time. I promise you, whatever I write I'll send to you first and anything you don't want to be included, I'll remove."

"Okay, thank you," Nigel said. "And thank you for being a good friend to our Lucy." Anne didn't look up. She just dabbed at her eyes with the crumpled tissue.

Camille got to her feet. "Thank you again for the tea."

"Do you want to stay for another cup?"

"No, I'm good," she told him. "I've got to get the next train back to London. But you've both been very helpful. And once again, I'm so very sorry for your loss." With that, she grabbed up her bag, headed out the way she came and closed the front door behind her.

As she walked the short distance back to Sevenoaks train station, her head was spinning with a flurry of conflicting thoughts and emotions. She felt sick and dizzy, but had a fire burning inside of her all the same. Fighting through the exhaustion, she pulled out her phone and sent Leila a brief message asking if she could meet her off the train.

The Ex

The best thing for Camille right now would be to go home and rest. Catch up on some much-needed sleep. But she couldn't go home. Not yet. Not now they were getting ever closer to the truth. If Lucy had met up with Mark on the night she died, then someone must have seen them together. Perhaps now the police would take their claims seriously.

Chapter 21

DI Richard Shaw considered the piles of paper on the table in front of him. Every so often he'd glance up from a printed-out screenshot of a Facebook community page or a Twitter feed and regard the two women in front of him with an incredulous expression on his face. But at least he was contemplating the evidence they'd brought with them. Or rather, what Leila had brought with her.

Once on the train back to London, Camille had called Leila and filled her in on everything Lucy's parents had said. That Lucy had displayed no signs of depression or suicidal tendencies and, more importantly, that she'd been meeting Mark the night before she died. He was the last person to see her alive. If that didn't warrant the police taking a closer look at him, then what did?

And Leila, being Leila, had gone to town with the evidence, printing off everything she had on Mark, everything she'd found out about the dead women and their links to him and each other. It was an impressive portfolio, presented in a clear plastic box file. But as DI Shaw continued to spread the papers out on the table in front of him, shaking his head intermittently, Camille saw how it might look to him. Like the workings of conspiracy theorists.

Still, the incredulous expression on his face had morphed into one closer to curiosity as he examined more of the evidence. Finally, he sat back in his seat and folded his arms over his chest.

"Very impressive," he said, although it didn't entirely sound like he meant it. "And you think this is ample proof that Mark Kennedy has something to do with the deaths of these three women?"

"Yes," Leila said. "It's clear as day. He killed them. I know he did."

"I see. So he killed Ophelia Andrews, who had enough alcohol and sleeping pills in her system to take out a rugby team? Or Lucy Meadows, who was discovered by friends hanging off her bedroom door with a belt around her neck?" He was leaning forward, reading off his own notes from a thin spiral-bound pad. "Or what about Charlotte Browning, who came home from the pub one night and tripped and fell down the stairs? He killed these three women, is that what you're saying?"

Camille swallowed and glanced at Leila, but her demeanour was unremitting. "Yes. That's what we're saying."

DI Shaw sucked back a deep breath, his chest expanding as he did. Tonight, under the stark fluorescent lights of the interview room here at Stoke Newington police station he looked younger than she'd first realised. In his mid-thirties, if she had to guess. Was that young for a DI? She wasn't sure. But if she was going to pursue a career in investigative journalism, she should probably do her research. The police were always involved somewhere down the line and she needed to bring her A-game if she was going to make it in her dream career. She did notice the DI was wearing a wedding ring, however, and the bags under his eyes said he'd been working long shifts. It was far from Sherlock Holmes' standards in terms of reading people, but she was getting there.

"Surely you can see why we're concerned," she tried. "These women's deaths are all linked by one common denominator. Mark Kennedy."

"No. They're not, Ms Fletcher. The women who died might have all had the same boyfriend – when they were all at university around the same time – but their deaths are not linked. And none of the investigating officers found any evidence of foul play."

There it was again. The same argument Harriet had given. But Camille wasn't having it.

"What about what Lucy's dad told me? That Lucy was meeting with Mark the night before she died. Has anyone even questioned him about it?"

DI Shaw sighed. "I can't disclose what's been written in police files, or, indeed, any aspects of the investigation. But I can tell you all areas were considered. Like they always are. And no evidence of foul play was recorded."

He said these last words whilst stabbing at the table with his finger. He was trying hard not to lose his patience.

"For fuck's sake!" Leila spat. "This is just typical of you people, isn't it?"

"You people?"

"The police! The Met! Jesus, you'd think you'd learn your lessons, but you don't. It's just an old boy's club. You don't care about justice for these women. You're not interested in finding out the truth. You just want to brush it under the carpet and move on with the least amount of fuss and paperwork." She pointed her finger at him. "But we see you, DI Shaw. We all see you."

Camille bristled with nervous energy at her friend's outburst. It needed saying. She believed that. But as the room fell silent, she had an awful feeling they'd gone too far.

"What about the fact we were followed?" Camille offered. "Both of us. And you saw that tweet from Ophelia. She thought she was being followed too."

"*Thought* she was. You don't have proof of any of this."

"Jesus," spat Leila. "Have you heard yourself?"

"Hey, let's try to stay calm," Camille said, glancing from Leila to DI Shaw. "Please. We need your help."

The man took another deep breath and exhaled loudly, but there was enough subtext behind it she suspected he was softening.

"We just want to make sure this doesn't happen to any other women," she added, keeping her voice low and calm. "I understand what you're saying. That these deaths have been investigated and no one thought they were suspicious. But people get things wrong, don't they? Even experienced police officers. Because what if we are right about Mark? What if he strikes again and again? When do you take this seriously? When Leila and I end up on a slab in a morgue? We could be next. And yes, that might mean we've got an agenda and a specific frame through which we're considering this evidence, but that doesn't mean we aren't on to something. What if he kills again and you've done nothing? Would you be able to look your wife in the eyes? Or your kids?"

It was a risk. She had no idea if he had children, but it appeared to pay off. In her experience, if you mentioned someone's kids, you often focused their mind.

DI Shaw blew out his cheeks, gathering the piles of paper together in front of him. "I'll tell you what I'll do, okay? I'll examine everything you've brought in and make some proper notes before taking it to my gaffer, to see if he thinks there's anything in it. But I can't promise anything. Do you understand?"

"Thank you," Camille said, glancing at Leila. "That's all we ask. Look at the evidence, maybe speak with Mark again about the night Lucy died and—"

"I said I can't promise anything," DI Shaw cut in. "I don't want you to think this means we're opening an investigation into Mr Kennedy, but I'll do what I can."

"Thank you."

Beside her, Leila snorted but managed a muttered, "Thanks."

"Right then," DI Shaw said, raising his arm to look at his watch. "It's getting late, so if there's nothing else, I'm going to ask you both to leave. I've got your numbers and I'll call you if anything comes up."

* * *

Outside the police station, Camille bounced from foot to foot to keep warm whilst she waited for Leila to use the bathroom. Things had gone better than she'd imagined with DI Shaw and, coupled with the cool night air, she felt wide awake and ready for action. What that action would entail, she didn't know, but she was slap bang in the middle of this mission and her entire being was eager for what came next. It was better than sitting around waiting for the inevitable.

Unfortunately, as Leila emerged from the police station, she had a drawn expression on her face and, from the way she was walking, it was clear there'd be no investigative work going to take place that evening.

"Are you okay?" Camille asked as Leila joined her on the roadside.

"I'm just feeling a little deflated. I thought we had him."

"We will get him. DI Shaw listened to what we had to say. And he seemed more open to the idea than last time. He said he'd look into it."

"He was fobbing us off, Cam. I'm certain of it."

Camille wasn't as adamant about that as her friend, but she let it pass. It was getting late and her initial burst of energy on leaving the station was now fading fast.

"Do you want to stay over at my place?" she asked, gesturing down the road. "It's only a short walk from here."

Leila closed one eye. "No. It's fine. Thanks. Where's the nearest station?"

"Hackney Downs. But if you're walking that far, you might as well come back to my place. Come on, it's safer if we stick together, too."

She hadn't considered this point before voicing it, but as the words left her mouth, she realised how true they were.

"We'll be all right," Leila said, nodding to a row of black cabs waiting across the street. "I'm going to jump in a cab. Want me to drop you off?" She seemed broken, like someone had drained all the vitality from her.

"Are you sure you're okay?" Camille asked.

"Yes! Stop asking me. Do you want a lift or not?"

She glanced down the street, hit with a sudden resolve. "No. I'll walk. It's only ten minutes and you're going in the opposite direction. Plus, we can't let that bastard get to us, can we? Otherwise, he's won."

Leila smiled. "Good point. Look, I'm sorry for being pathetic. I just feel shitty. I'm probably just tired or whatever. We'll catch up soon though, yeah? Tomorrow?"

"No problem." They said their goodbyes and Camille waited for Leila to cross over to the waiting taxis before turning around and heading for home.

As she walked down Amhurst Road, she was up in her head, thanking the cosmos for its help up to now and asking it once again to take care of her. She called on whoever or whatever was out there to help her step into her power and to continue watching out for her. It felt remarkably empowering as she strode along the deserted streets. Right now, she needed all the help she could get. These were trying times and she needed to stay strong both mentally and physically if she was to keep going.

She was near enough to the main road not to feel too isolated. But she'd only got a little way down the street when she heard the distinct sound of footsteps behind her.

Shit.

No.

Not now.

Please . . .

She slowed her pace, giving whoever was behind her a chance to pass by or cross over to the other side of the road. Like she would have done if she found herself walking too close behind someone on a deserted street. But they remained on her side of the road and gave no indication they were trying to get around her. In fact, the pace of their footsteps had fallen in line with her own. Camille held her breath as a million thoughts flew through her mind. Was this it? Had he come for her? She wondered if she could outrun him. Or even fight him off. He was tall and athletic, but the amount of adrenaline and nervous energy whipping through her system gave her cause to believe she'd not go down without a struggle. At the corner of Amhurst Road, she stopped. Maybe this was what was supposed to happen tonight. Maybe this was the cosmos' way. She was done running. Done with being scared. With fists clenched and her breath tight in her chest, she spun around to face the person following her.

"What do you want?!"

Chapter 22

Camille once read that if you ever suspected you were being followed, it was a good idea to face the person head-on, to look them in the eyes and call them out. The idea being that most attackers relied on the element of surprise and if you demonstrated that you knew they were there, they often panicked. But as Camille turned to face whoever was following her, she was surprised to see the road was empty. There was no one there.

She paused, attention flitting around the scene as she squinted into dark corners and dingy alleyways. But there was no shadowy figure present. Not a soul in sight.

She pulled out her phone, wondering if she should call the police, or even retrace her steps and tell DI Shaw her concerns. But tell him what, exactly? That she'd imagined footsteps? He seemed now, begrudgingly, to be on her side. She didn't want to spoil that goodwill by showing up at the station acting like some nervy kook. Besides, she'd just been talking about being followed, about her worries, so it was clearly in the forefront of her mind.

Shit.

Was this all in her head?

Had it always been?

There was surely a name for the phenomenon where you experienced things that weren't real because you were expecting them to be. Camille was susceptible to the idea of footsteps and being followed, so her tired mind had conjured them up.

But her eyes didn't lie.

There was no one in sight.

But as she took a right down Shacklewell Lane, she heard the footsteps again and this time she had no doubt. They were moving fast, too, the rapid flit-flit of rubber soles on concrete growing louder every second. As she turned around, she saw them. A dark figure with their head down on the other side of the road, heading the same way as she was. They weren't running, but weren't out for an evening stroll, either.

Camille let out a yelp.

In the darkness, it was hard to make out any features other than a black outline, but her heart and guts told her all she needed to know. And what they were saying was that she was in danger and she needed to run. Turning on her heels, she raced down the street, pulling her phone out and calling Anthony as she went.

"Pick up, Ant," she whispered, pressing the phone to her ear. "Please pick up."

In front of her were the Cotton Lofts apartments and as she got nearer, she saw two women letting themselves in through the security gate. Glancing over her shoulder, she saw the figure cross the street after her.

No. Please. No . . .

She ran over to the security gate as the women passed through to the other side. She just managed to shove her foot in the gap before it fully closed. It was heavy and hurt her instep, but she was able to slip through to the other side before letting the wooden gate swing shut behind her.

"Help me," she called out, but the women had already entered the building and didn't hear her. She returned her attention to the phone. "Come on Ant, where are you?"

She'd now found herself in a wide passageway that ran around the side of the building and opened out into a large communal space. Through the gloom, she could make out a small court-yard with raised planters and bench seating. Tall security fences surrounded the entire area. Which meant that, other than back the way she'd come in, there was no way out.

She glanced around her, frantic breaths billowing out into the chilly night air. She was ready to bang on the door to the apartments when the ring tone in her ear clicked off and a voice came on the line.

"Hey there, stranger. How are you? I just got back."

"Ant," she rasped, in a hoarse whisper. "I'm being followed. Again. I think it's him."

"Fucking hell, Cam. Where are you?"

"Not far from the house, the backyard of Cotton Lofts. But I'm trapped here." She spun around, searching desperately for a gate or a side door. He was out there waiting for her. She knew he was. He probably knew there was no way out and was biding his time. But then she saw something. "Wait, I've got an idea."

As she moved around to the rear of the building, a security light came on to reveal the industrial-sized refuse bin that had been pushed against a fence over in the far corner. If she could scramble up on top of it, she could get over the fence. From there, it would only take a few minutes to reach her house.

"I think I can see a way out," she told Ant. "I'm going to put my phone away, so I've got both hands free."

"Okay, but be careful," Ant said. "I've found you on the Find My Friends app. I'm coming to get you."

"Thanks," she said. "Hurry."

She hung up and stuffed the phone back in her pocket before running over to the fence and grabbing onto the lip of the bin. Her trainers scrambled for a foothold as she scrambled up on top, but eventually, she got both elbows up over the top and hauled herself up. As she got to her feet, she peered over the top of the security gate.

It felt like her heart had fallen into her stomach.

The dark figure was still there. They'd crossed over to the other side of the street and were standing facing the gate. On seeing Camille appear over the top of the security fence, they tilted their head to one side. Then, as if animated by a volt of electricity, they set off walking.

What was their game?

Had they given up?

Or did they know a different way around?

On the other side of the fence was a large concrete car park with spaces marked out in white paint, but no cars. Over to the left, she saw a patch of grass and a basketball court in front of another apartment block and in front of her, across the far side of the car park, an exit out onto the road. Cecilia Road. The road where she lived. She was safe. Almost.

The thought came to her that the dark figure could very well be circling around to the far side of the car park to head her off. If they knew the area well, it was a possibility. But she was also out of options.

Swinging her legs over the top of the fence, she lowered herself down and dropped the last metre onto the concrete. A burning pain shot up both legs on impact, but she ignored it and pressed on, running as fast as she could across the car park. Her whole body ached with tension and exertion, but she had tunnel vision, eyes fixed only on her escape route. Once she was out the other side, it was only fifty metres to her front door. She'd be safe.

Her feet pounded the concrete as she raced for the exit. She was almost at the roadside, ready to cross over when a dark shape veered in front of her. Hands grasped at her upper arms. She tried to scream, but her voice caught in her throat. She tried to pull away, but they were too strong for her. This was it. It was game over. She was going to die. She was . . .

"Hey, hey, Cami." The figure held her at arm's length and in the orange glow from the streetlight overhead she saw the recognisable face of her best friend and flatmate.

"Ant," she gasped. "Thank God. He was . . . He's . . ."

"Don't worry, hun, I've got you." He placed an arm around her shoulders and guided her across the road. "You're all right. You're safe."

"I thought I was going to die."

"Stop that," he said, pulling her towards him and gripping her shoulder. "But we need to get back to the house. I've got something I need to show you."

The Ex

"What is it?" she asked, not sure if she had the mental capacity to deal with anything else this evening. "Is it bad?"

"Depends how you look at it," he said, raising his chin to look back over her head. "It could be dangerous. But it could also give us the answers we need."

Chapter 23

Camille was still shaking as she took off her jacket and hung it in the hallway. Behind her, Anthony was taking his time locking the front door – Mortis and Yale locks – he even slid the top and bottom bolt home, which was something that they seldom bothered with. Whether this was for her peace of mind or because he, too, was worried, she couldn't be certain. But she was glad of it. The fact he was taking this as seriously as she was doing helped. It meant she wasn't going crazy.

"Are you okay?" he asked, squeezing her arm.

"Yes. I am now. But that was damn scary back there, Ant. They were definitely chasing me."

His mouth widened into a thin-lipped smile. "Do you think it was . . . him?"

"I don't know." She sighed. As she walked through into the front room, she turned back to face him. "If we're right about Mark, then why wouldn't it be him? But I don't know. I didn't *feel* like it was him. Don't ask me why because I don't actually know what the hell I mean by that. Sorry, I'm talking shit. I'm all discombobulated and up in my head, not thinking straight."

Ant followed her into the room. "That's understandable, Cam. Don't beat yourself up about it. Do you want to call the police and report it?"

She sat down on the edge of the couch. "I don't know. I don't know what to do. We've just been to the station, Leila and I. We gave them all the information we had."

"And?"

"Not much. I spoke with the same guy as before, DI Shaw. He seemed more open to the possibility that Lucy and the rest might have been murdered. He said he'd review the stuff we'd brought in and talk to his boss. I could call him, but I don't want to piss him off."

Ant glared at her. "You were almost attacked, Camille. If he gets pissed off by you reporting that, then he needs to rethink his career path."

"Yes. Fair enough." She shook her head, hoping to shake out some of the bad energy swirling around in there. It didn't work. "Can we leave it, please? For now, at least. I'll see how I feel in the morning."

"Have it your way." He moved past her into the kitchen. "I'll make us a drink, then I'll show you what I've found. Tea?"

"Do we have anything stronger?"

"There's a bit of this knock-off Amaretto stuff left."

"No. Tea it is, then. Cheers."

She sat back on the couch and closed her eyes. The pulse points in her neck and thighs were throbbing and as her adrenaline levels abated, she felt as if she might burst into tears. But she fought against it, gritting her teeth and balling up her fists. She had to stay strong. She couldn't let go of her power. Not now. No one was going to break her spirit. Not Mark, not some shadowy figure, not DI Shaw's reluctance. She had justice and virtue on her side.

As well as some excellent friends.

"Here you go, princess," Ant said, placing two mugs of steaming tea down on the coffee table and lifting his laptop off the couch so he could sit down beside her. "Now, then. Take a look at this."

He opened the laptop and logged in. As the screen flashed into life, it showed the last webpage he'd been on, a Facebook event page for something called *Your Questions Answered*.

Camille squinted at the screen. "What am I looking at?"

"Wait." He clicked on another tab and an online article popped up from the Barking and Dagenham Reporter. A photo of a man's face adorned the article, top right. It was a typical head and shoulders shot, the sort you might find on LinkedIn. Mark Kennedy. He looked older than the last time she'd seen him, but there was no mistaking those blue eyes or that supercilious smile. She read the headline at the top of the page.

'Golden' Mark Kennedy's next step towards becoming Conservative MP for Barking

She scanned the piece, reading how, after five years of working in the public sector, Mark was moving into full-time politics and hoped to stand as MP in the 2024 election. Apparently, he had big plans for the area and was committed to meeting the local people and bringing a grassroots approach to his policies. It was the sort of typical guff you heard a lot from new politicians, but he'd probably do well for himself. Just as long as no one from his past made life difficult for him.

She pulled her focus from the screen to look at Ant. "We knew this. Or suspected as much. What's new?"

"This is," he said, clicking back to the Facebook event page. "He's doing a meet and greet on Friday morning. Tomorrow. All welcome. Just turn up with questions and he'll answer them, that sort of thing."

She nodded. "You're an absolute star, Ant. This is what I've been waiting for. I asked Stephen if he could arrange a meeting between me and Mark, but this is even better. This way we catch him unaware. I must go. I must speak with him."

"You think you can do it, see him face to face? I mean, there'll be plenty of people around, so it'll be safe." He twisted around to face her. "But if you do this, Cam, then you're going to be well and truly on the guy's radar. Is that what you want?"

She wanted to tell him no. It wasn't what she wanted. But circumstances had transpired against her and she had to see this through. For Lucy and the others. And for her own safety and sanity. She had to know.

"If we're right about him, I'm already on his radar," she told Ant. "He knows what went down between me and him, he knows what he did. Thus, he also knows I could go public."

Ant nodded as he closed the laptop. "I'm coming with you, though."

"No. I want to go alone. He might speak more candidly if it's just me and him."

"You think? He's just going to admit he's been killing women? Easy as that?"

"No. But I want to look him in the eyes. I want him to see me. I want him to know that I know." She looked down to see her hands were once more balled up into tight fists, her knuckles white with the intensity. "He's a piece of shit, Ant. I see that more than ever before now. Even before he was a killer, he was an abusive rapist prick. I want him to know he's not going to get away with it any longer. Any of it."

Ant blew out a long breath. "You're scaring me now, Cam. I don't want you to put yourself into a dangerous situation. Or say something you can't walk away from. Remember, you've got no proof of any of this."

"The proof's up here," she snapped, tapping the side of her head with her finger.

They stared at each other. Ant's mouth opened and closed as though he wanted to say something, but he'd thought better of it. Despite her outward appearance remaining resolute and unabashed, Camille knew exactly what he was going to say. Because she felt the same. That what she'd just said was absolute nonsense. Ant was right. Without tangible evidence, she could get into a lot of trouble throwing around those sorts of accusations. Especially to someone like Mark.

"I'll be careful," she told him. "I'll be clever about it. Okay? But I've got to do this. I need to see him."

Ant twisted his mouth to one side, but she could tell he wasn't going to take her on. "Fine," he sighed. "But I am coming with you and that's the end of it. I'll wait outside if you want, but I'm not letting you go there alone."

"Fine. Thank you."

She leaned forward and grabbed her mug of tea. It was cool enough to drink and she gulped it down in a few mouthfuls. She hadn't realised how thirsty she was, but it wasn't a shock. She'd been neglecting her health for the last week, eating on the go, not hydrating enough. It wasn't good. It had to stop.

"I'm going to go to bed," she said, placing her mug down and getting up off the couch. "I'll see you in the morning."

Ant gave her a warm smile and an encouraging wink as she passed by. Yes. This is what she needed. A good night's sleep now and a proper breakfast in the morning. It would set her up well for the day. She needed to be in top form. First thing tomorrow, she would see Mark face to face after all these years.

Your Questions Answered.

It seemed like an apt title for the event. Because she had a lot of questions for 'Golden' Mark Kennedy. And she would not leave without getting some answers.

Chapter 24

It took Camille and Anthony forty-five minutes and two trains (the overground to Whitechapel and then the district line) to reach Barking, where Mark's meet and greet with his prospective constituents was taking place.

The venue was an old community centre, a short walk from the station and across the road from the grounds of Barking Abbey. The Facebook event page had stated an 11 a.m. start and things appeared to be in full swing when they got there a few minutes after. A woman with grey tied-back hair and pink cheeks welcomed them as they entered the building and asked them to sign in.

"Are you here to see Mark Kennedy?" she asked Camille as she finished signing her name on the clipboard.

She straightened up and passed the pen to Ant. "That's right. He seems very much what we need around here. A young go-getter with ideals." It was generic flim-flam, but it seemed to do the trick, eliciting a flurry of animated nods and winks from the woman.

"He's amazing," she said. "He's going to take this city by storm. Then the country. Then the world. Watch this space."

Camille smiled and flicked up her eyebrows before taking Ant's hand and leading him through into the main space. The room was almost full, surprising for a Friday morning, with at least a hundred people sitting facing a small stage, which was bare except for a metal podium off-centre, to the right. Whether this placement was deliberate, she wasn't sure. But Mark certainly wasn't dealing with subtlety. An enormous banner hung across the back of the stage with the words *Mark Kennedy, Member of Parliament for Barking 2024.*

"Nothing like being overconfident, is there?" Ant whispered as they headed for the back row and sat on the two seats closest to the end.

Camille considered the banner up on stage. It was a bold statement, but she kind of admired the impudence. And, really, what was the difference between Mark stating this and her writing in her manifestation journal that she was going to be a famous writer? They were both just putting the idea out into the world. Asking the universe for help. But as she settled into her seat, any vague admiration she might have felt crumbled to dust as the lights went up on stage and a voice boomed over the PA system.

"People of Barking, please welcome your future member of Parliament, Mark Kennedy."

A ripple of applause went around the room as the man himself strode onstage. He was wearing a dark navy suit and a grey tie. As he bounded up to the front of the stage and waved to the assembled throng, he looked trim and athletic and full of energy. His hair was cut short and parted to one side and his eyes sparkled under the stage lights. He looked good. But he always did. And that meant nothing.

As he moved over to the podium and thanked everyone for coming, Camille cast her gaze around the room, taking in the other people who had come here to listen to Mark and get their questions answered. With both Barking and nearby Dagenham and Rainham being historical Labour stronghold, he had his work cut out for him, but if anyone could convince these people of his worth, it was Mark.

As he spoke, she sensed the room relax. People were warming to him. He spoke with vigour and conviction, explaining his plans for the regeneration of the retail and commercial district. He would bring new jobs and opportunities to the town, he told them. He'd put Barking back on the map.

Camille hadn't intended to become so entranced by Mark's rhetoric, but that's what happened. Even Anthony's cynical asides halted after the first few minutes and he too seemed captivated by Mark's supreme oration skills. It wasn't so much what he was saying, but how he said it, the emotion he placed behind his words, the way he breezed over certain statements and took his time over others. Even when he wasn't speaking, the intense way he peered into the crowd had everyone in the palm of his hand. The whole thing was clearly very well-rehearsed, yet it appeared effortless. It was like watching a top pianist or athlete, someone at the height of their game, engaging in what they loved and making it look easy.

His speech ended to rapturous applause, much louder and more exuberant than the low energy smattering he'd received as he'd taken the stage. It seemed the people of Barking – those sitting here at least – had been won over. He left the stage with a triumphant wave as the grey-haired woman from the reception stepped forward and informed the gathered throng that the Q&A would begin in fifteen minutes and would last an hour.

"Bloody hell," Ant sneered, looking at his watch. "We've got to wait another hour?"

Camille wasn't relishing the idea, either. "Wait here," she whispered, peering across the room at the door Mark had disappeared through after his speech.

Before Ant could talk her out of it, she was marching over there. It felt like her heart was in her throat. A shiver of adrenaline shot down her spine as she approached the door.

"Excuse me, you can't go in there. Mr Kennedy is getting changed." She heard the woman's voice, but didn't turn to acknowledge her. Her focus was only on the doorway. On getting to Mark.

"Hello? Miss? There's no access down there for the public."

But the woman was too far away to block her. Without looking back, Camille pushed through the door, finding herself at the end of a long corridor. There were no windows and just one door halfway down on the left. At the far end, the passage turned down to the right and she could see light emanating from an unseen source. She could also hear music. Moving down the corridor, she edged nervously around the corner. At the far end of the next corridor, a door had been wedged open and beyond this, she could see a large, brightly lit room containing tables and chairs set out in a U shape. As she got closer, she could also see a person moving around and as she entered the room, they turned to face her.

"Mark!"

She froze in the doorway. Even though she was specifically coming here to see him, it was still a shock to be standing so close after all this time. Not to mention after everything she'd found out about him. He'd changed out of his suit and was wearing a pink polo shirt tucked into beige chinos.

"Camille?"

She swallowed, hoping the right words would form, but none did. Mark looked her up and down, an expression halfway between confusion and amusement forming across his fine features. It was as if he didn't know whether to welcome her or shout for security.

"What are you doing here?" he asked.

She cleared her throat and stepped forward. "I came to speak with you. I've got a few questions."

"Okay. Well, it's great to see you again." He didn't take his eyes off her as he walked over to her. He seemed perturbed. But why wouldn't he be? As he got closer, he shook his head in mock disbelief. "Look at you. How are you?"

Before she could answer, a whirlwind of bluster in the form of the grey-haired woman followed her into the room. "Mr Kennedy. I'm so sorry. I tried to stop her."

Gone now was the keen, affable nature she'd exhibited as Camille had signed in. She leaned against the doorframe and glared at her. "Miss, I told you there was no admittance back here."

"Glenda, it's quite all right," Mark said, holding up his hand and baring two rows of bright white teeth. "Camille here is an old friend of mine. She wanted to catch up in private. Isn't that right?"

Camille regarded him out of the corner of her eye before smiling at Glenda. "I am awfully sorry," she said. "I didn't realise I wasn't supposed to come back here."

"Did you not hear me shouting at you?"

"No. I didn't." She pulled an apologetic face but didn't care whether or not Glenda believed her. She was here now, and she wasn't leaving. "I'll only be a few minutes, then I'll leave Golden Mark to his people. Is that okay?" She glanced at Mark, then back at Glenda.

"It's fine, really," Mark said. "If you wouldn't mind delaying things out there for a while longer, Glenda, I'll be out as soon as possible. Thank you so much."

The woman gave Camille a stern look but shuffled off down the corridor. They waited for her to be out of earshot before either of them said anything.

"What are you doing here?" Mark asked. "Do you live in Barking?"

She narrowed her eyes at him. The question seemed genuine enough, but he was a good actor. He always had been. "No. I live in Dalston. I thought you knew that."

"Why would I?" He perched on the edge of the nearest table. "I'm sorry I've not kept abreast of what most of our old crew are doing these days. I'm a little ashamed to say I lost touch with everyone. Just about."

"Just about? That's funny."

He frowned at her. "Is it?"

She inhaled through her nose, holding the breath in her chest as she considered him. In turn, he looked back at her with an open face, those blue eyes of his wide and expectant.

"What would you do if I told you I know?" As she said the words, her entire body tingled with a fight-or-flight response. She hadn't intended on saying anything so forthright and as she heard herself, she was overcome with nausea. Regardless, she held her nerves, locking eyes with her ex-boyfriend, searching his face for any tells. Anything that would give him away.

"I know, Mark," she whispered, narrowing her eyes.

"What?" He was still smiling that Hollywood smile of his, but the tiny muscles at the side of his jaw were quivering like he was forcing it now. "What do you know, Camille?"

The way he said it made her blood boil. It was that same condescending tone he used with her towards the end of their relationship. The horrible, toxic prick.

"I know about Lucy and Charlotte and Ophelia. I know what you did."

He flung his hands in the air. "Oh my fucking Christ! Are you serious?" But the dramatics were fast done away with as he stepped towards her, stabbing a finger violently in her face. "Is it you? Writing those slanderous messages about me online? Because I swear to God, Camille, if it is—"

"It's not," she replied, standing her ground. Even if she'd wanted to run, her legs felt like they'd turned to stone. "But I've been doing some research of my own. I've met with Leila Bloom and Harriet Knight. Remember them, Mark? Remember what you did to them? What you did to all of us? You see, we've been talking, Mark. Sharing stories. And it's become clear that you've done quite a few nasty things in your past that you wouldn't want to be made public."

"Fuck you," he snarled. "This is ridiculous. Just a lot of bullshit rumours."

"Really? You raped me, Mark. I know that's not bullshit."

"What the hell are you talking about? When was this supposed to have happened?"

She squeezed her fists together. "That night after Stephen's birthday. I came back to your place. I told you I was too tired, too drunk, that I didn't want to . . . But you didn't listen."

She gasped. She'd never properly vocalised these things to herself before today, but as she did so now, vivid images of that night flashed up in her mind's eye.

"For heaven's sake, Camille. We were boyfriend and girl-friend." He spat the words at her. "And we were good together. Especially sexually. You liked it a bit rough now and again, as far as I recall. You're misremembering this. It's probably Leila Bloom putting ideas in your head. You know she's fucking mental, don't you? Totally crackers."

Camille flinched as another image flashed up in her memory. "You pushed me down on the bed," she whispered, her skin bristling as she relived the moment. "You held me there. You were laughing as I was telling you to stop."

Mark shook his head. The smile was well and truly gone now. In its place, an angry snarl. "You need to stop this. You need to shut your mouth, Camille. If you ever say these things to anyone else, I . . . I will ruin you. Do you hear me?"

She felt numb and dizzy. She couldn't feel her arms or legs. It was as if she was having an out-of-body experience, but in that moment, she also had no fear. Raising her head, she looked him dead in the eye.

"Have you been following me? Is it you? Or one of your henchmen? A hired heavy?"

"What the hell are you talking about, you ridiculous bitch?"

As Mark stepped forward, Camille's eyes darted to his hands. A normal person, when becoming angry, would make a fist, but he'd spread his hands wide like he was about to grab her. His long fingers were crooked and taut. He lunged towards her, but she cried out and he stopped.

"You did it," she gasped, stepping back. "You actually did it. You killed Lucy. And the others."

"Don't be stupid," he growled through gritted teeth. "You sound fucking crazy, do you know that? You sound like them. And all the others. Paranoid fucking halfwits who can't be happy with who they are, so are trying to ruin me. But it won't work, *darling*. Sorry. I won't let you or anyone else spoil what I've worked so hard for."

Camille was startled as footsteps echoed down the corridor behind her. Voices followed.

"I've told you, Mr Kennedy is busy!"

"Yes. And I told you I'm worried about my friend—"

She spun around as Ant and Glenda burst into the room. "Ant?"

"You all right, hun?" He straightened himself to his full height, eyes scanning the room. "Did he hurt you?"

"Of course I didn't bloody well hurt her," Mark spat before letting out the fakest laugh Camille had ever heard. As she turned back, his face had brightened with a wide smile. "We were just catching up, weren't we Cam? We're old friends from Oxford. Having a bit of a giggle about old times."

Ant curled his lip. "I know who you are, mate."

"Mr Kennedy, is everything all right?" Glenda asked. "I'm so sorry but this gentleman was insistent."

"It's fine, Glenda. But I really should get out there now and speak with the congregation." He picked a white sweater off the back of a chair and put it on before flattening his hair with the palms of his hands. "It was lovely seeing you again, Camille."

He held his hand out and, still feeling dazed and out of it, she took it. "Oh? Yes."

With that big smile still in place, he leaned in close. "And remember what I said, *Cami*. Anything you think you know is best forgotten. Otherwise, this won't work out well for you."

She held his gaze, hands gripping at each other's now like they were engaged in some weird battle. The winner being the one who could emit the most hostility whilst still submitting to social niceties. Mark won out, in the end. But it was probably how all politicians greeted each other.

"I suppose we'll get going then," Camille said.

"Yes. Probably best."

She let go of his hand, but before she could turn around, he leaned in even closer, speaking under his breath. "Those girls deserved everything they got," he whispered. "Don't end up like them, Camille. It's not a good look."

She gasped, darting her attention over to Glenda and Ant, but neither of them seemed to have heard. She looked back at Mark, whose eyes were as intense as ever. He stepped back and opened his arms wide.

"Well, I really must go and meet my people. Thank you again for dropping by. It was wonderful seeing you again. You look really well. We must not leave it so long next time." Then to Glenda. "Shall we?"

With a jiggle of her shoulders, Glenda reached for Mark's arm and guided him out of the room, leaving Camille and Ant to watch as they disappeared down the corridor. Once their footsteps had disappeared also, he turned to her.

"What happened?" he whispered. "Did you find out anything?"

Camille didn't look at him. "I'll tell you soon," she said. "But right now, I want to get out of here and as far away from that man as possible."

Chapter 25

"Oh, my days, Cami. Are you okay?" Leila yelled across the large pub, hurrying over to the booth where Camille and Anthony were sitting. They were in the Pendle Tavern a few minutes walk from Hackney Downs tube station, but apart from a few old boys nursing their warm pints, they were the only customers. As Leila reached their table, she threw her arms up. "Hun. You poor thing. You look really pale."

Ant had called Leila the second they'd left the community centre. He said they should all be together. He was right.

"I'm okay," Camille told her, lifting her glass of gin and tonic. "This is helping."

But it wasn't, not really. She kept shivering like she was cold, even though it was a warm day and her heart hadn't stopped pounding since they'd left Mark's event. What he'd said to her in that back room kept going around and around in her head.

She regarded Leila as she stood next to the table. Her face was like that of a troubled meerkat who'd just spotted a predator. Dark shadows ringed her dark eyes and her hair was still wet from whenever she'd showered last. This, coupled with the stains on her jumper and the fact the collar of her leather jacket was tucked in on one side, made her appear rather dishevelled. And not particularly well. Mark's words reverberated in Camille's head.

You know she's fucking mental, don't you? Totally crackers.

But they were his words and being who he was – what he was – she had to assume they were carefully picked, designed to cast doubt in her mind. Because that's what people like Mark did, wasn't it? They manipulated and lied for their own ends. She saw that more clearly than ever now. She might only be ninety-five per cent sure he was a murderer, but she was one hundred percent certain he was a narcissist and a gaslighter, probably with psychopathic tendencies.

"Camille?"

She snapped back to the present to see Leila leaning over the table, looking at her with expectant eyes.

"Sorry?"

"Do you want another drink?"

"No," she replied. "I've got plenty left. Thanks."

"Right. Let me get myself a large glass of something wet and you can tell me all about what happened with that evil prick."

Camille watched her as she walked purposefully over to the bar and waved for the server's attention. "Does she seem different to you?"

Ant twisted around to look, but when he turned back, he shrugged. "Not really. Why do you say that?"

"Nothing. Ignore me. I'm being stupid." She took a large gulp of her drink. The tonic was a little flat, but it meant she could sense the gin's presence more. She sighed. It was ridiculous to think Leila was anything other than what she was – a concerned woman, a victim of circumstance. Like her and Lucy and all the others, Leila's issue was she'd fallen for an abusive and manipulative man. A man who was doing all he could to ensure none of those women ever spoke about who he really was. She wasn't crazy. She was hurt and angry.

"Right then," Leila said, appearing with a large glass of white wine in her hand and shuffling into the seat next to Ant. "Tell me everything."

The table fell silent as Camille straightened her back and relayed what had happened at her meeting with Mark. Striving to stay as factual and unsullied by emotion as possible (like a good journalist would) she explained how calm he'd appeared at first, but how unsettled he'd become when she'd mentioned Lucy and the other women. As Ant and Leila looked on with open mouths, she reeled off everything she could remember – what he'd said, what she'd said and that he was about to attack her at one point. She explained how Glenda and Ant had disturbed them, before taking a deep breath and relaying what Mark had whispered in her ear before he'd stormed away.

"That son of a bitch," Leila whispered. She lifted her glass and gulped back a mouthful of wine. "He's playing with us."

Ant leaned back and rested his head against the wooden surroundings of the booth. "That sounds like an admission of guilt to me. What do you think?"

"Absolutely," Leila said. "He's silencing everyone who has anything on him. In the worst way possible."

Camille ran her fingers up and down the side of her glass, drawing lines in the condensation. Her friends were right, of course. But she had so many conflicting thoughts swirling in her head that she felt like she couldn't focus on any one of them. It wasn't just Leila who had given her cause for concern. She worried she was going crazy, too. Reality felt like it was slipping away from her. She felt sick and unsure of herself. But maybe that was what the sick bastard wanted. Maybe that was his plan.

She shook the unhelpful thoughts away and took another big drink.

Stay in the moment, Cam.

Focus on what you know to be true.

"Cami? Are you sure you're okay?" Leila asked, concerned eyebrows almost meeting over her scrunched up nose. She shook her head. "Oh, my girl. He's messed with your head, hasn't he?"

"Maybe. I don't know. It was scary. He was right there in front of me. The expression on his face . . . it was as if he despised me. Yet we loved each other once. Or I loved him, at least. But he used to be so kind. It's hard to marry up who he was with who he's become."

"Yes, but you have to," Leila said, sitting back. "He's evil, Camille. A threat to both our lives. We have to stop him."

"I know. We keep saying that. But how? He's rich and powerful and the police don't want to know."

"They *didn't* want to know," Leila replied, her right eye twitching. "But I've discovered some new information. Or rather, I remembered something Mark once told me. Did you ever meet his brother, Simon?"

Camille frowned. "No. Never. I didn't think they were that close."

"Not sure. But Simon Kennedy is an anaesthetist." She raised her eyebrows, glancing between Camille and Anthony as though waiting for a response. When none came, she carried on. "So . . . He knows about using sedatives. How to knock people out quickly and without a trace."

"Fuck me," Ant whispered.

"Exactly. So now Mark has motive and means. And in terms of his three exes who are still alive, he's now looking for opportunity."

Camille swallowed. "And I've just put myself slap bang in the middle of his radar."

"Don't be hard on yourself," Ant told her. "If he is out to get you, he'll find you whether or not you approached him first. Plus, if he was the one following you, then he already knows where you live."

The skin on Camille's arms prickled with heat energy as she and Leila both turned to glare at Ant. He baulked for a moment before his face fell. "Shit! Sorry, Cam. That came out really fucking badly. I didn't mean to scare you. I just meant you shouldn't beat yourself up about—"

"It's fine, Ant. Really." She reached over and grabbed his wavering hand. "I know what you meant."

"We will not be victims of that prick," Leila said, placing her hand over the top of Camille's and Ant's. "Not anymore. Never again." She gripped Camille's hand tight, her face rigid with emotion.

"But what's next?" Camille asked. "I don't want to sound like a broken record, but I feel we're going around in circles. What do we do?"

Leila lifted her hand and sat back in her seat. "Don't worry. I've got an idea."

"What is it?" Ant asked.

She took a large gulp of her wine and narrowed her eyes. "I can't tell you just yet," she said, eyes flittering around the room. "But it could stop Mark once and for all."

Camille and Ant exchanged a look as Leila drank down the last of her wine. "Sounds rather ominous," Camille said. "But don't do anything stupid, Leila."

She had a bad feeling growing in her stomach and she wasn't exactly sure what was causing it. It could be her growing unease about her friend's state of mind. It could be the fact her ex-lover had just threatened her life. It could be both those things and so much more besides.

"Righto, darlings, I've got to get off," Leila told them, placing her empty glass down triumphantly. "I love you both. Stay safe. Stay vigilant."

With that, she shuffled out of the booth and headed for the door. Once there, she turned and gave them a curt nod before disappearing out into the street.

"Did that all seem a bit odd to you?" Camille asked, turning back to face Ant.

"In what way?"

"I don't know. You don't think she's got some different agenda, do you?"

He twisted his mouth to one side. "This is Mark again, isn't it? Messing with your head?"

She shrugged. "Maybe. Yeah."

"She's probably a bit antsy, that's all," Ant said. "Isn't it understandable? Because I'll be honest with you, Cambo. You haven't been acting yourself recently either. Again, understandable."

"Yeah. You're right." She finished her drink. The last thing she wanted was to allow Mark to get to her. Because that was his plan. It was how narcissists operated.

Ant checked his phone. "Do you want another drink? I've got time for one more before I start my shift."

Camille stretched. "Do you mind if we don't? I'm worn out. I just want to go home and chill out in front of some trashy TV."

"Shall I come back with you? I can try to swap shifts with someone."

She grabbed her bag. "No, don't. I'll be no company. To be honest, I might go straight to bed. I'm knackered and I'm seeing Stephen tomorrow. I don't want to be a nervous, tired-out wreck."

Ant pursed his lips. "Oh, yes? A hot date, is it?"

"Don't be daft. We're just friends."

"Yeah, sure. Friends." He winked. "But I'm pleased for you. It'll be good to take your mind off all this madness for a while. I know heavy shit is going down, but I also think we're making each other paranoid, to be honest. If all you think and talk about is shadowy figures and killer exes, you start to see danger and evil everywhere. It's human nature, evolution at work."

Camille got to her feet and stood by the side of the table. "Are you going to be okay?"

"I'll be fine." He smiled. "Text me the second you get home."

"I will."

"Hey, Cambo." She'd turned to leave and had walked a few steps when Ant called after her. As she turned, he held up his fist and tapped it on his chest in a show of solidarity. "You've got this, sister. And it's not going to last forever. Keep your chin up and your eyes open."

She held up her fist. "I'll see you later, Ant."

It was still daylight outside and the journey back to the house would only take Camille around fifteen minutes if she walked fast, but as she left the pub behind nervous energy overcame her. It wasn't nice to feel this way. Paranoid. Hyper-alert. It was exhausting. This situation might not last forever, as Ant had said, but neither did she have forever. She'd already spent too long treading water in her life and right now it felt as if she was in quicksand, sinking fast. She needed this to end. And soon.

Quickening her pace, she hurried along the main street. Tonight, she'd be kind to herself, a hot bath and then an early night. Hopefully, after a good night's sleep, things would seem a little better in the morning.

Because, quite frankly, they couldn't seem any worse.

Chapter 26

The bed was warm and toasty and Camille snuggled into the folds of the thick duvet, wrapping her bare legs around the cushiony material. She'd been dreaming of a sandy beach, somewhere warm and peaceful, the salty sea lapping at her feet as she lay back with the sun on her face. In the dream she was a famous writer who'd been travelling the world, enjoying the rich offerings of the local areas in the daytime and writing all night, poring over her laptop with a bottle of local wine to hand. The world knew her as a truth-teller and an adventurer. Someone with the world at her feet and life in her hands. The way it should be . . .

She stirred, but the sleepy smile on her face remained. It felt as if she was in a glorious cocoon, a haven away from the harsh dangers of the outside world. Her mind was empty of thoughts, still fuzzy from the benign dream world where she'd been lounging these past ten hours.

A yawn stretched her gummed-up mouth but she didn't open her eyes. She didn't want to accept the new day just yet. As her awareness spread, she became aware of a tightness in her chest. It felt like it was telling her something. Was there something she had to do today, somewhere she had to be? She stretched as her mind warmed up and her consciousness flashed back online.

"Ah, shit."

Mark . . .

She propped herself up off the bed on one elbow and rubbed at her eyes. The grim and dingy bedroom in which she found herself only exacerbated the fact she wasn't on a sunny beach. She needed to clean up her environment. What was that saying? Tidy room, tidy mind.

Sitting upright, she swung her legs over the bed and reached for her phone. The time on the screen said 9:15 a.m. She'd slept well and was surprised to find the remembrance of her predicament didn't smash her in the guts like it had done the previous few days.

There was also a text from Leila saying she needed to talk. Camille closed it down without responding. She would call her, but not now. Today was a new day and, for whatever reason, she felt more positive than she had done in weeks. She wanted to stay that way. And whilst Leila was fast becoming a good friend, she was intense and abrasive and right now Camille needed calm.

She wondered if there had been insightful information in her dreams that only her subconscious had remembered – and this was why she found herself in this happier state of mind. If so, she was glad of it. The anxiety she'd harboured since discovering she could be Mark's next victim was, for now, only a small part of her reality rather than it totally enveloping her. Instead of feeling nervous and confused, she felt empowered. Maybe it had been seeing him face to face that had done it, but she was done with being afraid. If he was going to try to kill her, then let him try. She was ready. And she wasn't going out without a fight.

The Ex

Grabbing up the towel lying over the back of her chair, she headed for the bathroom. The house was quiet and still, but as she listened at Ant's door, she heard a dull rumble of snoring from inside. She smiled. He was a good friend. Normally, on a Friday night, he'd stay over at Tim's house after work. The fact he was here with her meant a lot.

She leaned into the shower unit and turned the water on as hot as it would go before stripping off and stepping inside. The searing jets pummelled her skin, but she enjoyed the experience, putting her head under the water and hoping to eradicate more of her demons in the heat and steam. As the water washed over her, she visualised her past troubles dropping away and a new determination filling her soul.

That bastard had killed Lucy and broken the hearts of Mr and Mrs Meadows. He'd robbed three sets of parents of their children. Three wonderful women cut down in their prime. Who would never marry, would never have children, would never achieve their dreams. It was so unfair. And for what? So he could keep his status as 'Golden' Mark Kennedy. So the world would never know what an abusive, toxic piece of shit he really was.

But Mark hadn't counted on Camille Fletcher stepping into her power so forcefully. Today the universe was well and truly on her side and she was going to ride this wave as long as possible.

She twisted off the shower and reached for her towel, wrapping it around her as she stepped out onto the bathmat. Her plan now was to get dressed and tidy her room. Then, once her environment was in order, she'd set to work doing what she did best. Writing. She'd procrastinated about it for long enough. It was time to start that article. She couldn't let Mark get away with this. The world needed to know the truth. If she couldn't take him down physically or legally, she'd do it with words. She'd weaponise her laptop and a fresh word document and expose him for what he was. There would be ways around the libel issue. She just had to be clever about it. Once the first article had been written and was out there, others would follow. She'd give a voice to his victims, write the stories they couldn't.

She was so caught up in her thoughts, excited about the possibilities of what could happen, that it wasn't until Ant opened the bathroom door and poked his head around it that she realised he'd been banging.

"Are you all right in there?"

"Yes . . . umm . . . sorry, did you need to use the toilet?"

"Well, I do. But I was knocking because your phone has been ringing for the last five minutes."

"Oh?" She pushed past him and hurried down the corridor to her room.

"It's rung about three times," Ant called after her.

She could hear it as she got to her bedroom door, that high-pitched chirping noise that was her phone's default ring tone but which she always meant to change. She got over to it as it rang off.

Damn it.

As she scooped up the phone and scrolled through the missed calls, there was no number stored.

Who was trying to contact her so desperately?

Her mind raced with possibilities. It was usually cold callers, sales calls that withheld their numbers. But for them to call three times in close succession seemed odd. And on a Saturday morning, too. She chewed on her bottom lip. Could it be Mark? But if so, where would he have got her number? She sat on the edge of her bed and placed the phone next to her on the pillow.

"Who was it?" Ant shouted through the door.

"I don't know. Probably someone trying to get me to upgrade my phone or something . . ."

She trailed off as the ring tone filled the room once more. This was it. She tapped answer and held it to her ear.

"Hello, Camille Fletcher speaking."

"Ms Fletcher." The voice was deep and steady. "This is DI Richard Shaw at Stoke Newington Police Station."

"Oh, I see. How is . . . How are you? I mean . . . Sorry, what can I do for you?"

The DI cleared his throat. "I'm calling you as a courtesy, Ms Fletcher," he said. "I thought you might want to know that we brought Mark Kennedy in for questioning yesterday afternoon . . ."

Chapter 27

A shudder ran down Camille's body and it wasn't just because her room was chilly and she was only wearing a towel.

"You arrested Mark?" she gasped.

"No," DI Shaw said. "That's not what I said, Ms Fletcher. We brought Mr Kennedy in for questioning. We had some lines of investigation we needed to clear up and he came to the station willingly and without caution."

"Yes, but did you ask him about Lucy and the others? Sorry, you probably can't tell me that over the phone. Is he still there?" The forthright energy she'd experienced on waking was still present and there was no way she was letting this drop. The police had him. He was going down. She lowered her voice. "Do you want me to come in and make a statement, DI Shaw?"

"No, I do not, Ms Fletcher." He sighed pointedly, as though he was trying to stay calm and wanted her to know. "My colleague and I discussed quite a few things with Mr Kennedy, actually. None of which I can go into with you either on the phone or elsewhere – and the upshot is he has strong alibis for all the dates in question."

"All three? Did you ask him about Charlotte, too?"

"All three, Ms Fletcher. Not that we are in any way considering these women's deaths to be suspicious. As I said, Ms Fletcher, this is a courtesy call. I know they were friends of yours and that might be hard for you to accept, but you must. It's very sad and unfortunate, but it's time to let this go. For your sake."

"Excuse me?" Camille stiffened as the words sank in. "Are you threatening me?"

Another sigh came down the line. "No, of course I'm not. I'm trying to help you. I am sorry for your losses, but it's time to move on, Camille. People will be watching you carefully after these allegations. Anything you write about Mark Kennedy, either on social media or your blog, will be pored over and if you slander him in any way, there will be repercussions. I shouldn't be saying this to you. Do you understand?"

So that was it. They were trying to silence her. She got to her feet and moved over to the window to open the curtains. Outside, it was a fresh spring day. The sun was out and a gentle breeze swayed through the trees that lined the lane at the end of the garden.

"Camille?" DI Shaw said with a growing impatience noticeable in his voice. "Do you understand what I'm saying to you?"

"Yes, yes, don't ask questions or the big men will get me. Just like always."

"I'm saying be an adult about this," DI Shaw replied. "I have two daughters, Ms Fletcher, seventeen and fifteen. I'm telling you this as I hope it will show you that I am not dispassionate to your concerns. But there is no case here for Mark Kennedy to answer to."

Out the window a small tabby cat walked regally along next door's fence, stalking an unsuspecting starling that was picking at a bird feeder a few metres away. "Fine. I get it," Camille told him.

"Good. And I am sorry. Now please, focus your energy elsewhere. I don't want to hear from you again."

He hung up and the line went dead. Camille held the phone to her ear, regardless. The cat was about to pounce on the starling, hunkering down and wiggling its bum in readiness. Camille gritted her teeth and didn't breathe. Maybe this was the universe showing her the way. If the starling succumbed to its predator's advances, then that was the way the world was, and she had to accept that. The bigger and more ferocious animal always won.

The cat pounced, but at the last minute, the starling flapped its wings and flew away from the feeder, leaving the tabby to fall awkwardly onto the ground. As the starling soared across the endless blue sky, the cat slunk into the undergrowth with its head down. Defeated.

"Hmm," Camille said to herself. "There you go."

She closed the curtains and dried herself off. As she did, she felt an overriding sense of pride that it was only anger and resentment now prickling the small hairs on the back of her arms, whereas once it was fear and trepidation. This experience had already changed her. She was stronger and more confident in who she was. And what she had to do. She dressed in her old joggers and an oversized t-shirt and headed downstairs.

"Who was it?" Ant asked, not looking up from the TV as she entered the front room.

"The police," she said.

That got his attention. He glanced at her, coffee mug poised centimetres from his lips. "And?"

She shook her head. "Nothing like that. Not really. It was DI Shaw, the same officer as before. He said they'd interviewed Mark, but he has strong alibis for all the dates in question. So they won't be pursuing any other lines of enquiry. Basically, he was ringing to tell me to leave it alone."

Ant sipped at his drink. "I see. But having an alibi doesn't mean anything, right? Surely he's going to cover his tracks. And didn't we already wonder whether he's got people working for him? I imagine someone in Mark's position—"

"Don't, Ant," she said, moving past him into the kitchen. "It's not helping." She flicked the kettle on and selected one of the upturned mugs on the draining board. She was hoping for a few minutes to collect her thoughts on the matter, but he followed her in.

"You can't just leave it. You'll be living in fear for the rest of your life. If you have information that could ruin him, he isn't going to let that go, is he?"

She reached for the jar of coffee off the shelf above the kettle and placed it alongside her mug. "I don't know, Ant." She puffed out her cheeks and exhaled a long, deliberate breath. She hoped it might unravel some of the pent-up emotion tightening her chest, but it didn't. "The truth is, I don't know what to think right now. I'm angry and frustrated and have a million conflicting ideas dancing around in my head. I'm questioning everything – Mark, myself, Leila."

"Leila?"

She shrugged it off. "I don't know. It's like ever since she came into my life, it's been a rollercoaster ride." She lifted her phone and opened the last text she'd received from her new friend. The one she still hadn't replied to. "But maybe she's one of those people who needs lots of excitement in her life, who thrives off of it."

Ant stepped back and cleared his throat theatrically. "Erm, are you saying she's a drama queen? That she made all this up to – what – add more flavour to her life? Your ex-boyfriend is killing women if you'd forgotten."

Camille sighed. This wasn't coming out as she intended it to. "I haven't forgotten. And I'm not saying that. At all. I love Leila. She's great. It's just . . . We don't know her that well." She screwed the lid off the coffee and grabbed a spoon, scooping a large helping into her mug. As she moved, she felt Ant's eyes on her.

The kettle clicked off the boil and she poured water into her mug. The air in the kitchen had turned sour, but she didn't know how to clear it, so she said nothing. He continued to watch her as she bent down to open the fridge and take out the carton of milk.

"All I'm saying is—" she started, turning to look at him and hoping more words would follow "—that I'm worried . . ."

She trailed off as her phone chimed in her pocket. Saved by the bell. Pulling it out, she saw the caller ID was once more showing as unknown. "This is probably the police again," she said, holding the screen up for Ant to see.

"Well, you need to tell them you aren't going to . . ." He trailed off as she held a hand up to him so she could answer it.

"Hello?"

"Am I speaking with Ms Camille Fletcher?" It was a man's voice, but not the one she'd been expecting. This person was older and more well-spoken than DI Shaw.

"Yes, that's right," she said. "And who are you?"

"My name is Ralph Harrington-Jones from HJBC Law. We represent our client, Mr Mark Kennedy. I believe you are aware of him?"

His tone was polite, but she sensed a threatening undercurrent in the way he said *believe.*

"Yes, he's an old friend of mine. *Shh.*" She pushed Ant away, who was getting in her face, mouthing for her to tell him who it was. Swerving around him, she walked into the front room and perched on the arm of the couch. "What's this about?"

"I think you know what this is about, Ms Fletcher. But on the assumption that you are someone who hasn't quite grasped the enormity of their situation, let me spell it out for you. Mr Kennedy is a high-profile figure who will soon be part of the British political establishment. You cannot be throwing around ridiculous unsubstantiated accusations. I have this morning completed the requisite forms to apply for a restraining order against you, which I am almost certain we shall get. After this, if you come within a hundred metres of Mr Kennedy, you will be breaking the law. If you try to contact him in any way, you will be breaking the law. Do you understand what I'm telling you, Ms Fletcher?"

Camille bristled; a sneer twitched at the side of her mouth. But what could she do? What could she say? He had her.

"Yes," she muttered. "I understand."

"Good. And further to this, Ms Fletcher. We know the sort of outlandish claims you and your friends are currently making regarding Mr Kennedy. He categorically denies having anything to do with these poor women's deaths and was happy to speak to the police yesterday afternoon regarding these matters. But this must stop. Now. Mr Kennedy has been so traumatised by this experience that he's had to take a few days away from his campaign to recuperate somewhere in the countryside. Somewhere private."

He's traumatised?

The mendacious bastard.

Harrington-Jones continued. "If you don't want to be sued for slander, then please stop this pointless and far-fetched crusade. We have people monitoring your online output, Ms Fletcher. If we see anything libellous written about Mr Kennedy and these women, then we shall take matters further. Do you understand?"

"Yes," she croaked before clearing her throat. "Yes, I understand."

"Good. Then we'll leave it there. When Mr Kennedy returns from his holiday, I shall inform him he has nothing further to worry about. I hope I don't have to speak to you again, Ms Fletcher. Good day."

He hung up, leaving Camille sitting on the arm of the couch staring into the middle distance. A hot rage flooded her system, but she had no clue what to do with it. She felt trapped and stupid, like a small child who didn't have the mental or verbal capacity to deal with its predicament.

"What was that all about?" Ant whispered from over her shoulder.

Camille chucked her phone onto the couch cushion. "Mark's lawyers," she said, sliding off the arm of the couch and flopping back on top of her phone. "Telling me to back off or they'll take me to court for slander. He's getting a fucking restraining order against me. As if *I'm* the dangerous one."

Ant placed Camille's coffee down on the table and took her place on the arm of the couch. "They're trying to silence you."

"They've succeeded." She swung her legs onto the floor and sat up. "What can I do now? I wanted to write an article. I wanted to expose him."

"You still need to. Fuck them."

"No. It's over, Ant. He's too powerful. But maybe this is a good thing. They say he's got strong alibis on the days Lucy and the others died."

"Yes. And you know what I think about that."

"But maybe this is him taking a different approach now. Silencing me with lawyers. I'd rather he do that than him or one of his cronies doing it with their hands. Permanently." She reached for her coffee but made no move to drink it. Instead, she placed it on her lap and wrapped both hands around the mug. It was warm and comforting and sometimes you had to be thankful for the little things.

"What about Lucy and Ophelia and Charlotte? Are we just going to let their families think they fucked their lives up the way they did? You said yourself how broken Lucy's mum and dad were. They're going to go to their graves thinking their little girl killed herself."

"What if it's the truth?"

"What if it's not?"

Camille looked away. Was he right? Despite her obstinance on the phone, Mark's lawyer had left her feeling anxious. If it was fear alone driving these thoughts, then she was doing exactly what Mark wanted.

"Remember what he said to you, Cambo. That doesn't sound like the sort of thing an innocent man says."

Camille sniffed. She could still hear Mark's words in her head, the nasty way he'd rasped them in her ear.

Those girls deserved everything they got . . .

Don't end up like them.

It's not a good look.

"If you ask me," Ant went on, his voice rising with emotion. "All this means is that he's scared you're getting closer to the truth. Involving lawyers is basically an admission of guilt. And you don't know what to think? Come on, Cam."

She stared into her coffee. He was right. She'd been second-guessing herself, questioning her own sanity as well as that of her new friend. But this was him. Using his toxic ways to invade her thought processes. Gaslighting her from afar. She hadn't known what to think. But she did now. Ant was right. This wasn't over. Not by a long stretch.

Chapter 28

Mark Kennedy killed three of his ex-girlfriends – Lucy Meadows, Ophelia Andrews and Charlotte Browning.

He did this to stop them from selling their stories to the press or revealing information that would damage his political career.

He is a manipulative and self-serving man, but also extremely intelligent. Somehow, he made their deaths look like the result of a suicide or an accident.

He may or may not have people working for him. In the last two weeks, Leila Andrews, Harriet Knight and Camille Fletcher have all been followed home on at least one occasion.

They continue to feel threatened.

Camille stared down at the notepad on her lap. It wasn't a comprehensive account, but it was a start. A way of getting her thoughts out of her head and onto paper so she might organise them better.

Because whilst she agreed with Ant, that she needed to stay with this story and get to the truth, she also needed to keep herself sane and stable. She'd never been very good at compartmentalising opposing aspects of her life, but she hoped this might be a start. If she was ever going to have a career as an investigative journalist, she had to view the cases she was working on dispassionately. Otherwise, you made mistakes, missed important facts.

So, in the spirit of this, she'd felt it would be useful to get everything out of her head and down on paper before meeting up with Stephen. This way she could enjoy a pleasant evening without her anxiety weighing her down. Perhaps it was easier said than done when you had your friend's death and the possibility of your own demise pressing down on you, but that was her hope, at least. Then she'd revisit her notes tomorrow. Refreshed and with a clear mind. She'd read often how, if you were troubled, it was important to put space around your problems and return to them at a later date. That way, you could approach them from a different perspective and hopefully get a new insight into what to do next.

With this in mind, she closed the notepad and placed it next to her on the couch. The time on her phone screen showed 16:35. She was meeting Stephen in Soho at seven and she was already cutting it fine. It was time to get ready for her date.

No.

Wait.

It wasn't a date.

She couldn't think like that.

Despite her growing feelings towards Stephen, that she'd like him to be more than a friend, she had to play it cool. She suspected he felt the same way about her, but she wasn't certain. The last thing she wanted was to reconnect with him, only to mess it up.

She'd lost too many friends recently.

* * *

It was ten minutes past seven when she got to the venue where they'd arranged to meet, a small bar near Old Compton Street and Charing Cross Road, called, simply, The Bar on the Corner. But that was good. Simple was good. It was what she needed.

She entered and stood in the doorway for a moment to allow her eyes to grow accustomed to the gloom. She couldn't see Stephen anywhere as she wandered over to the bar, scanning the room as she went. In the visualisation exercise she'd gone through on the journey over here, he was already waiting for her, waving excitedly as he spotted her across the room. But the reality was she was the first to arrive. Still, it was another learning point, she told herself. What was it Tony Robbins said? Swap your expectations for appreciation and you'll never be unhappy. Something like that. She wasn't a massive fan of Robbins (she preferred her self-help gurus to have a gentler, more feminine energy) but it made good sense.

So here she was, without expectation, happy to be out of the house and meeting with Stephen. For once, she would leave all her troubles at home. All the unanswered questions, all the anxiety and confusion would still be there tomorrow. But tonight was about relaxation and having fun. It was about letting her busy mind settle so that inspiration would once more have room to grow. Plus, on a more fundamental note, it had been a hellish couple of weeks. She deserved to kick back a little and have fun.

Vowing to herself she'd stay present and in the moment, she raised her head and smiled as the young barman sauntered over to her.

"Can I get you a drink?" he asked.

"Yes. Can I have a Manhattan please?"

"Sure. How would you like that?"

"Perfect. Thank you."

She smiled to herself as he nodded his approval and glided over to the other side of the bar. A perfect Manhattan. When she'd first heard someone ask for one, her initial response had been to double-take. She'd assumed they were being particularly rude and arrogant with the bartender.

Make me a drink and make sure it's bloody perfect!

These days, of course, she knew the term referred to a half and half mix of sweet and dry vermouth that accompanied the bourbon, but it still made her chuckle when she thought about it.

Who was it who'd first asked for one in front of her?

Was it Erica?

Her shoulders sagged.

Shit. No.

It was Mark. Of course it bloody was. They'd laughed so much at the time when she'd explained her mistake. But thinking about it now, he probably was being rude and arrogant.

Bloody hell. Why did it always come back to him?

She screwed up her eyes, telling herself to stop this at once. She was out on the town. He didn't get to invade her thoughts. Not tonight.

"Here you go." The barman's deep voice snapped her back to the moment. "A perfect Manhattan."

"I hope it is," she told him with a flick of her eyebrows.

He returned the gesture with a crooked half-smile. "Of course." He followed up with a wink, causing Camille to giggle girlishly. "That'll be sixteen pounds when you're ready."

The giggling stopped. Jesus. It had been some time since she drank in central London and she'd forgotten how expensive it could get. Lifting her bag onto the counter, she was scrambling around for her purse when she felt a presence beside her.

"I'll get this."

She looked up into Stephen's smiling face. "Hey, its you." He winked. Her second one in as many minutes. "Thank you. Are you sure?"

"It's the least I can do after being late," he said, nodding at the barman. "Can I have the same, please?"

The barman offered a brief salute in response and Camille turned to face Stephen. "Thank you, you're very kind."

"I don't know about that," he said. "But I'm thirsty and I am sorry for being late. My bloody Uber never turned up. I had to jump in a black cab."

"You take cabs everywhere." She picked up her drink and took a sip. It was strong and spicy and . . . well, perfect. "Quite the big spender, aren't you?"

"I know, it's terrible. And so bad for my carbon footprint. But it's a special occasion, isn't it? I thought I'd push the boat out." There was a glimmer of mischief behind his eyes, so she couldn't tell whether he was being entirely serious. But as his drink arrived and he passed the barman his card and asked him to open a tab, she reminded herself to relax. Things happened for the right reasons if you let them. The universe was in charge.

The next few hours flew by in a whirlwind of deep conversation, plenty of joking around and lots more cocktails. As the evening turned into night, and the house lights dimmed and the music volume rose, they even engaged in a little dancing. Camille hadn't danced for what seemed like forever and despite the busy room and lack of an actual dancefloor, she moved around her partner with joyful abandon. This is what people meant when they talked of losing yourself in the moment. In this space of benevolent thoughtlessness, nothing else mattered: not Mark, not her lack of career, not even Lucy (God rest her soul). For the first time in a long time, Camille felt free and happy.

And probably quite drunk, as it happened.

As they stumbled back to their table, she fell into Stephen's arms and her lips were planted on his before her brain and reason caught up with her. He kissed her back with a passionate, open-mouthed kiss, pulling her into him at the same time. He smelled amazing and was a good kisser, too. Camille closed her eyes, sinking into his firm embrace as his hands caressed the small of her back and the top of her bum. It felt like they were kissing for hours and no time at all. When Stephen finally pulled away, they smirked gleefully at each other.

"I wasn't expecting that," he purred.

"Really? But was it okay?"

"It was more than okay." He leaned into her, his hot breath tickling her neck and sending shivers down her back. "Do you want to come back to my place?"

She stared into his eyes as he leaned back and waited for an answer. Normally they were blue, but his pupils were so dilated because of the dark room (and for other reasons, she hoped) it gave the impression that his whole iris was black. She lifted her chin as she considered his question. Of course she wanted to go back to his place. She would like nothing more than to lose herself in him.

He continued to hold her gaze, neither of them blinking as the space between them fizzed with a tangible erotic charge. She wanted to kiss him again. God, how she wanted to kiss him. She wanted to kiss him and never stop kissing him. But was this a good idea? When your ex-boyfriend was readying himself to kill you, it was probably a bad time to start a new relationship. But then when was a good time these days? If you waited for life to be on an even keel, you'd be waiting forever.

Stephen tilted his head to one side and smiled.

"Yes, I'd like to come back to your place," Camille whispered. "Let me text Ant and tell him I won't be home." She was smiling as she pulled her phone out of her jacket pocket, but her euphoria soured as she saw the notification on her screen. A new message from Harriet.

"What is it?" Stephen asked.

"Harriet. You know, Harriet Knight. Another of Mark's exes. It's the first time I've heard from her since we met. I wonder what she wants." She tapped open the message to find just five words.

Can you call me please?

She glanced up at Stephen, feeling very sober suddenly. "Give me a second, please." She slipped off her stool and headed for the door. "I need to make a call."

She found Harriet's number straight away before weaving her way through the bar and out onto the street, where the cool evening air chilled her bare skin and sobered her up even more. She didn't dare take a breath or even allow herself to imagine what Harriet might want as the dial tone chirped in her ear.

She picked up after two rings. "Camille. Are you okay?"

"Yes. I'm fine. What's going on?"

"What do you mean?" she asked. "Where are you?"

Camille glanced down the street. It was still relatively early and this part of London didn't get into full swing until gone midnight, but there were a lot of people around. "I'm out. What did you want?"

"Oh God, you don't know, do you?"

It felt like her heart had dropped into her stomach. "Know what?"

"I haven't heard the full story; I've just seen it on Facebook, that's all. I thought you'd know more, which is why I asked you to call."

Camille bounced from foot to foot. It was chilly outside, but this was out of impatience. The adrenaline firing in her system was dealing with the cold. "What's going on, Harriet?"

"Oh hun, it's Leila. She's dead."

Chapter 29

Camille was standing on the curb side staring at her phone when she heard Stephen's voice behind her.

"Hey, is everything all right?" He walked over and draped her jacket over her shoulders. "You must be freezing out here with just that thin top on."

She might have been freezing, she wouldn't have known. Right now, she couldn't process anything.

"Leila's dead," she whispered, without looking up.

"I beg your pardon?"

"Leila Bloom. Harriet just told me. She's dead."

Stephen placed a gentle hand on her shoulder and turned her around to face him. "Are you sure?" he asked, stooping to meet her gaze. "How? When?"

She frowned. "I don't know. She didn't say." Shaking her head, she looked up into his eyes. "I need to go home. Is that okay? I'm sorry."

Stephen nodded. "Sure. I'll call an Uber." He already had his phone out and the app open and she didn't have the energy to stop him. Plus, she wanted to get home as soon as possible. She watched on as Stephen tapped furiously at his phone before looking at her with a warm smile. "We're good. There's one literally around the corner."

The car arrived and they jumped in the back without another word said between them. As the car negotiated Soho's one-way system, Camille opened Facebook on her phone and found Leila's profile. With wide, unblinking eyes, she scanned the feed. But there was nothing there. The last post was from almost eighteen months ago and was brief, Leila talking about going to the pub for the first time since the pandemic started. Camille went back to the home page and typed Leila Bloom's name into the search feed. This time she got what she was looking for: three posts from people who knew Leila and who had tagged her. As her heart threatened to beat its way through her ribs and out of her chest, she perused the Facebook posts, eyes falling on certain words and phrases.

My darling sister and best friend . . .
Lost her battle with depression . . .
Heartbroken . . .
Can't believe it . . .
You went through with it . . .
At peace now . . .
Be kind . . .

Camille glanced up as what felt like a sledgehammer hit her in the guts. Through the window, the bright lights of Angel whizzed past as they headed towards Islington. She'd be home soon but had no idea what she was going to do when she got there. A heavy weight of emotion bubbled below the surface of her awareness but didn't reach her eyes or mouth. The tears felt trapped inside of her, blocked by the confusion and anger filling her system.

"It was suicide," she whispered to herself.

Stephen, who'd been silent this whole time, lost on his own phone, looked over and as their eyes met, he offered her a reassuring smile. "Looks that way. Poor thing. Did she give you any sign?"

Camille turned back to her phone without answering. Did she give any sign? She was certainly troubled, but that was understandable given the circumstances. Unless . . . ?

No.

She squeezed the muscles of her upper body together to keep the thought from entering her being. Besides, according to his lawyer, he was out of town.

"We're almost in Dalston," Stephen said, leaning around the side of the driver's chair to look through the windshield. "Do you want me to come in with you?"

"Umm. I don't know."

"It's okay. I'll take you inside at least. I can get another cab later if I need to." He smiled again, but this time it was one of those smiles that was all lips and eyes but with little joy behind it. The sort of smile you offer to grieving widows at a funeral.

"Thank you," Camille replied.

They got the driver to take them right up to the house and once stopped, they climbed out in silence. Ant must have heard them arrive because he opened the front door as they walked down the path.

Camille met his gaze, stomach muscles quivering as she tried to hold in the sobs. "Have you heard?"

He nodded, pulling her in for a hug as she got to him. "Let's get you inside."

They shuffled into the front room, still in each other's arms and Ant settled her on the couch. She looked up to see Stephen had closed the front door and was standing in the doorway. It looked like he was hanging back, giving her space. She appreciated it.

"Do you want a cup of tea?" Ant asked. "Or something stronger. I bought a bottle of vodka the other day."

"God, no. I don't want anything. A glass of water, maybe."

"Coming up."

He hurried into the kitchen and Camille waved at Stephen. "Come in, sit down."

He did as she instructed but opted for the armchair a few feet from her rather than the seat next to her on the couch. He seemed uncomfortable, but why wouldn't he? It was difficult to know how to react to someone who'd received bad news. Terrible news. The worst news. Camille didn't even know what she wanted right now, so how could he? And the night had been going so well.

"What have you read?" Ant asked, reappearing and handing her a glass of water.

"Everything I could find," she said. "Harriet called to tell me. Then I went on Facebook. A few people implied she took her own life."

Ant let out a heavy sigh. "That's what it's looking like. I messaged a few people who were close to her, said we'd become friends recently and I was concerned. No one was that committal, but one girl intimated she'd been up and down for years. Bipolar, she reckoned. She also said it wasn't the first time that Leila had tried it."

Camille snapped her attention his way. "Really?"

"It's what she said."

"Oh god, that's so sad," Stephen added. "She always seemed such a happy-go-lucky kind of person. So full of energy. So full of *life*."

He was right. She did. But then how well do you ever really know someone? People were good at putting on a front, hiding themselves from the world. She'd done it herself. She still did. But it rarely helped.

The room fell silent as Camille sipped at her water, but next to her on the couch she sensed Ant bristling like he wanted to say something. She knew what it was.

Raising her head, she met his gaze. "Go on then," she said. "Say it."

"Well, it's a reasonable question, considering everything we know. Did he do it? Was it Mark?"

Camille darted her attention over to Stephen, who just shrugged and shot her back another smile of condolence. "It seems too much of a coincidence now. But if she was troubled . . . if she'd tried it already . . ."

"That doesn't mean she tried it again," Ant replied. "Fuck. We're all troubled, aren't we? That's the human condition. You'd be a fool not to be a bit troubled in this modern world, what with everything that's going on. But that doesn't mean she killed herself. How did she seem to you the last time we saw her?"

Camille frowned. "She seemed fine. Well, not fine, but focused. Like she had something she wanted to do. But not this. She can't have meant this."

"I don't think she did. This is Mark. It has to be."

"Do we know when it happened?" Stephen asked.

"They found her this morning. They think some time yesterday evening."

Camille closed her eyes, picturing the last message she'd received from Leila. She'd said she needed to speak with her. Was it a cry for help? Her reaching for a friend's hand in the darkness?

"I wonder if *Golden* Mark Kennedy has an alibi for this one," Ant added with a sneer.

"I think he does," Camille said. "His lawyer said he was taking a holiday in the countryside. Apparently, me confronting him about Lucy traumatised him and he needed a break."

She raised her eyebrows and nodded as Ant stared incredulously at her.

"That bastard. He's got an answer for everything, hasn't he? But this points to him even more so if you ask me. He's set it up to be out of town so he's not in the frame. But that means nothing. There's always a way around these things, isn't there? All it proves is he has an accomplice. He's pushing his luck now. Everyone makes a mistake eventually. A paper trail or something. We need to call the police, have them investigate his current whereabouts and—"

"No, Anthony!" Camille snapped. "I've been warned. If I say or do anything relative to Mark, he'll sue me. I could go to prison."

"Fuck me. So, you're just going to let him get away with it? You're going to let him win? And what if he comes for you next, Cam? What then?"

"Go to hell, Ant!" she yelled. "You don't know what I'm going through. You're not helping. At all. So shut up, will you? Please. Stop it."

Ant flinched dramatically, causing Camille to turn her back on him. She placed her head in her hands. She couldn't deal with this. There were too many questions and not enough answers. Too much confusion fogging her already inebriated system.

"I say we all need to take a step back," Stephen offered, his voice soft. "This is very sad news and we're all rather thrown by it. Let's not take it out on each other."

Camille sniffed. Anthony huffed. But a second later, he nudged into her. "Sorry, Cambo. It's just a shock, isn't it? I can't believe it."

"Me neither," she said, wiping at her eyes. "But I don't know what you want me to do. It's just me now. I'm all alone in this."

"You're not alone," Stephen told her. "Is she, Ant? You've got both of us. We're not going to let anything bad happen to you." He walked over and knelt in front of her, taking her hand in his. "Why don't I stay over? I'll sleep on the couch."

She squeezed his hand. "No, it's fine. You go home and get some sleep. Ant's here. I just want to go to bed." She wiped at her eyes with the heel of her palm. "I'm sorry about tonight . . . You know . . ."

"Gosh, Cam, you don't have to say sorry. Some other time. Are you sure you don't want me to sleep down here, though?"

She shook her head and released his hand. "I feel exhausted. I just want to sleep."

"Fair enough." He stood upright. "I'll get off then. Will you call me tomorrow, let me know how you are?"

"Of course."

"We'll be all right, won't we, kiddo?" Ant said, placing his arm around her shoulders.

"Yeah."

Ant got up to walk Stephen to the door and Camille wilted onto the couch, placing her head on the soft cushion and raising her feet to screw them into the corner where the arm met the backrest. A tear rolled down the side of her nose, but she made no move to wipe it away.

All at once, she felt more alone than she had done in a long time. It wasn't the boys' fault. Ant and Stephen were both great. But they didn't know what she was going through, not really. Four of Mark's ex-girlfriends were now dead. Three looked suspicious. Four was something else. And with only her and Harriet left, what did that mean? When was it her turn to die?

She screwed her face up as more tears filled her eyes. She didn't know whether she was crying for Leila or herself. It was a weird sensation, feeling so miserable and afraid at the same time. A shiver rocked her body, and she pulled her legs up to her chest, so she was in a foetal position. It was as if the scales had now fallen from her eyes and she'd found herself naked and vulnerable with nowhere to run. She sobbed softly as Ant came back into the room and placed a blanket over her.

"You okay, Cam?" he whispered. But when she didn't respond, he didn't push it. Instead, he turned off the main light and switched on the lamp next to the TV. He was a good friend and she was lucky to have him and Stephen. But whilst they might watch out for her, they couldn't guarantee her safety. No one could do that. And that thought was the most terrifying thing she'd ever had to deal with.

Chapter 30

The next few days were lived on autopilot. Camille woke up, washed, got herself dressed, but each task was carried out with no real thoughts passing through her mind. Stephen called around a few times to check on her, but she was in no mood for company. It was as if her mind had been working so hard over the last two weeks – assembling theories, trying to work out what was going on, what she should do about it – that it had finally broken.

She felt warm and fuzzy-headed as if her body was fighting off a virus. When any notions or thoughts did pop into her head (about Mark or Leila, say) she'd consider them, but as though once removed from the story. An observer, rather than someone slap bang in the middle of the situation. Other times she was overwhelmed, worrying that she was nothing but a phoney. She had wondered if poor Leila was thriving off the situation at times, but now she worried that was her projecting all along.

It was Camille who wanted the rumours about Mark to be true. If Leila's biggest fault was being overly paranoid, hers was much worse. She wanted Mark to be a murderer because it fed her own sense of drama and desire for a good story. But that was pointless now, too. She was too distraught to even open her laptop. And even if she could write, she wasn't allowed to. Mark's lawyer had sent through official documents stating she wasn't to come within one hundred metres of their client, plus a threatening letter that informed her she would be sued for libel if she linked Mark to the deaths of Ophelia, Charlotte and Lucy (the letter used their full names) in any medium, both online and in print.

Yet even with all this going on, there was still a small part of her that suspected not all was as it seemed. Mark was rich and powerful. He could easily have organised a cover-up. Was that what was going on? The more she considered that question, the less sane she felt. Her entire world had spun off its axis.

It also didn't help she'd been drinking too much – a bottle of wine every night for the last three nights. Ever since she found out about Leila. She'd asked Ant or Stephen to go to the shop for her, stating she was too scared to leave the house and, thankfully, they'd complied without question. Clearly, they realised she needed the crutch alcohol provided right now. Whether that was a good thing, she didn't know – or care. The wine helped her sleep and quietened her mind. Even the hangovers helped a little. She couldn't concern herself too much with the petrifying headfuck that was her life when she was focusing on not throwing up.

But this morning she'd woken early and dragged herself into the bathroom before even Ant had woken up. Because, despite her woozy state of mind, she knew it was Friday and at 11:30 a.m., at the West London Synagogue over in Golders Green, Leila's funeral was to take place. Because she was Jewish, they'd made the arrangements much sooner than usual. But, even then, her parents had had to jump through many legal hoops before the coroner would release their daughter's body.

Now showered and dressed, Camille was back in the bedroom making the final touches to her make-up and hair whilst Ant got ready downstairs. It wasn't going well. She leaned back from the small mirror she'd been using to apply her mascara and blew up her fringe. She looked an absolute fright. Even with copious amounts of foundation and blusher, her skin looked pallid and blotchy.

"Sorry, mate," she whispered into the ceiling. "I wanted to look more appropriate for your big send-off."

She was, however, glad they were laying her friend to rest sooner rather than later. The funeral would provide some closure and she hoped, after it was all over, she might claw back some semblance of herself. If there was any semblance left, of course.

She was startled as she heard a car outside and movement downstairs. Stephen had offered to drive, and it sounded like he'd arrived to pick them up. Before he knocked, Anthony opened the front door and she heard the two of them talking on the doorstep. It wasn't clear what they were saying, but the low bass tones of their voices sounded gloomy and monotone. Camille headed back to her room to get her bag and was distracted momentarily by the view through her window. The sky was a single washed-out blanket of light grey. No sun. Not even any birds. A fitting day, all in all.

"Camille, are you almost ready?" Ant called up the stairs. "Sorry, chick, I don't want to rush you, but time is ticking on."

The Ex

She checked herself in the full-length mirror hanging on the back of her door. She'd opted for black jeans and a black shirt rather than a dress. Leila would rather she felt comfortable than subscribe to any formal conventions. She had, though, washed and straightened her hair, which was a concession to how seriously she took this. She'd not even felt like bathing in the last couple of days.

"Here we go then, hun," she sighed. "Let's say goodbye."

It was hard to believe someone so fiery and full of energy could have done what Leila had done. But that didn't mean she hadn't done it. People hid things well and since Camille had heard the news, certain events – things Leila had said and done – had made more sense. It had been clear from the off she had issues, but Camille had assumed her troubled demeanour was because of the rumours about Mark and her desire to take him down. But maybe not.

"Camille . . ." Ant's voice carried up the stairs again.

"Coming." She grabbed the dark grey cardigan from off the bed and headed for the door.

* * *

It was a fifty-minute drive to Golders Green. Stephen began the journey attempting to make small talk but soon gave up when it was clear he was getting no real response from his companions. At the crematorium they found a bench near the back of the room and kept their heads down, letting Leila's family have their space. She had two brothers and her parents were both still alive and, whilst no longer married, they seemed close. Like Lucy's mum and dad had been. There was nothing like shared grief to bring people together. For a time, at least.

Harriet was also here and was sitting on the other side of the aisle at the end of a row. Camille hadn't spotted her until she was already settled, but as Harriet turned, they exchanged thin-lipped smiles and a brief wave, with Harriet mouthing that she'd speak with her after. As more people filed in, she felt Stephen's hand on hers and closed her fingers around his. It was good to have him here.

"How are you feeling?" he whispered in her ear.

She shrugged. "I'm not too bad. I just feel so sad for her family. It's horrible." She had so much more she wanted to say, but the service appeared to be starting. "We'll talk later," she told him. "I'm sorry for being so distant the last few days. I'll drag myself out of it. I promise."

The wink and squeeze of her hand she got in response told her everything she needed to know.

As the rabbi appeared at the front of the room and welcomed everyone, Camille sat back and tried to zone out. She was a spiritual person, not religious, but from what she could gather, neither was Leila. The difference was that none of Camille's family had any religion either. Indeed, she'd only been to a handful of church services in her life, her aunt's wedding when she was six, her grandma's funeral a few years later. That day was rather grim as well, her poor nan having died of cancer at sixty-nine, which was no age at all. But the sadness in the room today was something else. Wherever she looked, people were sobbing loudly and unselfconsciously. But why wouldn't they be? They'd lost someone very special. A strong, funny, clever woman cut down in her prime. And whether that was by her own hand or someone else's, right now it didn't matter. She was gone and the world was a worse place because of it.

Camille closed her eyes, feeling a shiver run down her arms as she recalled the last thing Leila had said to her.

Stay safe. Stay vigilant.

It was good advice.

She exhaled a wavering breath of emotion. It was strange. She was sitting here in the most crowded space she'd been in for a while, yet she felt so alone. But they didn't know what she knew. They didn't understand. All around her, people were mourning the loss of her beautiful friend whilst Mark was out there forging a successful future for himself. Whether he was to blame for Leila's death, she wasn't sure. She wasn't sure about anything anymore. But regardless, he was untouchable. No matter what she did, he had the upper hand. If she told anyone what she believed – what Leila believed – then at best she was a paranoid kook and at worst a libellous criminal. They'd lost. Mark had won.

It seemed the universe wasn't on her side after all.

Chapter 31

Following the interment, Leila's dad announced the family were holding a reception a few miles down the road, in memory of his beloved daughter. All were welcome, he said. Camille hadn't wanted to go at first, but Ant and Stephen had convinced her it would be a nice thing to do, with Stephen adding that it might do her good to socialise a little. He seemed worried about her and that was nice, she supposed, but it didn't help. In fact, today she was finding his caring nature a little overbearing.

But she needed to speak to Harriet, so after queuing to shake hands with Leila's family and offering her condolences, Stephen had driven them the ten-minute journey to the reception. The house was enormous, standing in its own grounds and with a wide driveway that curved up to the house from the road. Impressive stone pillars stood on either side of the main entrance. Inside, however, the house was dingy and dusty and the décor, despite being rather lavish, was old-fashioned. There was also a strange odour in the air that Camille couldn't quite place. She didn't think it a particularly apt or pleasant setting to say goodbye to someone so vibrant and sassy as Leila, but it was her father's home and big enough to fit the hundred or so mourners inside. In the dining room, there was a large table on top of which was laid out what Camille heard referred to as a consolation meal, which looked to be predominantly made up of eggs. Not that Camille had any appetite, anyway.

Whilst Anthony used the bathroom and Stephen headed for the kitchen to get some much-needed drinks, Camille wandered around the space. Rather than being open plan the way most modern houses are, the downstairs was divided up into a plethora of small rooms and annexes. A lounge here, a dining room there, plus a study, a library and what looked to be a games room for when the grandchildren stayed over. It was here where she headed. Most of the adult mourners had assembled into small groups and were talking animatedly with one another. Elsewhere others sobbed and were comforted by friends and family. She leaned against the doorway and took in the three small children who were sitting in a row with their backs to her and staring at the largest television she'd ever seen. On the screen, a small animated blue dog was bouncing on a larger dog's belly. Camille watched for a moment before turning back to the main room. She felt out of place. Except for Ant and Stephen, she didn't know anyone. But even if she had done, she had little to offer in terms of conversation other than basic aphorisms. But then she remembered. Harriet was here.

Raising herself on her toes she peered around the room. Harriet had appeared eager to talk in the crematorium, but perhaps she had left straight after.

Damn it.

She was wondering whether she should go somewhere quiet and call her when she saw a flash of dark brown hair across the room. It was one of those moments where the other person seemed to sense you were looking at them because as Camille walked over, Harriet turned and smiled at her.

"There you are," she said as Camille joined her.

They hugged and air-kissed and then stared at each other for what seemed like a long time but was probably only a second. Harriet was wearing a smart black two-piece and white blouse. She looked nice. But up close, she looked as worn out as Camille felt. She ran her tongue across her bottom lip, trying to get a read on Harriet. Today she seemed warmer, more welcoming. There felt to be more of a connection between them than the last time they met. Or maybe that was what Camille yearned for and she was seeing things that weren't there. It wouldn't have been the first time.

"Do you still think Leila and I are crazy for thinking Mark is doing this?"

A frisson of nervous energy pricked up the hairs on her neck. She had been planning on saying something much more generic, but the words had fallen out of her mouth before she could stop herself.

"Wow, you don't sugar it, do you?" Harriet swallowed and glanced about her before grabbing Camille's arm and pulling her to one side. "Listen, Camille, I never said you were crazy. I was just concerned for my family. I didn't want to prod any sleeping giants. But maybe now, yes, you might have something. It's getting a lot harder to put these poor women's deaths down to merely a coincidence. Four ex-girlfriends of Mark's. All dead."

Camille nodded. Never had being right felt so horrible. "Four dead. Two left. That means either one of us could be in his sights next."

Harriet inhaled through her nose, her chest rising and falling under her silk blouse. "Have you spoken to the police?"

"Have you?"

"No. I thought you and Leila were ..." She looked down. "Sorry. I've been shit. I do have a habit of sticking my head in the sand when life gets scary."

"You can't do that anymore," Camille said. She was speaking more bluntly than she'd normally do, but Harriet's flippant nature was getting to her. It was also solidifying a lot of ideas that had been spinning around in her head the last few days. "If we don't want to be next, we need to do something. But we must be clever about it. Because I have spoken to the police and they don't believe me. They say nothing suspicious has gone on. Tragic accidents or death by suicide – that was what the coroner reported for the first three. I imagine once the inquest is over, they'll rule Leila's death a suicide too. I heard they found empty bottles of vodka and sleeping pills next to her body. Because that's so much easier for them, isn't it? Less paperwork and man-hours. Makes you sick. I even got a nasty letter from Mark's lawyers and a restraining order."

"Shit." Harriet's eyes widened. "So, he knows you know."

"He does. So now do you believe me?"

"Maybe. Yet I have a real problem believing Mark Kennedy is following women along dark streets at night, or actually killing people. But ..." She held her hand up as if anticipating Camille's response, ". . . he could be hiring someone to do it. He's got enough money and the right contacts, coupled with his low moral compass and eagerness to succeed. It's not inconceivable he'd try to get rid of anyone who might stand in his way."

"He's not *trying* to do it. He is doing it." Camille glanced across the room. Stephen had emerged from the kitchen with their drinks and was looking around for her. "But you might be right. It looks like he's set up an alibi for Leila's death, too. Supposedly holidaying in the countryside."

Harriet pursed her lips. "He was always a clever bugger. And even at Oxford, he was happy to do whatever it took if it meant his own advancement. I remember once he—"

"—Yes, yes," Camille said, cutting her off. She didn't have time for nostalgia. "Don't worry, Harriet. I've been rather out of it since Leila died, but today has really woken me up. I will not let that bastard hurt anyone else. If it's the last thing I do, I'm going to . . . I'll . . . What . . . ?"

She trailed off as something flashed up on the TV screen in the games room. The cartoons had ended and a news programme was now showing. Stepping away from Harriet, she narrowed her eyes to read the headline at the bottom of the screen.

No.

It couldn't be?

The rumble of conversation faded away and her vision shifted from macro to micro as a wave of nausea overcame her. She felt like she was floating above herself. There was nothing around but her and the television.

Was she dreaming?

The Ex

Was this real?

Yet there it was, white letters on a red background at the bottom of the screen. Four words that flipped her entire being upside down.

Mark Kennedy Found Dead.

Chapter 32

"Turn it up," Camille mumbled to herself. Then, louder. "Turn it up." Behind her, Harriet was saying something to her but she couldn't focus. Ignoring her, she hurried to the games room and over to the television screen.

"Excuse me. Can you turn it up, please?" The three small children looked at her, their small mouths hanging open. Camille clapped her hands together to focus their attention. "I need to hear what the man is saying. Do you understand?!"

She hadn't meant to sound so harsh, but she'd clearly failed because one child started crying and a second later, all three of them were at it. Their wails echoed out into the next room.

"Oh, no. Don't do that," Camille said. "Please . . ."

"What's going on?" She spun around to see a woman standing behind her. "This is the kids' room. What are you doing?"

The woman appeared tired and angry like this was the last straw for her. Camille didn't want to make a scene, but she didn't have time to mess around.

"Are there any other TVs? I need to watch this."

The woman frowned but glanced over her shoulder. "Yes, there's another set in the study. Down this corridor, next to the kitchen."

She had to shout the last part as Camille was already heading there, winding around people holding paper plates and small glasses of wine. Without slowing down, she ran into the study and over to the small television that was standing on a small table in the corner.

It was a new flat screen set with no obvious controls and no remote control in sight. She slid her finger along the bottom of the screen and touched on a row of buttons. She pressed them all and the screen flashed on. Result.

She turned the volume all the way up as Mark's face appeared on the screen. It was a different channel, but this news was clearly of cross-channel importance.

Bright hope of UK politics dead at 33

She glanced behind her to see a green leather footstool, which she pulled towards her and sat on. Once settled, she turned back to the screen to see the newsreader staring solemnly down the lens.

"Colleagues expected Mr Kennedy to return to work yesterday after holidaying in Hertfordshire, but it appears he never even got there. Reports say he had been dead since last weekend and was only found this morning when his weekly cleaner arrived for work . . ."

"Who is that?" a man's voice asked.

Camille turned to see a stout old man standing in the doorway. He squinted at the screen.

"He looks familiar."

"Yeah . . . umm . . . not sure."

Camille turned back to the screen. There were too many thoughts smashing into each other behind her eyes to form a coherent reply. Dead since last weekend. Which means he died around the same time as Leila. Did she . . .? Or did he . . .? She wracked her brain. Did the timeline make sense? Did it add up?

She gulped back a shudder of emotion. Of course it didn't add up. Nothing added up. It was all too much to deal with. She needed some air. She stood and was heading for the door when Stephen appeared.

"There you are."

She pointed behind her at the television. "Have you seen?"

"Yes. I've seen." He held his arms out to her and she went to him.

"What do you think it means?"

He pulled her into his broad chest, muscular arms holding her tight. "It means maybe now we can move on. Put all this behind us."

She pushed him away, but held on, staring up into his kind face. *Put all this behind us?*

She wanted so much for that to be the case, but how could he say that? After everything she'd been through, how could she ever carry on normally without knowing the truth? She'd been followed home, twice. She spent every waking hour half-scared to death but trying to kid herself she was strong. Her friends had died and no one could tell her why. She needed answers.

Turning back to the news programme, she saw the camera panning across the outside of Mark's campaign headquarters in Barking. The voice-over was explaining how the authorities hadn't confirmed the cause of death, but she knew by now that could mean anything from the reporter not having the facts or there being a press blackout. Because how did a healthy man in his prime end up dead?

Was this what Leila had meant that day in the pub – about stopping Mark once and for all? Had she killed him and then herself to cover it? Camille grimaced as the thoughts formed.

No.

She wouldn't do that.

Leila hated Mark, but she wouldn't have stooped to his level. She wouldn't have taken another person's life. Leila might have been dealing with more issues than Camille had realised, but she couldn't accept she was a killer.

"Hey, Cam." She flinched as a hand gripped her shoulder. Stephen leaned in and whispered in her ear. "Let's go home. I don't think it's a good idea to stay any longer."

She didn't move her eyes from the screen, but he was right. The façade of the world had been peeled away and underneath the surface, all she'd found was darkness and confusion. "What about Ant and Harriet?"

"Here you go." He handed her the car keys. "You get in the car and I'll find Ant and tell Harriet what's going on."

She took the keys and forced a smile. "Thanks, hun. I appreciate it."

* * *

Back home, Ant went straight through into the kitchen but rather than fill the kettle as Camille was expecting, he came back with three glasses and a bottle of vodka. He handed the glasses out to Camille and Stephen and twisted off the bottle top. The vodka had been in the freezer and the bottle was translucent with frost, as if straight out of an advert. In silence, almost reverentially, Ant poured a large measure into each of their glasses before filling his own.

"To Leila," he said, raising a glass.

They chinked a subdued 'cheers' and drank. The vodka was ice cold and tasted like Camille had always imagined neat vodka to taste. Horrible. Like savoury chemicals. She swallowed it down regardless and glanced between the two men. Neither of their faces gave much away, but Stephen especially looked uneasy.

Ant sniffed. "Do we think it was suicide, then? Or what?"

"I don't know," Stephen replied, staring into his drink and swirling the liquid. "He was a confident guy with an enormous ego. I wouldn't have said it was his style. But if he was responsible for all those women's deaths, maybe his conscience caught up with him."

"Or he realised he wasn't going to get away with it," Ant replied. "History is full of arrogant, egotistical men who took their own lives when things stopped going their way. Most would rather kill themselves than suffer the indignity of going to prison."

He had a point, but Camille's reasoning felt skewed. She couldn't focus. For want of something to do, she took another big gulp of vodka. It didn't taste any better, but she swallowed it down without it troubling her tastebuds too much. Words were forming in her mind and travelling to her mouth. They wanted to come out, to be spoken into the world, but it scared her to let them. She took another drink, draining her glass, and went for it.

"What if Leila did it?" she said, looking at the floor. "What if she killed Mark and then took her own life?"

A silence fell between the three of them. She sensed Ant and Stephen exchanging glances, but she didn't look at them. She couldn't.

"Ah, Cam, I don't know about that," Stephen said. "It sounds like Leila was more unsettled than any of us knew. But she wouldn't do that. First, how could she?"

"I've been going over it since we left the funeral," she said. "The last time Ant and I saw her, she mentioned something about stopping Mark once and for all. I can't get her words out of my head. She would have had time after leaving the pub to get to Mark's flat, kill him, then go back home and . . . you know. Fuck. I can't even believe I'm saying this. I'm so sorry."

"Hey, it's fine. We're all upset and confused." Stephen placed an arm around her. "But did Leila even know where Mark lived?"

"I don't know. But she could have found out." She sniffed and gazed up at Stephen. "Did he ever reply to that email you sent him?"

He shook his head. "No. I got nothing. Mustn't have wanted to know anyone from his past. Even me." He sniffed. "Sorry, that sounded insensitive. I didn't intend it to."

Camille placed her hand on his arm and smiled. "Don't worry. When was the last time you saw Mark?"

He blew out a breath, his full lips quivering as he did. "Gosh, that's a question. Three years ago? Maybe four. It's funny. I had been thinking about reaching out to him again. I was settled and happy in my career for the first time and my mind had drifted towards reconnecting with old friends. You as well, Cam. I'm glad we did. But you know what? Maybe this puts everything to bed finally. I'm not saying we just forget about Lucy and Leila and the rest of them. We might never know whether they were tragic deaths or Mark was involved. But either way, he's gone."

As he said this, she noticed his left eye twitch and for a split second, there was a sadness in his expression.

"Are you sorry he's dead?"

He startled and looked at her. "No. I'm not. Well, only in the same way I'm sorry anyone is dead."

Jesus. She hadn't imagined him to feel sorry for the evil prick. But he and Mark had been best friends. They were almost inseparable at Oxford. Like brothers more than best friends. She couldn't blame him too much for nostalgia getting the better of him.

She shrugged. "I just wish it felt like closure. But he's got away with it. He might be dead, but Lucy's parents still think their daughter killed herself."

"But what if she did?" Stephen said. "We may never get the truth, but at least now the future is clear. You're safe. Harriet is safe. No one else has to die."

He smiled at her. And maybe what he was saying made sense. She glanced at Ant, who had been sipping his vodka in silence.

240

As their eyes met, he shrugged. "I don't know, Cam. I'm completely worn out by it all. My head is all over the place."

She knew how that felt. She was about to tell him as such, but a loud banging on the front door startled her.

"Who the bloody hell is that?" Ant gasped, placing his drink down.

"It's okay," Camille told him. "I'll get it." A sinking feeling in her guts told her it was for her, anyway.

She walked over to the front door and took a deep breath before unbolting it top and bottom and twisting the Yale lock open. As the cool air from outside was sucked into the hallway, she revealed DI Shaw, framed in the doorway. Another police officer, a woman, was standing behind him, but Camille hardly noticed her.

"Good evening, Ms Fletcher," DI Shaw said in a low voice. "I wonder if we might ask you a few questions."

Chapter 33

DI Shaw and his colleague (who Shaw introduced as DI Louise Johnson) sat side by side on the couch, staring at Camille. She leaned forward on the armchair with her elbows on her knees and rubbed at her temples.

"It's a simple enough question, Ms Fletcher," DI Shaw said. "Do you remember what you were doing last Saturday?"

"If you can't recall right now, that's fine," DI Johnson added and as Camille lowered her hands, she shot her a smile. Was this what they called 'good cop, bad cop'?

"Everything is a bit of a blur right now," she sighed. "I've not been sleeping well. Plus, I've just come back from my friend's funeral where I found out about Mark, and . . . well . . . I've had better weeks." She swallowed and let out another sigh. "But last Saturday, yes. I was with my friend Stephen. He's upstairs with my housemate. He can tell you."

DI frowned. "You were with him all day?"

"In the evening. From seven."

"What about the daytime?" He flipped through the notepad he was holding. "We haven't got an exact time of death for Mr Kennedy. It's not as precise as it is in the movies. Sometime on Saturday, we think. But it could have been earlier."

"In the daytime, I was with Anthony. My housemate. Who's also upstairs."

"You were with him the whole time?"

"Yes." The muscles across her shoulders tightened as she realised this wasn't entirely true. They'd been together in the house for most of the morning, but he'd gone to work around 1:30 p.m. She inhaled abruptly as she remembered something. "I was here. At home. You rang me, remember? To tell me to stay away from Mark. Which I did."

She was speaking to DI Shaw but looking at DI Johnson. It was probably exactly what they wanted – for her to feel closer to the female officer so she'd open up to her – but she seemed the most affable and responsive and, right now, Camille would take anything she could get.

"I called your mobile, Ms Fletcher. You could have been anywhere."

"Do that thing you can do. Triangulate my phone signal or whatever it's called. You'll be able to find out I was here when we spoke."

DI Shaw arched a single eyebrow before returning to his notepad and scrawling something down. "What about the rest of the day?"

"I was here. Then I got ready and went to meet Stephen in Soho. Again, check my phone. You'll see. You can have it if you want. If that makes it easier."

"That won't be necessary," DI Johnson said. "Thank you, Camille."

"Why are you asking me all these things? Do you think I killed Mark?"

DI Shaw cleared his throat and glanced at his partner. Neither of them answered.

"How did he die?" she asked. "I'm assuming it wasn't natural causes."

DI let out a long deliberate sigh like he had done on the phone almost a week earlier. The subtext seemed the same now as it was then. He was losing patience, trying to stay calm.

"I can't say too much about it," he said. "It certainly looks like Mr Kennedy took his own life, but we're trying to rule out the possibility of foul play."

Camille sneered and wasn't bothered if they saw it. "If it was suicide," she said. "It was probably because people were getting too close to the truth and he felt he only had one way out."

DI Shaw looked her in the eye. "When was the last time you saw Leila Bloom?"

"What do you mean?"

"It's a simple question, Ms Fletcher. When did you last see her? Or speak to her?"

"You think she's got something to do with Mark's death. Jesus. Her family buried her today. Have a bit of respect."

DI Shaw didn't falter, maintaining strong eye contact. "Did you know she was stalking Mr Kennedy?"

"Excuse me?"

He went back to his notepad. "Does the name Douglas Mathers mean anything to you?"

Douglas Mathers.

It sounded familiar.

Was he someone from university?

"That was the fake name Leila was using for a campaign of hate against Mr Kennedy. We found a laptop at her flat. My colleagues discovered Ms Bloom had set up at least ten fake accounts, but Douglas Mathers was the main one she was using to spread malicious rumours and slander about Mr Kennedy. Chiefly that he was behind the deaths of Charlotte Browning, Lucy Meadows and Ophelia Andrews."

What the fuck?

She tried to swallow but her throat was so dry it hurt. Her head felt like it was going to explode.

"Were you aware she was trolling Mark in this way?" DI Johnson asked.

"No."

"Because this is very serious. If you did—"

"No!" Camille yelled. "I didn't know. All right?" She slumped back in the chair, wishing the house would cave in on her.

DI Johnson sat forward. "I know this must be hard to hear. But it seems Leila Bloom was quite a troubled person. She appears to have grown obsessed with Mr Kennedy."

"He treated her like shit," she muttered in response. "He was toxic."

"But no one deserves the targeted harassment that she engaged in. And now he's dead, around the same time as she took her own life. You can see how it looks."

Camille shot DI Shaw a disgusted sneer. "So *now* you believe something weird is going on? It takes a *man* to die under suspicious circumstances before you investigate, is that it?"

"I don't know how many times I must tell you, Ms Fletcher. None of those women's deaths were anything other than tragic accidents or suicides. I can show you the coroner's report, the inquest verdict. It's all there in black and white."

"Really?" It felt like her sneer had curled halfway up her face. She didn't know whether she was angry, distraught, or broken-hearted. Shoving her hands under her legs, she took a deep breath, resisting the urge to flip the coffee table over.

"It's time to leave the conspiracy theories alone, Ms Fletcher."

DI Johnson touched her colleague on the arm. "It sounds like you may have got caught up in some of Leila's fantasies as well, Camille. Would that be fair to say?"

"Oh my God! Is that what you think, that Mark was the innocent party in this? Do you think Leila hounded him to suicide? Or that she killed him, then killed herself?"

"That's what we're trying to find out."

"Do you think she killed Lucy, too? And the others?"

DI Shaw narrowed his eyes.

Jesus.

He did think that.

But why? It made no sense. Yes, she hated Mark, that was clear. But so what if she pretended to be someone else whilst she got the word out about what he was doing? It could be just her way of protecting herself and . . .

Shit.

This all began after Douglas Mathers commented on Lucy's Facebook page. If Leila had started those rumours, then what did that say about her? Was she really someone who'd seen

Mark for what he was and was doing what the police couldn't or wouldn't? Or was she as deluded and troubled as DI Shaw was making out?

Camille let out a sigh. There was so much emotion behind it that it felt like all the energy had left her body. Her brain hurt. It was as if the answers to these questions were hidden behind a thick wall, somewhere deep in her subconsciousness. She knew they were there somewhere, but she couldn't get to them.

On one hand, she had to admit it looked bad for Leila. But she still couldn't believe she was capable of killing someone. Not Mark, and especially not the other women. It didn't make sense. But that would have been Mark's plan – make it look like those accusing him were kooks and psychos. It was how gaslighters operated.

She shook her head. It was all too much to deal with. "Am I under arrest?" she asked.

The police officers stiffened. "No, you're not under arrest," DI Johnson replied. "We're in the dark as much as you. We're only trying to piece together what we know while we wait for the coroner's report."

"For both Mr Kennedy and Ms Bloom," DI Shaw added, tapping his notepad. "I am sorry for the loss of your friend. I know you've had a lot to deal with recently and I can understand how it looks. But you need to keep your head down and let us do our jobs. Okay?"

The nod she gave him was a reluctant one, but a nod all the same. Because what else could she do?

"We'll leave it there for now," DI Shaw said, getting to his feet and holding his hand out to Camille as she made to get up. "You stay there. We'll see ourselves out. And can I ask that you don't leave London for the next few days? We may need to speak with you again."

She looked up at him. "Leila didn't kill anyone."

He smiled, and for a moment she saw something approaching humanity in his eyes. "She killed herself, Ms Fletcher. You have to accept that."

"I don't know if I can."

He gave his partner a sharp look as she joined him at the door before pointing a finger at Camille. "You can't be thinking that anymore, Camille. Stop it. Go live your life."

She looked away. That's what she intended to do. But it didn't mean she was going to let this drop. The truth was still out there, and she was going to uncover it. That was her purpose now. She'd do it for Leila and Lucy and all the other women who'd died. And for her own sanity as well.

Chapter 34

After the police officers had left, Camille sat in silence for a few minutes until she heard footsteps on the stairs. A moment later, Stephen poked his head around the doorway.

"Have they gone?"

She nodded, biting her lip lest any emotion escaped. Right now, it could go either way in terms of how she dealt with the intense swell of despondency and indignation bubbling in her system. She feared once the floodgates opened, she might never stop crying or raging, or both.

"Did you hear what they said?" she asked.

"Not really. We were on Ant's computer looking for news about Mark. He's still up there." He sat down on the far end of the couch, motioning for her to join him. She didn't move.

"Leila was Douglas Mathers," she told him.

He looked confused. "Who? What?"

"It was a fake account. So she could troll Mark anonymously. They said she was stalking him, carrying out a campaign of hate."

Stephen held his hands up. "What does that mean?"

"I don't know. But it was Douglas Mathers – Leila – who first made the link between Mark and the dead women."

"Shit. So does that mean—?"

"It means either she made it up or she was cleverer than all the police put together." She didn't look at him. She had no idea why she was being so horrid. It wasn't his fault.

Thankfully, he didn't seem fazed. "Which do you think it is?"

"I want to think she was clever."

He steepled his fingers together, pressing them underneath his chin. A deep frown creased his forehead. "But if that's not the case … it means things have taken a dark turn somewhat. No?"

"What do you mean?"

"Don't get me wrong. Things are dark enough with all these poor women dying. But don't you think it might be a good idea – for your own health – if you put all this behind you? I don't want you to end up the same way as Leila."

"I won't, will I? If Mark's dead."

He closed his eyes like he was in pain.

Camille glared at him. "You think the same as the police. That Leila killed Mark and then herself."

He shook his head. "I don't know, Cam. I just want you to be happy." He rocked onto his feet. "Shall we have a drink?"

She shrugged. "Yeah. I think I need one."

"Coming up." She watched him as he walked into the kitchen and grabbed two glasses and the bottle of vodka off the counter. On returning, he poured them both a large measure and held a glass out to her. "There you go."

She accepted it and they sat in silence for a few minutes, sipping at their drinks and occasionally meeting each other's gaze. Camille had been attracted to how assertive and unwavering

Stephen was. But all at once he seemed nervous, like he had a lot he wanted to say but didn't know how to begin.

Finally, he spoke. "I can't believe Mark's dead."

She froze, about to take a drink. She hadn't been expecting that.

"You sound upset."

"No. I didn't mean that." He flattened down the front of his shirt with his hand. "But I was close to him. He was a big part of my life. And even after we stopped being friends, I always knew he was there."

"Can you still think fondly of him after everything that's happened? Everything that you know to be true?"

When she said this, Stephen's mouth twitched to one side. It was a subconscious movement and if she'd blinked, she'd have missed it, but it was there. Whether it was an involuntary spasm or his internal workings coming out in his physicality, she wasn't sure, but she didn't like what she saw. Was he humouring her? Or was there something else?

She observed him as he drank and rubbed his jaw. He had a kind face and had been a rock for her these last few weeks. It was true she was falling for him, but if he didn't share her beliefs concerning Mark and the dead women, that could change everything.

"Are you sorry he's dead?" she asked.

He swallowed and a grimace creased his features. "No. I'm not. He wasn't the man I thought he was."

Camille took a sip of her drink. The more she drank, the better it tasted. "You're right. He wasn't a nice man, Stephen. Even before you factor in the possibility he murdered four women – he was a toxic person. He took what he wanted from people, when he wanted it, without caring how much he damaged them. He was horrible."

Stephen frowned. "Did he take what he wanted from you?" When Camille looked down and nodded, he made a sound like all the air had been let out of him. "Ah, fuck. You mean he . . .?" A second nod confirmed it and he hissed into his glass. "That bastard."

Another silence fell over the room, even more awkward than before. Camille drained her glass and held it in her lap, running the pad of her thumb around the rim and eyeing the bottle on the table. Was another drink a good idea? It would help her sleep if nothing else.

"Do you actually think he killed himself?" Stephen asked.

"The way you say that you might as well ask me if I think Leila killed him?"

He shrugged and looked sheepish. "Well?"

"I don't know. I really don't know." The bottle of vodka was looking more and more tempting.

"Listen, I know you still want answers," Stephen said. "But it could be all over if you want it to be."

She turned her attention back to him. "How can it?"

"If Mark was killing his exes, then it's over. He's dead. Even if he was paying someone to do it for him, that stops too. You stop paying someone, they stop working for you, especially someone who does that sort of work. Leila's dead. There'll be no more conspiracy theories to chase after. We can move on."

Camille stiffened. Stephen's words felt like needles in her heart, but they woke her up just as much. A rush of determination flooded her system. "They aren't conspiracy theories and I won't move on," she told him. "Not yet. I have to keep going. I have to find out the truth. For Lucy and Leila, and those poor girls I never met. For them, and their families. And for me too. I won't stop until I know what happened to them."

She met Stephen's gaze. He looked worried. He looked afraid. But his expression was probably closer to concern. Or even dismay. Because why wouldn't he want her to move on? They were standing on the cusp of a new relationship. Who wanted their new partner's time to be taken up obsessing over a story with so many twists it could tie them up for years? But she had to do it. If he cared about her, he'd understand. They'd work something out.

Stephen smiled, perhaps realising at the same time he had no chance of changing her mind. "Okay," he said. "You do what you have to do. I'll support you."

"Thank you."

She was reaching for the vodka bottle, hoping another drink would strengthen her resolve, when hurried footsteps thundered down the stairs. The two of them looked up as Anthony burst into the room. He had his laptop under his arm and he looked as if he'd seen a ghost. His whole body was shaking with impatient energy.

"There's another girl," he gasped.

Camille and Stephen looked at each other, then back at him. "What?"

"We thought we knew about all of Mark's exes. But I've been doing some hardcore digging for the last hour and I've found another one. Sophie Lawrence. They were childhood sweethearts, together for almost three years. I think she's the missing piece we've been looking for."

Chapter 35

Ant's words hung heavy in the air before crashing to the floor like a carpet bomb and wiping out any conversation or thought processes that might have been going on before he burst into the room.

Another girl?

Camille's mouth flapped, searching for words that didn't want to appear. In the end, she made a noise like a strangled owl and threw her arms up to indicate to Ant he should continue.

He grinned excitedly and sat down on the edge of the coffee table. "Myspace," he said as if this would explain everything and have Camille and Stephen high-fiving him in celebration.

"What?"

Ant placed the laptop on his knees and laid his hands on the lid. "Okay, let me start from the top. For the last few days, I've suspected there was more to this than we thought. That there had to be someone else in the picture. I don't know why; it was just a feeling I had. So, I started doing more research. I found the page for Mark's old school on Facebook and messaged a few people that were in his year. But then I had a brainwave. Myspace. Everyone had a Myspace, right?" He nodded at Camille and Stephen for them to agree, which they did. "Exactly, but with the onset of Facebook, it fizzled out. People moved on. The founder, Tom, realising this, sold the company for a ridiculous amount of money, but the new owners changed the entire interface. So much so that even those people who were still clinging on lost all interest. But here's the thing. Since it changed over to its new look, most people assumed their old accounts had been deleted. Or they were so obsessed with the new social media flavour of the month that they forgot they even had a Myspace account. And now hardly anyone uses it. It's a forgotten relic of a different era. But there're loads of historic accounts still on there. You've both got accounts I bet you'd forgotten about. I'd also bet you don't remember the login details, so you can't close your account down even if you wanted to. And guess who else still has an account?"

"Mark," Camille gasped.

"That's right. Mark Kennedy."

Stephen sat forward. "That's very impressive."

"Tsk, please." Ant held his hand to his chest. "I've got plenty of experience. Anytime someone at work meets a new guy, they always come to me. Usually, I can find all their socials and anything juicy about them in a few minutes. I should be a private detective. I'd be amazing."

"Who is she?" Camille asked. "The childhood sweetheart. Have you spoken to her?"

"Not yet." He opened the laptop and clicked a few keys before turning it around to show them the screen. "These photos are all from Mark's page. Look at him. He's about sixteen or seventeen in most of these."

Camille squinted at the photos. They were standard shots, the first selfies of their day, probably taken on a digital camera and showing Mark in various poses. In his bedroom, up a tree, on a beach somewhere. His hair was longer and messier than she'd ever known it, but the cocksure smile gave him away.

"And this is Sophie Lawrence," Ant said, clicking through a few more photos to one of Mark and a young girl with long dark hair, parted down the middle. The two of them were staring into the camera and pouting and Mark had his arm around the girl. "There're loads of photos of the two of them," Ant said, clicking through at least ten more shots.

"I've never heard of her," Stephen said. "I thought he would have mentioned her to me if they were together for – what was it – three years? And you found out all this in the last few hours?"

Ant ran his tongue across his bottom lip. "I've been looking into it for the last couple of days, but I didn't want to say anything until I knew for definite." He looked at Camille with a concerned expression. "There's been too much hearsay and rumours flying around. I wanted to have the facts in place before I mentioned it."

"Fair enough," Stephen replied. "And . . .?"

Anthony twisted the laptop back around and closed the lid. "They went to the same school. I found an old friend of Mark's sister, a woman called Bridget Aspinall. She's very posh but seems nice enough. Loves a bit of drama from what I can gather. The perfect source for something like this. She's been more than happy to share what she knows." He leered at the two of them, clearly enjoying himself.

"And what does she know?" Camille snapped. "Come on, Ant. Spit it out, will you?"

"Well, according to Bridget, this Sophie was Mark's first proper girlfriend, and they were inseparable, did everything together. She was besotted with him. But she was also a year younger, so when he left for university it all messed up. They stayed together for a while, but as we all know, Mark was a good-looking guy. Bridget said as soon as he got to Oxford, his head got turned and that was it. He dumped Sophie."

Camille twisted her mouth to one side. "Did she take it hard?"

Ant raised his eyebrows. "You could say that. But it's not the worst of it. Being best friends with Mark's sister, Bridget was privy to a lot of private family stuff. It turns out Mark had got Sophie pregnant just before he left for university. Although Bridget said it might have been a ploy by Sophie to hang onto him. Trap him with a child sort of thing. She said she was the type."

"Bloody hell," Stephen muttered. "So, what happened?"

"Bridget isn't exactly sure. She heard Sophie lost the baby rather than having a termination, but either way, the baby didn't happen and Mark left."

"Jesus." Camille reached for the vodka and poured herself a glass before taking a big gulp of the clear, viscous liquid. She hardly tasted it now. Her mind spun with dark notions and twisted ideas. "Do you know what she's doing now?"

"I don't think she's doing anything. Bridget said that losing the baby hit her hard. Apparently, she tried to take her own life and has been in and out of mental hospitals for the last ten years."

He placed the laptop on the coffee table and sat back, allowing what he'd told them to sink in. Camille stared into space, the rim of her glass resting on her lips. She understood what Ant was implying with this discovery, but it was hard to get her head around.

"Do you think it could be her?" she asked, almost speaking to herself.

"Don't you? Bridget said she bumped into her a year ago. She was talking about Mark like he was still her boyfriend. It would make sense if she started removing the competition. Those she thought had taken her man."

"But murder?"

Ant shrugged. "Hell hath no fury . . ."

Camille drained her glass. "Bloody hell. Do you know where she lives?"

"Bridget said she still lived in the same house she grew up in. Somewhere in Maidstone. I've got the address. Her parents are both dead now." He narrowed his eyes. "Are you going to see her?"

"I've got to. I need to know." Beside her, Stephen exhaled. She turned to him. "You don't want me to?"

"I want you to be safe and I want you to be happy."

"I know you do," she placed her hand on his. "I'll be careful."

"I'm coming with you," he said.

"And me," Ant added.

"Are you sure? You don't have to."

"Absolutely, I'm sure," Stephen told her, getting to his feet. "I'll get off and come back first thing in the morning. I can drive us down there."

"Thank you." She stood and went to him. A big part of her wanted him to stay, but it was better to wait until she could put this awful period behind her before exploring their relationship further. That way, they'd start from a place of calm. That was important. The universe knew. "Drive safely." She reached up and kissed him.

As he pulled away, he smiled. "I'll see myself out. You get some rest and I'll see you tomorrow. About nine?"

"Perfect."

She watched as he walked through into the hall and waved as he opened the door and disappeared into the night. Standing in the middle of the room, she suddenly felt very vulnerable and a little ridiculous. But it was settled. Tomorrow she'd visit this mysterious Sophie Lawrence woman. Mark's first girlfriend and possibly his killer. She lowered herself back onto the couch and reached for the bottle of vodka.

When did life get so messed up and scary?

Chapter 36

The sky was overcast and it felt like it could rain any moment as Camille ventured down the garden path towards Sophie Lawrence's front door. It was a nice enough looking house, with flowers in the garden and lead on the windows. But this also meant it was hard to see through into the rooms beyond.

As Camille reached the bright red front door, she looked back, seeing Ant and Stephen watching her from inside Stephen's BMW. They'd wanted to come with her to speak with Sophie, but she'd insisted the initial meeting should be her alone. The last thing they wanted was to scare her off. Ant gave her a thumbs up and she turned back to face the door.

Here goes nothing.

She grabbed the brass knocker and clanked it hard against the wooden panel before she talked herself out of it. She stepped back and waited. Nothing. No sound of movement. She knocked again. As she turned back to the car and shrugged her shoulders, the relief she felt told her everything she needed to know. Maybe *this* was the universe looking out for her. Sophie wasn't home. There were no answers to be found here. So maybe it was time to focus her attention elsewhere. She'd go home. Live her life. Feel blessed she was still alive and had good friends around her.

She decided to knock one more time to make sure. But as she reached for the knocker, she heard the clunk-click of the door being unlocked. It opened as far as the security chain would allow and a woman peered out through the gap.

"Yes. What do you want?"

"Hi. Are you Sophie? Sophie Lawrence?"

"Who wants to know?"

She was well-spoken but her voice had a nervy, brittle quality to it, as if she needed to put more breath behind her words.

"My name's Camille Fletcher. I know this is a bit out of the blue, but I believe you used to know Mark Kennedy. I wonder if I can speak to you about him."

Sophie raised her head, one bloodshot eye peering out at Camille, looking her up and down. "Camille Fletcher. You were his girlfriend at Oxford."

"Yes. That's right." She was taken aback by the statement, but it would have been easy enough to have found out via social media. It wasn't too much of a red flag. It didn't stop her from asking, "Can I come in?"

Sophie shut the door without replying, but a second later it opened again, fully this time, to reveal the whole of her. Despite the passing of fifteen years, she looked almost exactly like she had done in Mark's Myspace photos. Her dark hair was long and parted down the middle the same way she'd worn it as a sixteen-year-old, except today it needed a good wash and a comb running through it. She had the same slight build, with square shoulders and slim hips, but her face looked drawn and tired where it was once full of life. It was as if the muscles that helped a person to smile had atrophied, leaving her with a permanent, jowly scowl.

"You'd better come in," she said, raising her chin to look over Camille's shoulder. "Are those two men with you?"

"Yes, they're my friends," she said, glad of their presence more than ever. "But they'll stay in the car."

Sophie muttered something under her breath and stepped to one side to allow Camille to enter. As she stepped into the house and Sophie closed the door, a heavy wave of despair washed over her. The house was gloomy and the air stale. If Sunday afternoon was a place, this house would be it.

"Come through," Sophie said, hurrying past her along the corridor. Camille followed on behind, glancing into the front room as she passed by. Net curtains hung in the window and a busy-patterned sofa clashed awfully with the brown and orange swirls of the carpet. To finish the look, china ornaments of small dogs adorned most of the surfaces, whilst washed-out prints in gold frames hung on the walls. If an old person lived here, it would be nothing out of the ordinary, but Sophie was the same age as Camille. It all seemed so incongruous and rather sad.

They continued to the end of the hallway and through into the kitchen. Here too the fixtures and fittings looked old and worn out like they could have been here since the sixties. The wooden units and Formica surfaces were discoloured from years of nicotine smoke, the same as the walls and ceiling. It was like looking at the room whilst wearing orange sunglasses.

"Do you want tea or coffee?" Sophie asked.

"No, I'm fine," Camille said, eyeing the mugs lying in the dirty washing-up bowl. "I just want to ask you a few questions, if that's okay."

Sophie moved over to the table on the far wall. She pulled out a chair and sat down before gesturing for Camille to do the same. As she walked over and took a seat, she sensed Sophie scrutinising her.

"What's this about then?" she asked once Camille was settled. "Something about Mark?"

Camille exhaled slowly, in an attempt to ground herself. "That's right. I take it you heard about what happened?"

"I saw it on the news."

"Yes, of course." She smiled but got nothing in return. "The thing is, I'm not sure how much else you know, but there've been quite a lot of suspicious deaths recently. I've lost two good friends in the last month and two other women have died as well. All of them ex-girlfriends of Mark." She didn't take her eyes from Sophie as she spoke, but the woman didn't flinch or look shocked or even react at all.

"Lucy Meadows." She sniffed. "She was your friend, wasn't she?"

Camille tensed. "Yes. That's right."

"She killed herself, didn't she?"

"You heard? And about the others? Ophelia Andrews and Charlotte Browning." When Sophie didn't respond, she carried on. "Didn't you think it was rather odd that so many of Mark's exes had died?"

"Maybe. But now he's dead too," Sophie added. "What of it?"

Camille clasped her hands together under the table. "Can you tell me about you and Mark?"

"Why do you want to know?" she asked, her inflection rising above a monotone for the first time. "Why should I tell you a damn thing?"

Camille remained still, working out her best line of response. She didn't have to bother, though. Before she found her words, Sophie carried on.

"You don't know how hard it was for me," she said, fixing Camille with a hard stare. "I loved Mark. I thought we were going to be together forever. That's what he told me. But no. He goes to Oxford University and starts sleeping around with loads of other girls. He said he'd wait for me. He was going to take a year out and we'd go to university together. As a couple." She stared at something over Camille's shoulder, not blinking. "He broke my heart. Destroyed who I was as a person. I had everything going for me. I was going to study English. I wanted to be a writer. I was good."

She shook her head and Camille resisted the urge to tell her she was a writer. Looking at this broken soul, with her wired eyes and down-turned mouth, it was hard to imagine her as a young woman full of vitality and dreams.

"I wanted to keep the baby," she said, almost in a whisper. "It was a part of me and a part of him. Even though he said he didn't want to be with me, I was ready to have it. I could feel it inside of me by that point. They said that was unlikely, but I could. But no. Mark was angry. He said if I had the baby, it would devastate his life and career plans. He said he wouldn't stand for that." She continued to stare straight ahead, fingers picking at the skin around her thumbnail. "One night he came around here, to the house. He sat where you're sitting right now. He told me he was sorry and that he loved me and that he wanted us to have a great life together. But for us to do that, we had to be free. If I got rid of the baby, he said we could go travelling for a year after university. All around the world. We'd have an amazing adventure, he said. Just me and him. Then when we got back, we'd settle down together and start a proper family. I can hear him saying it even now in my head. He was so convincing. So, I had an abortion. I killed my baby. And do you know what Mark did?"

She moved her gaze back to Camille, her mouth twisted in a cruel snarl. Camille suspected she knew the answer, but she didn't want to say it. "What did he do, Sophie?"

"He waited until I went into hospital and then went to Thailand. For three months. He didn't even call to see how I was. Being over fifteen weeks pregnant, I had to have surgery. I was still bleeding two weeks later when I saw photos of him with Charlotte Browning." The hatred in her voice was palpable. As she spoke Charlotte's name, her hands bent up into claws. At that moment, Camille realised Sophie could easily be the sort of person she desperately hoped she wasn't. Someone so full of resentment and spite she could commit murder. Multiple times. Scanning the kitchen, Camille's gaze fell on a large kitchen knife lying on top of a butcher's block next to the sink.

"It was a girl, by the way," Sophie said. "The baby. A little girl. Part of me, part of him. I'd have loved her. Even if I didn't have him anymore. But no. He took her from me, too. There were complications with the surgery. I won't be able to have children now. Not that anyone would ever want to breed with someone like me."

She sniffed and flicked her hair over her shoulders. As she did, Camille flinched, eyes darting from her to the knife and back again. "I can't even imagine the pain you've been through," she said. "I'm so sorry."

"Are you?" she said. "Why don't you write a blog post about how sorry you are?"

Camille inhaled slowly through her nose and told herself not to panic. Sophie knew who she was and what she did, it didn't mean she was a killer.

"I had to watch as he went from girl to girl. All of you were so much prettier and richer than me. I saw you on his Facebook photos, having a great old time at university while I stayed here with a hollow belly and my dying mother for company. How did you find me, by the way?"

Camille straightened her spine. "Oh, umm ... A woman called Bridgit. She said she knew you and was a friend of Mark's sister."

"Evelyn. I see. Did she tell you I was crazy? That I tried to kill myself?"

"No. She didn't," Camille lied. "I'm sorry to hear that."

"Are you? It might have been better for you if I succeeded."

The way she said it was throwaway, but her words winded Camille. She lifted her hands onto the tabletop and gripped the sides, ready to move. "What do you mean by that, Sophie?"

"I don't mean anything by it."

Camille glanced at the door, at the knife. "Sophie, have you done something bad? Have you hurt anyone?"

"Depends on how you look at it."

"My friend, Lucy," Camille said, shifting her weight onto her feet, gripping the sides of the table tighter. "Did you hurt her?"

"If you ask me, those preening bitches deserved everything they got," came the snarled reply. She glared at Camille. "You have no idea how I felt, having to watch the father of my baby parading around with all his new conquests. It made me sick. The doctors say I have a medical condition, that my brain function is all wrong, but he made me like this. Him, you and all the others. I had to look at you all, day after day, while I stayed here with mum."

Camille didn't take her eyes off Sophie. The way she was sitting, it didn't look like she was about to attack her, but who knew in these situations? Clearly, she wasn't well.

"That must have been awful for you," Camille said. "But why did you keep looking if it made you sad?"

"Don't you understand? He made me. He had my heart and soul. I gave them to him. He never gave them back." She slammed her open palm down on the table. "Him and his stupid whores having a good laugh at my expense. Is that right? Did you? Did you think it was hilarious that poor barren Sophie was pining for him while you were gallivanting around university, going to parties, having sex? Is that why you're here now? To mock me. To see how fucked up I am?"

She screwed up her face as though she was going to cry, but no tears came. Her eyes remained closed as Camille raised herself from the table.

"Listen, Sophie. I probably should get going," she said, softly.

It had been a mistake to come. She felt unsafe. Whether Sophie had it in her to kill, she wasn't sure, but something wasn't right and she needed to leave.

"Yeah, go. Just like everyone always does." Her eyes snapped open, but she made no other movements as Camille backed away from the table towards the doorway. "Did you get everything you came for, Miss Lifestyle Blogger? You going to go back to London to have a good laugh about me?"

"No. Not at all," Camille said. "Mark hurt me too. He wasn't a nice man. We all experienced how horrible he could be. But Lucy and I and the others, we aren't to blame for what happened to you."

"Do you think I killed them?"

Camille stopped in the doorway. "Did you?"

Sophie let out a high-pitched noise, which Camille assumed was her attempt at bitter laughter. "Wouldn't you like to know?"

It was pointless continuing anymore. The woman was twisted with the pain of her existence and wasn't going to give her a straight answer.

"I'm going to go now, Sophie. I'm sorry I bothered you."

"Yes. Go. Fuck off. Stupid fucking whore."

Suddenly, she was off her chair and storming across the room at Camille. "Get out of my house. Do you hear me? Get out!"

She had her hands raised, fingers bent, ready to claw at her. Camille turned and hurried along the hallway with Sophie following behind, screaming at her.

"You don't deserve to live! You don't deserve happiness! None of you do!"

Camille reached the front door and desperately grappled at the lock. Her hands were shaking and her palms were wet with nerves. "I'm sorry!" she cried over her shoulder. "Don't hurt me! It's not my fault!"

"It's all your fault!" A hand grabbed at her hair, yanking her back whilst another pulled on her shoulder. Sharp nails dug into her flesh as she worked on the lock. "I'll kill you!"

Another sharp jiggle and she got the lock open. As she yanked the door open she shoved back against Sophie and knocked her to the floor. As Camille leapt for the safety of the outdoors, she saw Stephen standing on the path a few feet away. He opened his arms and she ran into them.

"What's going on?" he asked. "We heard shouting."

Camille glanced back to see Sophie clambering to get up, still yelling threats and obscenities. She grabbed Stephen's hand and pulled him along towards the waiting car.

"I just want to get out of here," she said. "Now."

Chapter 37

Stephen wanted to take Camille home after her ordeal with Sophie, but she felt too rattled to be in the quiet of the house, even with Stephen and Ant there. She needed people around her, noise. There was safety in numbers. In the end, Stephen dropped his car off at their house in Dalston and the three of them walked to The Huntsman up the road.

Camille knew she'd been consuming a lot of alcohol lately, especially for a supposed lifestyle blogger, but maybe she wasn't that anymore. Her life had got too serious to go back to writing about green juice and mindfulness. Besides, after the day she'd had, a drink was needed. It would help settle her nerves. A few drinks would help even more.

They shared a bottle of Pinot Noir, which disappeared remarkably fast. Camille was all ready to order a second when Ant got to his feet.

"Work beckons," he said, rolling his eyes.

"Oh no," Camille cried. "Can't you ring in sick or something?"

"I wish. But no." He regarded her with a serious face as he pulled on his jacket. "Are you going to be okay?"

"Yeah, I am," she said. "Sophie Lawrence is a very troubled woman, but I don't believe she's a killer."

"It would make sense though," Ant said, gathering up his phone. "She certainly sounds like someone with a grudge. That's a good motive right there. Plus, she knew all about you. And the others."

Camille finished the last of her wine. He had a point. But right now, she was too exhausted to go over it again. She planned to relax and take her mind off all the horrible business of the last few weeks. She needed a few days of self-care and rest. Maybe then she could approach the situation with fresh eyes. Perhaps even start writing her article.

Ant was still staring at her as he adjusted the collar on his denim jacket. She shot him a grin. "I'm fine, mate. You go to work. I'll see you later."

"I won't be home late." He winked at her and Stephen. "You be good now, kiddies."

They watched him leave and then Camille turned to Stephen. "Thank you," she said. "For coming with me today. For humouring me through all of this."

He frowned. "I'm not humouring you, Camille. You've had a lot to deal with these past few weeks. I'm just glad I can help."

"You are helping." She touched his hand. "Will you excuse me? I need to use the bathroom."

"Of course." He sat upright and pointed at her empty glass. "Do you want another?"

As she stood up, she felt a little woozy, but she'd not eaten properly today. "Not a bottle. I'll just have a small one. Actually, make it a medium. But then I should get home. I'm so tired."

"No worries."

The Ex

She headed for the bathroom, sensing Stephen's eyes on her as she did and giving her hips a little sass as she walked alongside the bar. The wine helped. In the bathroom, she stopped at the mirror to check her hair and make-up before heading for one of the free cubicles. Despite feeling more ballsy and assured than she had done in some time, she still took the time to tear off strips of toilet roll and laid a ring of paper around the toilet seat before sitting down. After all, she wasn't an animal. And she was too exhausted to hover.

Whilst she peed, she closed her eyes, the effects of the wine diluting the anxious thoughts enough that she even felt a smile forming. It had been terrifying sitting in Sophie Lawrence's kitchen, but now, with a little perspective, she found it hard to feel anything towards the woman but pity. She seemed too frail, too broken by life to be any kind of killer. But then, it takes all sorts. And how much can you tell from first impressions? She stretched her neck to one side. Maybe she would try DI Shaw one more time and give him the lead on Sophie. After that, she was done. She'd stay vigilant as a testament to Leila, but she was damned if she was going to let fear control her another minute longer.

She finished and flushed the toilet, heading over to the sink to wash her hands. Yes. She'd give herself a few days off, enjoy some time with Stephen, and then she'd get down to some writing. Whether she wrote this story or something else entirely – she still had that fluff piece to finish – she didn't yet know, but that wasn't important. That she was writing at all was what mattered. It had been far too long. She might even buy herself a new laptop for the process. She deserved it. This was Camille Fletcher reborn. A better, more focused version of herself. The person she always knew she could be.

Back in the main bar, Stephen had bought them both large glasses of wine. She scolded him about it but was secretly glad.

"How are you feeling?" Stephen asked as she sat down.

She flicked her hair back over her shoulders. "Still a bit shaky when I think about it. So, I've decided not to think about it! For now, at least." She reached for her glass of wine but perhaps she was shakier than she'd realised because, rather than grabbing hold of it, she knocked the whole thing over. The next she knew Stephen was leaping to his feet with a red stain seeping out across the lap of his jeans.

"Shit!"

Camille was up on her feet in a jot, hurrying over to the bar to get a stack of paper napkins, which she took back to Stephen. "Here you go," she said, handing them over and resisting the impulse to dab at his crotch herself. "I'm so sorry. What a klutz."

He glanced at her and shook his head, but he was smiling. "I think this might be my cue to leave."

"Oh bugger. I tell you what, why don't you come back to my place? I'll wash them for you. You can put on a pair of Anthony's or something."

"No. I'll get a taxi back to mine and pick my car up tomorrow. I don't want to impose." He'd rubbed at his jeans until the napkins fell apart, but there wasn't much difference. "It's fine. Really."

"No. I insist," she said. "It's only around the corner and it's the least I can do. Please. I want you to come back."

He looked at her and his eyebrow twitched. "Well, if you insist."

"Yes. I do. Now come along, we can't have you standing there looking like that."

* * *

Luckily, it was getting dark as they left the pub. Not that Stephen seemed to mind about the massive wine stain across his crotch. They even joked about it on the way back to Camille's and were both in good spirits as they reached the front door. Before she unlocked it, she turned to him with a smirk spreading across her lips.

"You know you're going to have to take those off for me when we get inside."

He raised his head. "Well, it'd be hard to wash them with me inside them."

"Exactly. I think we need to get you inside something else."

"Really?" His eyes grew wide and she gasped, shocked with herself.

"I meant get you inside a pair of Anthony's trousers," she blurted. But as she turned back to the door and unlocked it, a sly grin formed. Maybe she wasn't that shocked.

The house was warm as they got inside. Camille ran straight upstairs to Ant's room whilst Stephen went through into the kitchen to fix them another drink. She found a pair of grey jogging bottoms in his top drawer and carried them downstairs. As she entered the front room, Stephen was coming back with two glasses of Coca-Cola.

"I hope there's something strong in there," she said.

"The vodka from before. At least it might taste a little more pleasant now." He handed her one of the glasses and in exchange, she hung the joggers over the crook of his arm.

"Here you go. Put them on."

"Thanks." He placed his drink down on the coffee table and headed for the door. "Back in a minute."

"You can get changed here, you know," Camille said. "I didn't have you down as a shy boy."

Stephen grinned. "I like to keep some dignity, ma'am. Back in five." With that he disappeared upstairs, leaving Camille to sink onto the couch and sip at her drink. It tasted a little bitter, but it was nice enough and she wasn't drinking entirely for the taste. She'd decided tonight was the night for her and Stephen and a little Dutch courage was needed. As she considered what was about to happen, a shiver ran down her torso. It had been some time since she'd been with anyone sexually, but she'd held Stephen at arm's length for long enough and since making the decision to go for it, she ached for him. It would be so good to feel something other than fear and anger and paranoia. She took another large gulp of the drink as she heard footsteps on the stairs and adjusted her position so she was facing the door as Stephen entered. As he entered the room he stopped, glancing down at the grey joggers he was wearing, then up at Camille with a lop-sided grin.

"What do you think? They're a bit tight."

"Yes, they are," she said, trying not to stare too readily. "Come here. Sit down."

The Ex

He was holding his jeans in his hand. "Where do you want me to put these?"

"The washing machine is through there," she told him. "But it makes a real racket. We don't need to put it on yet. I'll sort them later."

The glimmer in his eyes informed her he'd caught her drift. He placed his folded jeans on the coffee table and sat on the couch beside her. She handed him his drink. "Thanks." He let out a loud sigh. "What a crazy time. So much pain and upset and yet here we are."

"You said it. It's good though, isn't it? It feels right."

He rubbed at the side of his nose. "It does." He let his head loll onto the back of the couch and closed his eyes. "It really does."

Camille tilted her head to one side. He looked so sexy sitting there with his eyes closed and a half-smile playing across his full lips. "What is it?" she asked.

He chuckled to himself. "You know the ironic thing is, I don't think Mark would have made it, anyway."

"Excuse me?"

"His political career," he said, opening his eyes and turning his head to look at her. "He was too egotistical. Too power-hungry. People see through it these days. He was a nice guy back in the day. But he wasn't the golden boy he liked to make out. He looked worn out most of the time. The TV make-up hides it. But in the flesh . . . not so much." He sipped at his drink. "Sorry, we don't need to talk about him. Tonight is about us. Cheers." He held up his glass and Camille clinked hers against it, both staring into each other's eyes as they drank.

"If I never hear about Mark Kennedy ever again, it'd be too soon," she told him, draining her glass. She held out her hand, waiting as Stephen finished his drink and he handed her his glass. "Same again?"

"Please."

She got up off the couch and sashayed into the kitchen in the hope he'd turned to watch her. But as she got to the doorway, a wave of wooziness overcame her and she had to stop and lean against the wall to steady herself. That would teach her to drink on an empty stomach. One more and she'd suggest they go upstairs. She was ready. She was more than ready.

The cool air from the fridge roused her a little as she opened it to get out the bottle of coke and carried it, along with the two glasses, over to the counter under the window where the vodka bottle was standing. She poured out two decent measures and topped them up with the coke. As she did, she thought about what Stephen had been saying about Mark. It made sense he still had him on his mind. They were best friends after all but she wished he'd shut up about him. She straightened up and noticed her reflection in the kitchen window, illuminated by the fluorescent light above. It was like looking at a ghost, but as she was looking, her vision warped and blurred.

To counter the effects of the alcohol, she grabbed an upturned pint glass that was sitting on the draining board and filled it up with water from the tap, drinking the whole thing down in a few gulps. She held onto the worktop as she continued to stare at the ghostly representation of herself in the window.

"Are you okay in there?" Stephen called out.

"Yeah. Fine. Coming." She nodded at her reflection, but the movement only made her feel worse.

Come now, Cami, pull yourself together. A gorgeous guy is sitting on your couch waiting for you to ravish him. You deserve some joy in your life after all this misery and pain. So go get him.

She picked up the glasses, ready to join Stephen when she paused. Something had just hit her. A realisation. Like a sledgehammer to the guts. She raised her head to take in her reflection.

"What the fuck?"

Chapter 38

Camille gripped the glasses of vodka and coke tight as the room spun. It felt like the universe had just ripped out her soul. She felt sick and dizzy, confusion clouded her thoughts. She shook her head, trying to focus.

"I thought you said you hadn't seen Mark in over four years?" she called out.

"Yes. That's right," came the reply. "I thought we weren't talking about Mark."

"Only, you just said that he looked old up close. You implied you'd seen him recently."

Stephen laughed. "No, I didn't. I haven't."

Camille leaned over the sink and screwed up her eyes. "'The TV make-up hides it, but in the flesh ... not so much.' That's what you said." A flurry of troubling thoughts revolved in her mind, but she was struggling to grab onto any of them. "Have you seen Mark recently, Stephen?"

"No," he called back. "Why are you being weird? Come back in here and we can talk properly."

But Camille had just remembered something else. From a week earlier. At the time, she'd had a fleeting thought that something wasn't right, but had dismissed the notion before it had time to form properly in her mind. But now the realisation hit her. She let go of the drinks and as they crashed to the floor she turned, stumbling into the worktop on her way to the door.

"How did you know where I lived?" she asked. "When we got that Uber back here from Soho, the night Leila died. You sorted it on your phone, but I never told you the address. You knew already."

She stopped in the kitchen doorway as Stephen stood up from the couch. He looked at her with a strange expression on his face, halfway between lust and hate. Camille gasped as her eyes fell on his hands and on the black latex gloves he was wearing.

"No," she said. "You."

He grinned. "Me."

"I don't . . . I don't get it. Why?"

It felt like the walls of the room were zooming away from her, leaving only her and him alone in space. Nothing else mattered. Nothing else was real.

"Why what?" Stephen asked, adjusting one of the gloves and snapping the elastic around his wrist. "Why am I wearing these? Why am I here?"

"Why any of this?" Camille stammered, gasping for air as more truths dawned on her. "You killed Leila. And Lucy."

Stephen shrugged. "Guilty, I suppose."

"You suppose?" She was finding her voice again, the confusion and shock that threatened to overwhelm her surpassed by a massive surge of adrenaline. "But why me? It's over. Why are you doing this?"

"You ask a lot of questions, Camille," he said, wagging a black latex finger at her. "It is rather annoying; you need to watch that. But that's also one reason why I can't let you live. You're a meddling cow. You wouldn't have let it go. Ever. Even with Mark dead, you'd still be sticking your nose in, asking questions. I can't have the police sniffing around. You have to go. I'm sorry."

He screwed his fist into the palm of his other hand, flexing his biceps and broad shoulders as he did.

"Please, Stephen, you don't have to do this. I don't know why you're doing this, but you don't have to. It can stop. It can all—"

"I have to do it!" he yelled, spittle flying from his mouth. "Can't you see? I've come too far now. You know too much. You're too close."

Camille grabbed hold of the doorframe. Her legs felt like jelly. "What did Lucy or any of those women ever do to you? I don't get it."

"It wasn't for me. It was for him. The fucking bastard!"

Camille gripped the wood tighter. "What? But you said you hadn't—"

"I loved him," he said. "I've always loved him. I still do, the stupid prick." He screwed up his face, his usual calm demeanour twisting into a sinewy-necked rage. "I would have done anything for that beautiful boy. We had a thing, you see. A few years ago, when he first moved back to London. It was one night. One amazing night. I was drunk, but he was drunker and back at his place we kissed. Well . . . we did more than kiss. I took the lead, but he didn't stop me. He wanted me. I could tell. I could damn well tell!"

282

The Ex

He slammed his fist into his palm, making Camille jump. She opened her mouth, gasping for the right words. But what did you say in these situations? Besides, her tongue felt fat and despite the pint of water she'd just drank, her throat was dry.

"For a few wonderful hours I thought that was it," Stephen went on, red-faced now, foam forming at the corners of his mouth. "All those years loving him in secret. I thought we could be together. I thought he felt the same. But when he woke up the next day, he was disgusted with himself. And me. He pushed me away. Said it was a massive mistake. Said it could never happen again and that no one could ever know. But I knew. I KNEW!"

He moved around the side of the couch but didn't come any closer. She eyed him without blinking, trying to work out what to do. Could she get past him? Make a run for it? She let her left hand fall by her side, feeling her phone in the pocket of her jeans. If she could get to it without him seeing . . .

"He ghosted me after that," Stephen said, rubbing his forehead with the back of his thumb. "I lost the man I loved and my best friend all at once. I was a pariah to him. A dirty secret he didn't want to face. But then, after a while, I started to ponder all the other skeletons in his closet, all his other dirty secrets. We've all got them, haven't we? But Mark had more than most. You know that, *Cami.*"

The way he said her name, full of bitterness and spite, it was like he was a different man from the one she'd been falling for these last few weeks. Despite the flight or fight response tingling in her limbs, she still couldn't quite believe what was happening. After everything they'd been through, everything they'd talked about, he was the one they'd been looking for all along. She tensed her shoulders, gaze drifting to the doorway on the other side of the room. If he turned away, even for a moment, she was going for it. It was her only option.

"Stephen," she whispered, fixing him in the eyes. "Please don't do this. Please don't hurt me. We can sort something out."

He laughed. "I don't think so. You see, I was right. All you little hussies did have things on Mark. It was obvious. I knew what he was like with women. He used to tell me. I knew he liked to get a bit rough. And in this current climate, with all the woke posturing and the '*Me Too*' stuff, he'd be cancelled before he got anywhere. It'd come out. You said it yourself, you wanted to ruin him. Well, that's your answer right there, Camille. My big why. My big fucking why. I did this to show Mark how much I loved him. How much I cared about him. I thought that if I got rid of his skeletons, he'd see how important I could be to him. We could be together. A team. Me and him, like we used to be. Like I wanted us to be."

"You're crazy." It was the wrong thing to say, but it was all that came to her. Because he was. Clearly. Properly crazy. When she looked into his eyes, gone was the kind, supportive man who she thought cared for her. In his place, she saw a monster forged by animosity and malice.

He bit his lip and shrugged. "Maybe I am crazy, but that's how life makes you sometimes." He glanced down at his hands and at that moment, she saw her chance.

Pushing away from the doorframe, she placed all her weight onto her right foot, attempting to veer around the side of him.

The Ex

He saw her coming and lurched forward, but she had a split-second advantage and managed to move past him, her shoulder skimming along the wall as she went. She grabbed for the side of the bookcase, using it for purchase as she pushed off towards the door, negotiating her path like she was a bumper car at the fair. But Stephen had twisted around and was reaching for her. She felt a hand grabbing at her shoulder, but she shook him off. She was almost away from him; another few steps and she'd be in the hallway. The front door was closed, but she'd only put the Yale lock on. It would be tight, but she could make it. Once outside, she had a chance. There'd be other people around. But as she was moving for the door, she felt his hand close around her arm, fingernails digging into the thin skin of her wrist. He yanked her backwards and the room spiralled into a brown blur of colour and form as her feet buckled underneath her. She twisted through the air, seeing the edge of the coffee table in her peripheral vision as it zoomed up to meet her. As her head bounced off the table, she could only process the pain briefly before she lost all sense of who she was and why she felt so terrified. Then the light of her consciousness wiped to black. Then there was nothing.

Chapter 39

Even before Camille had opened her eyes, she knew something was wrong. Even before she remembered who she was and what she was doing prior to being knocked unconscious, her body was telling her to move. Her legs tingled with adrenal response hormones and the muscles in her chest and stomach were contracted, ready for action.

Shit.

Gasping back a mouthful of life-force, she opened her eyes. She was in her front room in the house she shared with Anthony. Home. So far, so good. But as she glanced to her right, she saw Stephen sitting next to her and clutched in his black-gloved hand, a kitchen knife.

As she turned her head slowly to better look at him, he smiled and pressed the tip of the blade against her throat. His eyes were cold and unforgiving. No kindness there now.

"You stupid bitch. Did you really think I was going to let you get away that easily? This isn't my first rodeo." His voice was unsettlingly calm. He glided the cold steel of the knife along her jawline and tutted theatrically.

"Please, don't hurt me." In contrast, her own voice wavered with emotion. She swallowed, feeling the knife-edge digging into her skin as the muscles in her neck moved. "I won't tell anyone."

"Hmm. If only I could believe that." He shook his head. More theatrics. "You've been a hard girl to get alone. I thought you'd be easy in every way. How wrong I was. I was planning to give you a similar send-off as I gave Charlotte. I don't think it would be beyond most people's scope of believability if you were to drink a few too many glasses of wine and end up falling down the stairs, do you? But no. After waiting all this time to make my move, that gash on your head from the table could pose a problem."

He paused, perhaps waiting for her to answer. But she didn't reply. Her throat was sore and she felt numb. Like all her nerve endings had retracted.

"It's a shame for Anthony," Stephen said. "He seems like a nice guy. But I may have to go with a house fire. That's all I can think of that would cover it and keep the narrative to the way I want it. I hope he's got contents insurance."

"He hasn't." It seemed like a dumb thing to say, given the circumstances, but there was subtext behind those two words.

Fuck you.

Stephen chuckled to himself, picking up on her indignation and relishing in it. "Oh, dear, you never saw this coming, did you? I can only imagine what's going through your pretty little head right now. But don't do anything else stupid, you hear me? If you play the game my way, it'll be a lot easier and a lot less painful for you. The rohypnol you ingested about ten minutes ago will take another ten to fifteen to properly kick in. After that, you'll be floating on a cloud. You won't know what the hell is going on."

Camille stiffened. Now it made sense. The wooziness, the way her limbs felt rubbery and disconnected from her body. It wasn't the wine at all.

"You're a fucking psycho."

He chuckled once more. "Maybe. They do say repressed sexuality can lead to trauma and mental health problems."

"Why are you doing this?"

"I've answered that already."

"No, you haven't. You're not doing this for him. You never were. You're doing it for yourself. You were jealous of us. Those close to Mark. Giving him what you never could."

She raised her chin as he pressed the blade against the thin skin of her neck. She was pushing her luck; she knew that. But if she was going out, she was going out speaking her truth.

"It must have killed you seeing him with us all, happy, loved up. And you in the shadows like some pathetic wretch. Unable to be who he really was. You're a coward."

She was also playing for time. Despite her body growing numb, she could still feel her phone in her left pocket. On the opposite side of where Stephen was sitting. If she could slip it out without him seeing, she might distract him enough that she could call the police.

"You don't know what you're talking about," he said and sighed a long, dramatic sigh. "But it's true I never really liked you. I put up with you so I could be close to Mark. Plus, it was university and I didn't have any other friends. And I was drunk most of the time. Charlotte and Ophelia, I didn't know that well, so killing them was a walk in the park. And don't get me started on that loud-mouthed twat Leila Bloom. But Lucy, she was a tricky one. She'd always been nice to me. Did you know she and I had a thing for a while?"

Camille frowned. "No. I didn't."

"Yeah, we kept it under wraps, but we were a couple for a few months. I tried so hard to fall in love with her. It would have been so much easier. But the longer it went on, the more I realised I was only with her because a part of me felt if I couldn't be with him then I'd try to act like him. Do what he did. Be with who he'd been with."

Camille inhaled slowly. "You were the ex she met that night."

Bloody hell.

This was on her.

Lucy's dad hadn't been able to remember the ex-boyfriend's name but had agreed it was Mark when she'd prompted him. That was sloppy journalism, leading the source. She should have been more thorough.

Stephen chuckled. "Guilty as charged. It was good to see her again though, albeit briefly. As I said, I struggled with that one, but I had to go through with it. By that point, I'd already done Charlotte and Ophelia. I'd jumped in with both feet, as they say. But I did care about Lucy. We got on. We could have been good together if only I'd . . . If I was . . ," He jerked his head away and snorted. "It doesn't matter now, does it?"

"But why not come out? Why not step into who you are as a gay man? No one would have cared. We'd have all celebrated you."

"Pfft, easy as that? Do you know what it would have done to my parents if I came out? They're old-fashioned and strict with it. They'd have disowned me. Cut me off. Then, after graduating, I went straight into investment banking. And fuck me if that isn't a world of alpha wolves. I needed to fit in. I had to."

"I'm sorry you felt you had to live like that," she told him.

She wasn't sorry at all but as he'd been talking, she'd worked her phone out of her pocket and it now lay, out of sight from Stephen, on the couch cushion beside her. She glanced down at it and, careful not to move anything but her index finger, slowly tapped out the access code. Next to her, Stephen was still bemoaning his lot, justifying himself for being a killer. It was all bullshit, of course, a poor me story that he couldn't escape from.

As the phone screen illuminated, she saw she had a notification. A message from Ant. Rather than risk the time it would take opening up the keypad and calling the police, she quickly swiped on the notification and – holding her breath lest the dial tone was audible – tapped 'Call this person.'

She gritted her teeth and waited, but there was no reaction from Stephen. He was too busy with his monologue to have noticed. She left the phone on and closed her eyes, saying a prayer to the universe that Ant would grasp what was going on.

"Did you kill Mark too?" she asked, cutting Stephen off and raising her voice to cover Ant's muffled tones as he answered. "If you loved him so much, why?"

"Why? Why? Why?" he yelled. "Jesus Christ, you're like a broken record!"

Camille flinched. "Haven't I the right to know? If you're going to kill me, I'd like to know the whole truth."

Stephen snorted and looked away, letting the knife drop for a moment. Glancing down, Camille repositioned the phone so the receiver could pick everything up. On the screen, the call time was counting down, showing Ant was still on the line.

"It was all your fault," Stephen muttered, turning back and raising the knife. "After you confronted him, he called me. Asked me to come to his flat. Which I did. I thought maybe he'd changed his mind about us, but no. He was shaken up. He told me what you'd said to him. I wanted to wait until my mission was complete before I told him what I'd done for him. But no. Once again, you stick your nose in and ruin everything."

"I didn't know," she said. Tears were running down her cheeks. She looked at Stephen. His face was bright red and his eyes were intense and demonic looking. "I was only trying to understand what was going on."

"Well, you'd got to him. He was concerned. And he's a clever boy is Mark – *was* a clever boy – it didn't take him long to conclude it was me who killed Lucy and the rest." He looked away and bit his lip, allowing Camille a furtive glance at her phone. Ant had rung off and the screen was black. She prayed he'd heard and understood. Stephen snapped his head back to glare at her. "I told him he had to keep it quiet. That I was doing it for him. For his career. Plus, he needed to keep me sweet. He's got a fiancée, you know? How would she take the news of his gay lover? How would the political world react? I know it matters less and less, but Mark was all about image." He twisted around in his seat so his whole body was facing her. Camille tensed as the knife pressed sharply at the skin of her neck. "Thing is, he didn't like being blackmailed. He got nasty. Very nasty. But to be fair, we both did. We fought. I'm not sure exactly how it happened, but he stumbled back and I fell on top of him with my hands around his throat. He looked so frail and helpless underneath me. So beautiful." He sniffed back and his face was wiped clean of emotion. "I crushed his windpipe. Watched him choke to death. After that, I dragged him over to the door, hung him from the handle and let myself out."

As Camille moved her head, she saw light trails coming off the lamp next to the TV. It was a strange feeling to be so unsettled and desperately tired at the same time. She wanted to close her eyes, but she clenched her fists and fought sleep with every inch of her being. If she fell asleep, she was dead. She glanced at the doorway. Her only exit. Could she make it? Her legs and arms felt less and less like they belonged to her.

"But it's over now, Stephen," she said, raising her hand to wipe at her face. "You don't have to do this. Mark's dead. I won't tell anyone. I swear to you."

"Hmm. Not sure I believe that, Miss Wannabe-Investigative-Journalist. Besides, I'm quite a completist about these things." He lifted the knife from her neck and examined it. "I've got to finish what I started. Otherwise, I'd never be able to live with myself. That might result from the whole trauma-mental illness thing, as well. OCD. Who knows?" He flicked his eyebrows and lowered the knife to rest the blade on his thigh, still gripping the handle.

Camille watched intently, eyes flitting from the knife to the doorway to Stephen. She had to act. Now. Another few minutes and the sedatives would have too much hold over her. She laid her palms flat on the couch and placed her feet flat on the floor, preparing to move. On the count of three, she'd go for it. It was her only chance.

One . . .

Two . . .

Before she got to three, her phone vibrated on the cushion next to her. She jumped.

Shit.

"What the fuck?" Stephen sat bolt upright, head snapping, to look at the phone. "You stupid bitch." He reached for it and as he did, Camille elbowed him in the face using all the strength she had. As his head flew back, she grabbed at his shirt, scrambling over the top of him to get to her feet. She stumbled as her legs almost gave way but used the momentum to propel herself across the room and through into the hallway. This was it. She was almost free. She could do this.

Chapter 40

"Get back here," Stephen yelled after her. But Camille wasn't stopping. At the front door, she grabbed at the lock. But her hands were sweaty and her vision blurred and distorted, so she found it hard to focus. Behind her, she could hear him getting to his feet. There was no time to get the door open. She snapped her attention up the stairs. The windows in both bedrooms looked out over the back garden. Could she jump to safety? As Stephen loomed nearer, she didn't have a choice. As she pushed off from the front door he was standing in the doorway, blood pouring from his nose. He grinned at her, exposing rows of pink teeth.

"Go to hell," she yelled as she staggered past and grabbed for the handrail. Her voice sounded like it was coming from underwater.

Come on Cam.

You can do this.

She hauled herself up the stairs, whimpering and gasping for air as she went. Every movement she made sent her head spinning and she worried she was going to fall backwards down the stairs.

Like Ophelia . . .

No.

Not going to happen.

Despite her growing fatigue and the fact her legs felt as if they were made of modelling clay, she kept on. Stephen was ascending the stairs behind her. Snickering to himself. A merciless predator stalking his prey. He was enjoying this, the evil bastard. And she'd been falling for him, ready to give herself to him. How could she have been so wrong about someone?

At the top of the stairs, she fell through the open doorway into her bedroom and landed on all fours. The light was off, so her vision was even more compromised. She twisted around as Stephen reached the top of the stairs.

"Well, here we are," he said, stepping forward so he was silhouetted in the doorway. "Camille's boudoir. And there was I thinking I would never get up here."

"Leave me alone," she screamed. Or tried to, at least. The words came out as a slur of noise.

She shuffled into the room, flailing around with her arms as Stephen approached. Her fingers found the leg of her bedside table and she grabbed it, books and face creams scuttling across the floor as she hurled it at him. But her throw was weak and her muscles weaker. It caught him above his left hip, before bouncing off onto the floor like it was nothing.

"That all you got?" he asked.

She scrambled forward, trying to get over to the window so she could pull herself up. But before she had a chance, he'd grabbed her leg. She spun over and kicked out with the other, but he dodged it and yanked her towards him. Her arms buckled beneath her and she smashed her head on the hardwood floor.

This was it.

She was about to die.

At least she couldn't feel any physical pain, but the existential torment made it feel like her heart was crumbling to dust. She was terrified, but she couldn't scream, frantic but without the ability to make her limbs do what she wanted.

Stephen dragged her across the floor and let go of her leg before stepping forward and kicking her in the ribs. She felt that. It knocked all the air out of her and most of her hope. Then he was on top of her, straddling her waist with those black latex hands around her throat.

"It could have been so much easier, Camille," he snarled, pressing his weight down on her neck, squeezing hard. "And a lot less painful. You brought this on yourself."

She squirmed and struggled beneath him, tensing every muscle she still had control of and thrusting her hips to get him off. But it was useless. He was too strong and heavy. She was waning fast. She thrashed her arms, fingers skating across the shiny floor, desperately searching for a pen, a glass, something she could use as a weapon. Stephen tightened his grip, literally squeezing the life out of her.

This was what dying felt like.

It was horrible.

She wasn't ready. It wasn't fair.

She was a young woman, in her prime. She had so much to give, so much to do with her life. It wasn't fair. It wasn't . . .

Her fingers touched something hard and she grabbed hold. Her hair straighteners. They must have slipped under the bed when she flipped the table. They were still plugged in, like always. As the room spun and faded to black, she brought the straighteners out from under the bed and plunged the hot ceramic plates into Stephen's eye.

He let go of her immediately, hands going to his face as he let out a terrible scream. He staggered to his feet, leaving Camille to roll onto her side, gasping for air and rubbing at her neck. But this was far from over. Opening her eyes as wide as they could go to try to combat the dizziness, she pushed herself upright, seeing Stephen stumbling back towards the door.

"You fucking bitch," he cried, hands holding his face. "I can't see. I need water."

With her last bit of energy, she grabbed at her bedsheets and dragged herself onto her feet. Stephen was still standing in the doorway as she launched herself at him, barging her shoulder into his exposed torso. She bounced off him onto the floor, but the force of the impact sent him staggering backwards across the narrow landing and over the top of the stairs. With hands still covering his damaged eye, he was unable to grab onto the handrail in time. As he lost his footing on the top step, he brought his hands down, but it was too late. He clawed at the air for a moment before letting out an anguished cry and tumbling noisily down the stairs. Camille dragged herself out of her room in time to see him hit the floor at the bottom, where he came to a stop. His body was twisted like a letter Z and his bruised, bloody face was motionless. She gasped for air, desperate to stay awake as the front door opened and Ant stepped through into the hallway. His mouth fell open as he saw

Stephen's broken form lying on the carpet and then looked up to see Camille lying with her head over the top step. She was just able to raise her hand, letting him know she was alive. Then, as the world finally twisted away from her, she closed her eyes and succumbed to the nothingness.

Chapter 41

Camille blinked herself awake, but a bright light overhead burned at her retinas and it took her thirty seconds or more to grow accustomed to her environment. She was lying down in a bed, but it wasn't her own. She glanced around, taking in the white walls, the pale blue curtain along one side of her and the suggestion of a window behind it.

"There she is. How are you doing, Sleeping Beauty?" She moved her head to the other side to see Ant sitting by her bed. He sipped from a cardboard cup. "I thought you were going to sleep forever."

"What's going on?" she asked, trying and failing to prop herself up. "Where am I?"

"Mile End Hospital. Do you remember what happened?"

"Oh, shit." She'd had no recall on waking, but the shock in his voice as he asked awakened her memories and the extent of what happened hit her like a kick to the ribs. "Stephen. It was him."

"Yes. It was." He blew air out the side of his mouth. "I still can't believe it. He had us both fooled."

This time, Camille managed to sit upright. "Is he . . .?"

Ant stopped mid-drink and shook his head. "No. I thought he was when I first saw him. But he's alive. He's pretty messed up, though. He's in another hospital. Under armed guard."

"Really? It's all over?"

He grinned. "Sure is, kiddo. Thanks to you. That was clever what you did, calling me. Luckily, I was already on my way home on the bus or I might not have picked up. I called the police as soon as I realised what was going on. They turned up a few minutes after I got home and arrested him. He's confessed to killing Mark and all three women. Leila, too. It wasn't suicide. He's going to rot in prison and it's more than the fucker deserves, if you ask me. Doing it for love? Bullshit. He enjoyed it. He was a psychopath."

Camille glanced about her. "Is there any water?"

"Yeah, here." He reached down and appeared a second later with a bottle. He screwed off the cap and handed it to her. "You've been asleep for almost eighteen hours, you know that? The rohypnol he gave you would only have lasted six to eight hours, the docs said. You must have been exhausted."

Camille sipped at the water. Wasn't that the truth? But it was over. It was all finally over. Still, the ramifications of what Stephen had done lay heavy on her soul.

"To think I was falling for him." She shook her head. "All those poor women. Dead. And for what? What did he achieve in the end? Nothing." She thought of Lucy's parents, how broken they were. She had wondered whether the knowledge that their darling daughter hadn't committed suicide would provide them with some comfort. But she saw now how stupid that idea had been. Someone their little girl trusted and liked had murdered her. There was no comfort to be found there. There never would be. She sneered at the thought of Stephen's smug face as he'd told her what he'd done. "I hope he dies in prison."

"Yeah, well, that's for the judicial system to sort out." Ant raised an eyebrow, suggesting he didn't hold out much faith. But there was some closure to be had here, Camille thought as she shifted her position. Even if it was simply that she could now look to the future. Plus, she had caught the killer and survived to tell the tale. She was stronger and more able than she gave herself credit for.

"My hair straighteners," she murmured, as more memories of what had happened came back to her. "I'd left them on."

"As usual."

She met his gaze. "Yeah, but it was lucky I had done. You can't be telling me off for that anymore."

"I bloody well can," he said. "We don't want you surviving a killer boyfriend only to die in a house fire."

"He wasn't my boyfriend," she replied. "And I don't want to hear about killer boyfriends – or ex-boyfriends – ever again!"

"We knew it though, Cambo. Didn't we? We knew there was more to it than what the police were saying."

She smiled. "We did."

Ant turned his head to the sound of footsteps outside the room. "Oh, here he is. Maybe you should remind him of that fact as well."

She followed his gaze over to the corner of the room to see DI Shaw standing in the doorway.

"Afternoon, Ms Fletcher," he said, rocking back on the heels of his shoes. "Can I come in?" She shrugged and he took that as a yes, striding over to stand at the end of her bed. "I think I owe you an apology."

Camille narrowed her eyes. She wanted to be angrier at him for what he'd done – or rather, what he hadn't – but her overriding emotion was relief. "I suppose you thought you were doing the right thing," she told him.

"That's very noble of you." He glanced at Ant, who stuck out his bottom lip. Camille guessed they'd already had words.

"Just as long as Stephen can't hurt anyone else," she said and yawned, a wave of weariness descending out of nowhere.

"You need to rest. I won't keep you," DI Shaw said. "You've been through a lot. I just wanted to come by and say I was sorry. And that you were right. I will take more heed in the future."

She smiled. She wasn't sure if that was true, but he was right about one thing. She did need to rest. Her eyelids hung heavy.

"I'll get off in a minute as well," Ant said. "Leave you to get some *more* sleep."

DI Shaw cleared his throat. "I am going to have to get you down to the station in the next few days, though. When you're up to it. I'll need a statement from you."

Camille settled herself back down on the pillow. "No problem."

"I'll be off then. Speak to you soon, Camille. And thank you."

She closed her eyes, listening to his footsteps as they echoed down the corridor. As a benign blanket of sleep wrapped itself around her soul, she felt truly content and unfettered by doubt for the first time since she could remember. It had been a tough year. Good people had lost their lives in the most horrific of ways and she wasn't sure how her experiences would affect her in the long term. But she knew she'd get through it. She was strong. She was brave. She was who she needed to be. Maybe the universe was on her side after all.

Chapter 42

Twelve months later . . .

The sun was shining down on Hoop Lane as Camille made the short walk over to the west side of the cemetery where Leila was buried. Camile had been here only once before since her friend had died, but she remembered the layout and found her headstone without much trouble. Someone had been here recently. Fresh flowers lay in front of the light marble plinth. Camille knelt and placed the bouquet she'd brought alongside the existing display, reading the inscription on the headstone as she did.

Leila Ruth Bloom.
Beloved daughter and sister.
Taken from us too soon.

There was also something written in Hebrew that Camille didn't understand.

"Hey, you," she whispered, squinting into the sun and raising her hand to cover her eyes. "I'm sorry I've not been to visit for a while. I've been busy." It surprised her how normal it felt, speaking to Leila this way. In fact, it felt good. She felt close to her. "I did it, Leila. I wrote my book."

Not only that, as of this week, she'd also secured herself a literary agent. A lovely woman called Kath Stringer, who was optimistic she could sell Camille's book (working title, *Linked by Love, Killed by a Coward*) to one of the big five publishing houses. The only thing was that Kath thought the title could be better, so Camille was currently brainstorming ideas with her creative team.

"I've done you justice, don't worry," she told Leila. "Everyone will know how amazing and gorgeous and funny you were."

Whilst the book dealt with Camille's first-hand experiences, she'd written it as a tribute to Stephen's victims. It was their story as much as hers. Even Sophie Lawrence. Camille had contacted her again after Stephen's court case and she'd agreed to an interview. This time around, she was a lot nicer and more accommodating. Years of pain and trauma had built on her existing mental health issues, but she was on new medication and looking to the future. Camille had promised to keep in touch. She hoped to help her over the coming years in whatever way she could.

Stephen had received a life sentence with a minimum term of forty years. He'd be almost seventy if he ever got out. It should have been longer, but that's the way the law worked. Ant reckoned he'd have a tough time of it inside. Inmates didn't take kindly to men who murdered women. But Camille tried not to think about that. It was bad karma. Plus, she didn't want to waste another second thinking about that evil prick.

She got to her feet, still looking at Leila's grave. "Kath thinks we could sell the film rights to the book, too. A documentary or maybe even a Hollywood film. But I don't know, it's a long way off." She wiped at her eye. "I really miss you, mate. We didn't get enough time together. I hope wherever you are, you're having a laugh and clutching a large glass of Pinot."

She bowed her head and thanked the universe for her life, for her friends, for being the lucky one.

"I've got to get going," she told Leila, stretching her shoulders back. "I won't leave it so long next time. I promise."

She turned and headed back towards the cemetery gates. She had felt a little guilty at first – about making money, and hopefully a career, from all the pain and death she'd experienced. But she'd made peace with that fact. She wasn't writing for fame or fortune. If those things came along as a result, so be it. But she'd written this book for those strong young women who never had time to finish their story. She was adamant that, despite any edits a publisher might request, she'd fight to keep it a testament to them rather than a salacious real-crime book. It had also been agreed with Kath that a share of all profits would go to the women's families. It was the least she could do. Many of the women's families had given interviews and passed on photos for her to use in the book.

The sun was warm on her cheeks as Camille got to the main road and took a left towards Golders Green tube station. Yes. Life felt good and for the first time since leaving university, she had real purpose. She'd got through this experience, not only alive but with a greater sense of who she was and what she could deal with. And there was no way she was going to waste her life any longer. Not one day. Not one second. She was living for four other women as well now. She wouldn't let them down.

About the Author

M.I. Hattersley grew up in Yorkshire, UK, and has spent the last couple of decades balancing creative work with a long list of mind-numbing day jobs. He's toured Europe with a rock 'n' roll band, trained as a professional actor, and founded a theatre and media company. He now writes psychological thrillers and domestic suspense novels, drawing on years of experience with intense people and unpredictable situations.

About Embla Books

Embla Books is a digital-first publisher of standout commercial adult fiction. Passionate about storytelling, the team at Embla believe our lives are built on stories – and publish books that will make you 'laugh, love, look over your shoulder and lose sleep'. Launched by Bonnier Books UK in 2021, the imprint is named after the first woman from the creation myth in Norse mythology. Embla was carved by the gods from a tree trunk found on the seashore; an image of the kind of creative work and crafting that writers do, and a symbol of how stories shape our lives.

Find out about some of our other books and stay in touch:

X, Facebook, Instagram: @emblabooks
Newsletter: https://bit.ly/emblanewsletter